MW01087406

BREAK
AWAY

Now it's time to make my move.
No more fouling out.
This time, I'm going to score.

HEATHER M. ORGERON

BREAKAWAY
Copyright © 2017 Heather M. Orgeron
ALL RIGHTS RESERVED

ISBN-13: 978-1979259217
ISBN-10: 1979259216

No part of this publication may be reproduced, transmitted, downloaded, distributed, stored in or introduced into any information storage or retrieval system, in any form or by any means, whether electronic, photocopying, mechanical or otherwise, without express permission of the publisher, except by a reviewer who may quote brief passages for review purposes.

This book is a work of fiction. Names, characters, places, story lines and incidents are the product of the author's imagination or are used fictitiously. Any resemblances to actual persons, living or dead, events, locales or any events or occurrences are purely coincidental.

Edited by
Edee M. Fallon, *Mad Spark Editing*
www.madsparkediting.com

Cover Design, Interior Design & Formatting by
Juliana Cabrera, *Jersey Girl Design*

www.jerseygirlandco.com

OTHER TITLES
BY HEATHER M. ORGERON

Vivenne's Guilt
Boomerangers

For anyone who's ever fallen in love with a friend and wondered: What if?

CHAPTER ONE

Colton (Age 13)

IT WAS MY THIRTEENTH BIRTHDAY, AND MOMMA WAS FINALLY letting me have my first boy/girl party. Well, technically Alex had been at every party I'd ever had, but she didn't count. Alex was...well, Alex. We'd been friends since we were in diapers and our mothers best friends since they were just little girls. We'd lived next door to each other our entire lives and still had sleepovers every weekend. She was like a sister...only *not*.

Anyway, the boy/girl party was a really big deal. Momma said we could have it in the pool house and promised not to bother us as long as we behaved. Allie and I had spent the entire day prepping, and I thought she was as excited about it as I was, but there I was...chasing her scrawny butt through the yard back to her house. Most of the time, Al was really cool, but she *was* still a girl, and sometimes she even acted like one.

"Alex," I called after her, "would you just freaking stop and talk to me?"

"I hate you, Colton Fowler!" she screamed without looking back as she climbed the porch steps and disappeared through the front door, slamming it so hard the whole porch rattled. *Girls!*

What I really wanted to do was turn around and go back to my party, but I would have gotten in trouble for making her cry, and maybe it bugged me just a little too. Once she was inside, I stopped running and slowly made my way to the front door, which of course was locked. I rolled my eyes, grumbling under my breath as I rang the doorbell and waited for Mrs. Mack to let me in.

My hands started to sweat when I heard the heavy footsteps approaching the door.

"Hey, Colton," Mrs. Mack said, trying and failing to hide a smirk. "What'd you do this time?"

"Hell if I know." I shrugged then jumped back when her hand flew out and swatted my arm.

"Watch your language, young man."

"Sorry," I mumbled, rubbing out the sting.

"She's in her room, Colt. Go on up." Mrs. Mack stepped back so I could pass. "If her door's locked, there's a bobby pin in the vase on the hall table," she added with a wink.

I nodded then ran across the house and up the stairs to Allie's room. I didn't bother checking to see if it was locked. I knew it would be, so I grabbed the pin on the way and popped the door open.

"Colton!" she screamed, covering herself with the T-shirt she was preparing to slip over her head.

I should have turned or left, or done anything but stand there with my mouth hanging open, but that's precisely what I did. Just. Stood. There...Staring. I hadn't seen Alex naked in years. Our mothers had put an end to that when we were around five. Alex was tiny and not really developed, but seeing her topless and her boobs...*Alex had boobs?* Little ones but *boobs.* That was the moment it truly hit me that Alex was a girl. A real one. A real one with *boobs.*

"Ugh!" she growled, turning her back to me while she pulled the shirt on. "You are such a jerk."

—

Alex turned back around, shooting me a death glare. "Uh, sorry, Al."

"Have you ever heard of knocking, pervert?"

"I, uh..." I didn't know what to say. This was *weird*.

"Just go back to your party with your stupid friends and stupid Marci." She threw herself face down on her bed, and her body started to shake with sobs.

Shit. My eyes began to water. I hated that she could make me cry with only a few tears. "Don't cry, Allie." I sat on the side of her bed and stroked the long brown waves of hair strewn across her back. "Don't be embarrassed. It's not like you have big ones. I mean, it's just like when we used to take baths together." I shrugged, trying to make her feel better even though seeing her naked still had me feeling *strange*.

Like she'd suddenly become possessed by a demon, she popped up in bed and leveled me with eyes that looked like they could burn holes right through me. "You...Colton Fowler, you are a *fucking* asshole!"

I'd never heard her say the f-word before. It sounded so foreign coming out of her mouth. I was shocked. I didn't like it at all. "What's wrong with you, Alex?" I asked, standing. "You're acting like...like a *girl*."

"Newsflash, I *am* a girl, or haven't you noticed? That's right, you've been too busy trying to kiss Marci. Oh, but she has big boobs, right? I'm just Alex. Scrawny, *boobless* Alex!"

Marci does have a nice rack...I knew better than to say that right now.

"Your boobs are nice too, Allie." My voice shook with that admission.

Alex blew out a long breath. "Just. Go. Home."

I grabbed her shoulder and turned her 'til she was facing me again. "I'm not leaving 'til you tell me why you ran out of the pool house crying. Al, all of our friends are still there, probably playing spin the bottle without us now."

"Good," she pouted. "I don't wanna play that stupid game anyway."

—

3

Ahh. "Is that why you left? Because you don't wanna play?" I pushed her hair behind her ears. "You don't have to kiss anyone if you aren't ready, Al."

Her head shook, and her voice trembled. "You forgot..." The tears began to spill over again. I was *really* not liking this girly side to Alex.

My heart was pounding because I didn't know how to fix this. How to get out of this awkward situation with my best friend. "I forgot what, Al?"

"You were gonna k-kiss her, Colt," she whispered, sniffling.

"So?"

"So...we promised to learn together so neither of us would be bad at it. You were going to kiss her first. Then you would know how and I...I would be left out."

The conversation we'd had a few years ago suddenly came back. The two of us watching *My Girl...*We'd promised then that we'd be each other's first kiss, just like Veda and Thomas. My throat thickened and my pulse sped up. "I'm sorry, Allie. I did forget. Do you still want to?"

She stared at me with her big brown eyes that were glistening with the tears she was fighting as she chewed her bottom lip. "Nah, just go. It's weird now."

But now I really wanted to kiss her, and it was obvious that it meant a lot to Alex. So, I didn't leave. Instead, I sat beside her on the bed, and my stomach roiled as I scooted closer. I lifted a hand to her face and with my thumb swiped a tear from beneath her eye. My entire body trembled as I leaned forward and pressed my lips against my best friend's.

Her hands were suddenly on my shoulders and then around my neck. After a few soft pecks, I went in for the kill, poking out my tongue and tracing her salty lips. She opened her mouth, and I shared the wettest, sloppiest, most uncoordinated first kiss there probably ever was with my best friend. It didn't last long, but it was enough to change *something* between us. After that kiss, there were times I saw her differently. Lying in the same bed no longer felt as innocent as it had in the past, and

—

4

as we grew older, there were times that I was outright jealous seeing her with other guys. It was stupid. Alex and I were not together, and we'd never kissed again after my thirteenth birthday. But there were many, many times I'd regretted that kiss over the years. Maybe, if it hadn't happened, things wouldn't have changed...

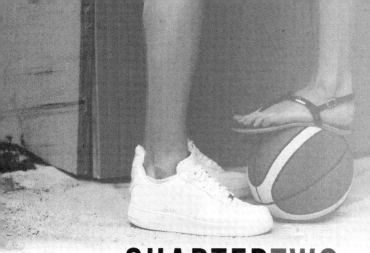

CHAPTERTWO

Alexis (Age 15)

"ALLIE, YOU LOOK SO BEAUTIFUL, BABY," MOMMA SAID, LIFTING her fingers to her lips as tears trickled down her cheeks.

I rolled my eyes and scoffed before mumbling out my thanks and walking past her into the hall.

"I mean it. Colt's a fool."

"For the last time, Mom, I don't like him like that!" I shouted, stomping down the stairs in my heels. I felt like a baby giraffe trying to walk in the damn things.

I finally looked up from my feet when I reached the bottom step, and there he was...Looking like a damned *GQ* model, in the foyer chewing his lip to keep from laughing at my embarrassment. *Great!*

My face warmed. "Hey, Colt," I called as I stepped onto the marble tile. "Where's Marci?"

He coughed. "She...uh. She's meeting us there."

"Us?"

"It's our first homecoming, Alex. I thought we'd ride together?"

Well, at least he hadn't completely ditched me. It had been hard having to share my best friend with his new basketball teammates and the girls who fawned all over him at school. *Skanky bitches.* I felt him slowly slipping away, and I hated it.

"A goddamned fool," Mr. Fowler agreed as he walked out of the kitchen with my father trailing closely behind. "Alexis, you look lovely, honey."

I cleared my throat and looked up at Mr. Fowler. "Thank you, sir." He was a big black teddy bear of a man, and had always treated me like his own.

Then my own father walked over, wrapping me in a tight hug, and whispered, "A damned fool," into my ear, and I'd had enough.

I glanced over to Colton, whose head was now hanging in embarrassment, and felt my blood begin to boil. "Why do y'all do this to us? Why do you have to make everything so weird just because we're in high school now? Nothin's changed! We don't like each other like that, okay? Stop trying to mess up our friendship. He's like my brother. It's gross." I felt that lie churn in my stomach. "Just...just...stop it, okay?"

All four of our parents mumbled and nodded, and Colt looked like he was about to punch someone. Why'd our parents always have to ruin everything?

I walked over to my best friend and reached for his hand, tickling his palm with my newly manicured fingers. "Sorry, Colt."

With a tight-lipped smile, he shrugged. "Don't worry 'bout it, Al. Like you said, it'd be like dating my sister." He forced a laugh. "Gross," he agreed, scrunching his nose.

Ouch. That stung. The truth was that I'd slowly been developing feelings for Colton over the last few years and I hadn't known what to do about them. Our parents teased us endlessly about how we'd been betrothed from the womb. Our mothers thought it would be the coolest thing ever to have their children wed. Our fathers had played ball together in school. They were ridiculously close, all four of them. They'd never monitored the two of us very closely because honestly, I think they'd have been over the moon if a relationship ever formed between us. But one hadn't. Apart from that one kiss, Colt never showed any interest in me, and I tried for all I was worth to hide the immense attraction I had for him.

I'd always thought Colton was beautiful, with his dark caramel skin and light green eyes. His hair was a mop of silky brown curls, and those dimples could melt the panties right off a nun. His muscles were becoming more defined. Somehow, my friend had turned into a sexy man-boy, and I wanted him. I wanted desperately to be on the receiving end of those flirty smiles he reserved for all of the other girls. Girls who I knew were only my friends to get closer to him. I wanted the stolen kisses and admiring looks. I wanted to be more than one of the guys, and I had to get over it or I'd end up losing my best friend completely.

I dropped his hand, feeling awkward. "Let's just go."

Mrs. Fowler drove us, trying to lighten our mood on the way, to no avail. Colt was pressed up against his door behind her seat and me against mine on the passenger side. We didn't speak to each other. Not one word. I'd never felt so uncomfortable with him in all my life.

As she pulled up behind the line of cars waiting to drop their kids off, his mom glanced at us in the back seat with a toothy smile. "You two lighten up. They were just teasin' ya. You only get your first homecoming once...Make the most of it, huh? I'll pick you two up at eleven. Have fun!"

When the car finally rolled to a stop in front of the gym doors, I bolted as fast as humanly possible. Bile churned in my stomach. It felt like we'd just had a huge fight, only we hadn't. I headed straight for the bathroom, the one place I knew he couldn't follow, to fix my makeup and dry my eyes, and as luck would have it, bumped right into Marci and her two minions,

Jessica and Lacy.

"Hey, Alex," Marci chimed with feigned excitement. "I take it Colton's finally here?"

Forcing a smile, I widened my eyes in a lousy attempt to keep the tears from falling in front of her. "Yeah, he's somewhere around." I hated that my voice broke.

"Great! You know I love you, right?" she asked, placing a tentative hand on my shoulder. I could sense there was more coming.

I swallowed the lump forming in my throat, nodded, and smiled. "Mmhmm."

"Just...don't take this the wrong way, okay?" she asked, smoothing her poufy pink skirt.

I didn't even try to hide the eye roll as I crossed my hands on my chest. "What, Marci?"

"Well, he's *my* boyfriend...yet he's always with *you*. I think maybe it's time you find a boyfriend of your own..."

Lightbulb. Why hadn't I thought of that myself?

I smiled the first and last genuine smile I'd ever offered Marci Mayweather. "You know what, Marci...I think you're right."

After she and her entourage left the restroom, I stared at myself in the floor length mirror. I looked good, and I knew it. My royal blue dress was form fitting with an open back. The bodice was covered in sequins, and the skirt was short and lined with layers of tulle. Coupled with my four-inch silver pumps, my legs looked amazing. So, maybe I didn't have much going on in the boob department, yet...but my ass was to die for, and I owed it all to the rigorous workouts it took to uphold my position on the school's track team.

I opened my silver clutch and applied a little more lipstick and the smoky-eye I'd spent hours practicing at home. Then I released the pins in my hair and let it fall in a cascade of dark brown curls almost to my waist.

I didn't know when I'd become that pathetic girl pining away for her best friend. But it ended tonight.

—

When I walked out of those bathroom doors, instead of hiding from the boy who'd been my very best friend for all of my life, I'd take my rightful place beside him. I wasn't going to lose him over a stupid crush. Colton was mine first, and as long as I kept those feelings in check, he'd be mine forever.

"Hey, guys," I called as I walked confidently over to Colton and our usual crowd, who were huddled near the DJ booth.

Colt visibly did a double take. "Hey, Allie, where you been? I was lookin' for ya." He eyed me skeptically.

With a coy smile, I leaned in closer to whisper into his ear, allowing my lips to *accidentally* brush his skin. "Restroom." The manly scent of his cologne almost made me falter...almost.

He placed his hand on my bare back, and every nerve ending in my body sparked to life. He leaned in close, and I could smell the mint from the gum in his mouth. It took all of my resolve not to melt into a puddle at his feet. "I like your hair down like that." His warm breath caused a chill to move throughout my body.

I shook it off and ruffled my hand into his curls before placing a kiss on his cheek. "Thanks, bro," I said, stepping to the side.

"Alex..." Colt's teammate, Ryan, purred. "Lookin' good." He roved his eyes up and down my body. Normally, I thwarted all of his advances—all of anyone's really; *God, how pathetic was I?*—but I smiled and returned his perusal.

"You don't look too bad yourself, Ry."

From the corner of my eye, I could see the confusion on Colton's face. He'd just have to get used to seeing me with guys the same way I'd had to get used to seeing him with girls. Our friendship was too important to lose over hormones.

"You wanna' dance, Alex?" Ryan asked, reaching for my hand.

I think I shocked myself along with everyone else in the

crowd when I smiled and answered, "I'd love to."

I'd be lying if I said I didn't notice my own pain reflected in Colton's eyes on the dance floor, but in some twisted way, it felt good. There he was with Marci in his arms, and for once I wasn't feeling the sick pang in my chest alone. He felt it too. I could tell. And I'd bet he felt it a million times worse than me because I'd had years to adjust to it and he was only just learning what it felt like to watch the other half of your heart in the arms of someone who wasn't you.

I tried to focus on Ryan, to feel those familiar butterflies when he touched me. But he didn't even spark an ember. Nothing. I felt nothing when he pulled me tighter to his hard chest. Not even a flutter as he trailed his strong hands up and down the naked skin of my back and when he licked the seam of my mouth and dove in, giving me my first kiss since the one I'd shared with Colt in my bedroom two years before, I had to fight the urge to retch.

It was awkward at first, but when I saw the pissed off look on Colton Fowler's face, it suddenly became bearable. I got really into it, digging my nails into the back of his shirt. I gave as good as I got and felt a triumphant smile curl my lips as Ryan groaned into my mouth. So maybe it wasn't fireworks and butterflies. Maybe it paled in comparison to the innocent, inexperienced kiss I'd shared with Colt on my pink floral comforter. I could become addicted to the way it felt to make my best friend jealous. I think I just had...

Ryan and I had worked ourselves into a steady rhythm, and after the third slow dance we'd spent with our tongues down each other's throats, I felt a tap on my shoulder. In my mind, it was Colt. He'd had enough and was coming to stake his claim on his girl...*his girl being me.* I'd have to reconsider all of this getting over Colt nonsense that I'd only just committed myself to. I smiled as I pulled my lips from Ryan's and turned to find a blinding white light shining right in my eyes.

"That's enough," Principal Hart said sternly, lifting Ryan's hands up from where they'd wandered to my bottom. "Let the girl breathe."

My face warmed as our friends did little to hide their laughter. Mr. Hart also played ball with our fathers, and I knew I'd be hearing more about this later. *The joys of growing up in small-town Texas.* "I'm really disappointed in you, Alexis," he said, drawing his brows together. "And, Ryan, have a little more respect for the ladies, huh? Keep your hands above the waist, or I'll be calling your parents."

Ryan chuckled. "Yes, sir," he responded with a salute. "Sorry, sir."

Mr. Hart nodded then turned his attention to Colton, who looked like he could breathe fire. "Colton, don't let your friends disrespect her," he said pointedly, as if he were my keeper. I hated that everyone made him feel responsible for me.

"No, sir," Colt responded, glaring at Ryan.

For the remainder of that evening, I felt the tension between us like a living thing. However, I didn't let that little embarrassment put a wrinkle in my plans. I flirted and danced with our friends all while the warden seethed beside me. Oh, he didn't say anything. He didn't have to. His disapproving looks and the way he didn't leave my side said more than he could have. Eventually, he'd get used to it. He'd learn to hide it just as I had. Until then, I'd enjoy his misery.

The ride home was quiet. Colt sat a little closer to me this time, but he didn't speak. I stared out of the window with a giddy smile on my face as I answered all of his mother's questions about the night. I may have gushed a little about how much I liked Ryan to rub salt in the wound. Hey, he'd been flaunting Marci and all of his other girls in my face for two years. He deserved to suffer a little.

I'd be sleeping over at Colton's tonight. We'd been spending the night at each other's houses since we were toddlers. It'd become the routine for our parents to alternate weekends with us. It gave them kid-free time to do their own thing, and Colt and I were always together anyway.

Colt stormed off to his room as soon as we got home. Mrs.

—

Fowler asked if anything had happened and I told her that I thought he and Marci had got into it. I couldn't tell her the truth, although she'd probably have been proud.

"I'm so glad you had such a great time, honey. I was starting to wonder if you'd ever get into boys," she teased. "Although, you know, we'd still love you, even if you liked girls...It would just make your betrothal a little harder to sell." She winked.

"I'm not a lesbian, and I'm not marrying Colt. The sooner you all get that through your heads, the better."

She giggled, wrapping a long tendril of my hair around her pale finger. "Stop fighting fate," she whispered, kissing my forehead. "You two were made for each other...You'll see," she added, slipping her finger from my hair and walking off to her room before I could argue.

I huffed out a frustrated breath as I marched up the stairs. The butterflies that had lain dormant for most of the evening were stirring up a frenzy in my tummy. I rapped my knuckles lightly on Colt's door. When he didn't answer, I let myself in, noticing he'd already pulled out the trundle from beneath his bed. The trundle we had yet to use. We'd always slept together in his bed or in mine. *He must be really pissed.*

I listened to the steady spray of the water from the shower through his bathroom door, and a waft of his soap filled his small room. I sat on the edge of his bed, feeling dejected... longing for the days when we were still innocent kids making mud pies and riding our bikes up and down the dead-end street for hours and hours.

The bathroom lock clicked, and I sat up straighter, plastering a smile on my face to disguise the hurt. "Hey," I whispered.

Colton walked over to his dresser, grabbed one of his undershirts and a pair of boxer shorts from the drawer, and tossed them next to me on his bed. He looked so sad, and I almost regretted the entire night. But then I remembered all the times I wore that same look. All the times he hurt me, and I got those emotions in check real quick.

"Hey," he said quietly. "Bathroom's free."

—

14

I rose from his bed, my heart sinking to my toes, as I walked past him into the bathroom that was still steaming from his shower. I wished he'd have grabbed my arm and pulled my body to his, finally confessing that he too felt all of the same things for me that I'd been feeling for him. But he didn't. After shutting and locking the door, I sat on the edge of the tub, silently releasing all of the emotion that I could hardly contain any longer.

I slipped out of my dress and into his clothes, bunching the collar of his shirt into my hand and holding it to my nose, breathing in his familiar scent...wishing that things could be different. That there really was such a thing as fate. That the two of us really were destined to be together. That it wasn't all just a bunch of bullshit that our parents had been feeding us since we were babies. I wished that they hadn't planted those romantic ideas in my head. That it didn't hurt so much to love him. Most of all, I wished that he'd loved me back.

When I was sure that he was asleep and I wouldn't have to explain my red, swollen face, I crept out of the bathroom and found Colton quietly snoring on the trundle. *He'd left me his bed.* His body was curled into the fetal position, and his beautiful face turned toward the door.

Reluctantly, I climbed into his bed *alone* and stared at the bare skin of his back that had somehow begun to change from a boy's into a man's without my permission. I fought the urge to crawl down there and lie next to him. He wouldn't push me away. But I respected his new boundaries, because one of us had to be strong enough to set some, and with tears soaking his pillow, I fell asleep to the familiar cadence of his quiet breaths.

—

CHAPTER THREE

Colton (Age 17)

"IF YOU BRING CHELSIE, I'LL BRING DEAN," I OFFERED. IT WAS THE end of our junior year, and our families were getting ready to go on our yearly trip to Alex's grandparents' beach house in Pensacola. I knew she had a thing for my buddy Dean, and as much as it grated on my nerves, I also knew it was the only way to get her to bring my new girlfriend, Chelsie.

She sucked on her teeth, shaking her head. "I really don't like that girl, Colt." But I could tell she was starting to reconsider. I could get Allie to do anything with the right motivation.

"Come on, Al..." I begged, sticking out my bottom lip. "Please? I *really* like her."

She rolled her eyes. "You *really* like her big tits," she accused.

I laughed. "I do..." I couldn't lie to her any more than she could to me. It was pointless. So, I stuck with brutal honesty. "I'd really like to look at her big tits in a bikini for two weeks too," I said, waggling my eyebrows.

Oomph. The book that was just in Alex's hands came flying at my chest. "Pig."

I shrugged my shoulders. "Guilty."

There was only one girl I'd ever had feelings for, and she was shooting daggers at me from the foot of my bed. I'd given up on the idea of us a few years ago when I realized that she didn't share the same feelings. It sucked, but I would take Allie any way I could. Even if it was only as friends. I still had the best parts of her, and I made up for the physical stuff with whatever girl tickled my pickle at the time. Currently, the position of pickle tickler belonged to Chelsie Montgomery, a blond, busty cheerleader that Allie barely tolerated. She gave good head and worshiped the ground I walked on. I needed a distraction from Alex if I was going to survive two weeks looking at her in a bathing suit. Last year, I'd nearly died of blue balls. True story.

"Why's it have to be her? What about Jeanine? You seemed to get on pretty well at Ryan's party last weekend, and I actually *like* her. What's so special about Chelsie?"

I raised my brows. "Besides her tits?"

"Colton!"

"Fine...she, uh. She has good *ball handling skills*," I teased, sucking in my bottom lip. Hey, she asked.

Her face turned beet red. "Stop with the basketball humor. It's not funny."

"*Blocked* by my best friend," I pouted.

Her eyes rolled up in her head.

"Come on, Allie, it's a little funny."

She rewarded me with an evil glare. It was time to pull out the heavy artillery. I reached out my arms, pretending to stretch, and grabbed hold of her foot and began tickling her mercilessly. Alex fell back onto the bed, and I climbed over her, straddling her waist with my knees as I tickled her ribs.

She bucked and writhed beneath me, and as she rubbed against my crotch, I began to envision what it would be like to make love to my best friend. I tried not to think about how I knew she'd respond to my touch. How she always had.

Her hands began slapping at my chest, drawing me from

—

my thoughts. "Get off, I'm gonna pee!" she shouted. "Fine! Fine! You win, Colt. Just stop it."

"You'll invite Chelsie?" I asked for clarification as I stopped the assault, but didn't let her go.

She was gasping for breath as she answered, "Yes, goddamn it. Get off of me. And you better bring Dean."

Dean...Fuck. "Deal."

Dean aggravated the ever-living shit out of me the entire twelve-hour drive to the beach. All he talked about was Allie and how he couldn't wait to get his hands on her. I should have won some sort of award for not beating his fucking face in. This never got easier.

When we finally arrived at the beach house, I couldn't get out of my parents' 4Runner fast enough. The girls hadn't arrived yet, so I helped unload our bags then excused myself to the bathroom to splash some water on my face in preparation for what was sure to be a grueling couple of weeks.

I heard a light knock on the other side of the bathroom door where I sat on the lid of the toilet, hiding from Dean. "Who is it?"

"Colton Fowler, you'd better get your butt out here before this girl drives me crazy," Alex grumbled through the door.

I smiled at how miserable we both were with our *friends* as I unlocked the door and pulled it open. "Wanna come hide in here with me?" I asked, peeking my head out into the hall. I grabbed her hand and ushered her into the small bathroom then shut and locked the door, resuming my position on the lid of the toilet.

"Colt, she's terrible. You owe me. Seriously, she never shuts up, yet she somehow never really says anything either. You sure know how to pick 'em," she said, throwing her hands in the air.

"I have no interest in her ability to hold up her end of a

—

conversation, Al."

Her face was stricken. "But why, Colt? Why do you date these idiots? You can do so much better than a brainless pair of tits."

"I have better."

She shook her head. "No. *Noooo*, Colton. That girl is *not* better. She could be the worst of them all."

Perched on the commode with my head in my hands, I uttered the most honest words I'd said to my best friend in a very long time. "I don't mean her..."

Allie's face screwed up in confusion. "Huh? You lost me, buddy."

I ran my hands through my hair and raised my eyes to meet hers. "I have you for all of that, Al."

I watched her throat move as she swallowed hard and just stared at me. I stared back, trying to force the words that I'd been choking on for so long, but couldn't. And just as I was working up the nerve to say fuck it all and confess my feelings, there was a bang on the other side of the door.

I brought my finger to my lips, instructing Alex to keep quiet. "Yeah?"

"There you are, Colty..." I stifled a laugh as Alex shoved her finger in her throat and exaggerated a gag. "I've been looking all over for you."

"I'm here. I'll be out soon. Go put on that little red bikini for me?"

Brainless giggled through the door. "Okay. Hurry up. I'm dying to see you!"

"She's *dying* to see you, *Colty*," Alex mocked and then burst out laughing.

"Unless you want to explain to Chelsie and Dean why we're locked in the bathroom together, you'd better be quiet."

That shut her up.

Allie looked at me expectantly, clearly waiting for me to finish what I'd started before the universe reminded me of why it would be a terrible idea to confess my feelings to a girl

—

who clearly didn't feel the same. I'd lose her. I couldn't lose her, no matter how much it was hurting me to hold on.

"You should go," I whispered, gesturing toward the door.

Her face fell as she turned the lock, hesitating for a moment as she allowed me one last chance to finish what I'd started. If I'd known then the way the rest of that trip would go, I'd have fallen to my knees and laid my heart at her feet. I'd have made a complete fucking fool of myself and risked it all before it was too late.

Alex and Dean couldn't have hit it off better, and I was consumed with jealousy as I watched the two of them making out on the beach a few yards down the shore from where Chelsie and I were lounging. I had a gorgeous girl lying topless beside me, and I couldn't peel my eyes from my best friend.

Our parents had been taking off in the evenings and leaving us to our own devices for a week now, and each night I watched my girl fall harder for the schmuck I'd brought along for her entertainment. I'd hand delivered the guy who would snatch my heart right out from under my nose, and there wasn't a damned thing I could do to stop it.

I'd seen Allie with lots of guys in the past, and none of them made me burn the way this one did. Because, somehow, I knew that this was *different*...

"Colty, will you rub some lotion on my back?" Brainless asked, pulling me from my murderous thoughts.

"Sure," I answered indifferently as I grabbed the lotion and mindlessly rubbed it into her sun-kissed skin. She was drop-dead gorgeous and more than willing, but I couldn't bring myself to want her anymore.

I tried to lose myself in her sick body, but all I saw was long, dark hair and chocolate brown eyes looking at Dean the way she usually reserved for me. I spent the rest of vacation counting the days 'til we returned home, hoping that everything would revert to the way it was before. But, of course, it never did.

"Oh my God, Colton...Thank youuuu," Alex sang as she danced around my bedroom braless, in a tiny tank top and the shortest fucking shorts I'd ever seen. *Did she always sleep in such revealing clothes?*

I forced a tight-lipped smile. "Don't mention it."

"This was the best vacation *ever*...right? Did you and Chelsie have fun?"

My stomach gurgled. I was going to be sick. "Yeah, Al. It was great."

"You just...well, you don't seem all that excited."

I buried my face in my pillow. "Just tired, Allie. Can you shut off the light and get to bed, please?"

"Really? But we just got home...Don't you wanna talk?"

I forced a laugh. "Al, what I really want...is to go to sleep." I was so tired of hearing how much she liked Dean. I just wished she'd shut the hell up about him already.

She huffed. "You're awful grouchy for a guy who just spent the past two weeks playing with the world's greatest pair of tits," she teased, poking out her tongue.

Alex was a talker, and usually, I was more than willing to listen to her endless drivel. Tonight was not one of those nights. I was barely holding it together. "Alexis Mack...the light, please?"

"Fine," she growled. "You didn't pull out the trundle. Should I do it, jerk?"

She was pissed, and I was a mess. "Just get in with me," I said, lifting the comforter.

A shocked expression crossed her face before she switched off the light and scurried into bed beside me. We hadn't slept together this way in a few years. But, tonight, I just wanted the old us back. I wanted to hold her in my arms and pretend that nothing had changed...that everything hadn't just changed.

—

"This is nice," she whispered, snuggling into my chest.

I smoothed her long hair back and placed a kiss at her temple. "Yeah, Al...it is."

CHAPTERFOUR

Alexis (Age 18)

I HAD JUST FINISHED ADJUSTING MY CAP AND PINNING IT INTO place with a few bobby pins when I heard a knock on my bedroom door. My heart leaped in my chest as I rushed to open it.

He was so beautiful. I took a moment to look him up and down. His vibrant eyes and gorgeous smile. That white-blond hair peeking out from the sides of his cap. *How'd I get so lucky?*

"Dean!" I squealed, rising up onto my toes and wrapping my arms around his neck. "I can't believe we're graduating."

He smiled. "You look beautiful, Alexis."

"Thanks, babe."

Dean and I had been together for almost a year now, and he still made my heart flutter. I thought that I was doomed to spend my life pining after Colton Fowler until I met Dean. This past year had been a fairytale. I had the perfect boyfriend. He was kind and attentive, and he made my heart dance. He was all of the things I thought I'd never find.

My phone pinged. It was Colt's message alert. I disentangled myself from my boyfriend and padded across the room to check my phone. It was a picture of the two of us on our first day of kindergarten. A smile moved across my face as a tear dripped from my cheek to the screen.

Colt: We did it, Al. Yay!

Allie: You made me cry, ass. I love it.

Colt: Sorry, Allie. See you soon.

I hugged my phone to my chest, smiling like a fool. I'd completely forgotten that my boyfriend was even in the room.

"Must've been some message...What'd Fowls want?" Dean asked with a sour look on his face. I hated that the guys all called him that. Dean knew it too. Colton was a brilliant basketball player, and his jealousy was unbecoming.

"Nothing," I answered, smiling. "Let's go."

We walked hand in hand down the stairs where my parents, along with Dean's and Colton's, were waiting—all three of our mothers with cameras in hand.

Colton walked in a minute later, and they ushered us all out to the front yard to snap a million photos.

After Dean and his parents left, Colt grabbed my hand, tugging me toward the oak where our mothers had photographed us together on the first and last days of every school year. Tears pricked my eyes as we laced our fingers and smiled at our mommas, ending a lifelong tradition.

"I'm going, Al."

No. "I'm sorry, what?" I asked, trying to make sure I'd heard him correctly.

"I'm going to California...to play ball. It's a full ride and a great opportunity. I can't pass that up."

"But I thought you said you were going to take the offer from Texas State?"

He shook his head. "I have to go...Please don't be mad, Al."

My lip trembled. I couldn't help it. I swore I wouldn't make him feel guilty no matter what he chose, but he was choosing wrong. I dropped his hand, backing away, my head violently shaking from side to side. "No."

"Alexis, don't do this to him," my father warned.

I looked up at his sparkling green eyes, and it was all too much. Just...too...much...

"I'm sorry, Allie," he offered in a broken whisper.

I looked around at all of our parents, who'd obviously already known and were just waiting for me to fall apart.

"Shitty timing, son," Mr. Fowler growled at Colt.

"Alexis, it's time to go," Momma called, motioning with her head toward the car.

Tears ran down my cheeks as I continued to stare into my best friend's anguished face. He reached out his hand to touch my cheek, and I recoiled. From his expression, you'd swear I'd just shoved a knife into his chest. Good. Because fuck him for springing this on me before graduation. We were supposed to stick together. That was always the plan. He didn't get to call the shots.

"Let's go," I rasped, ripping my gaze from Colton's.

I avoided Colt for weeks. It was childish and just plain stupid, but I was hurt and scared. And truth be told, I didn't know how I'd manage life without Colton in it.

He texted me every day...and I left those messages unanswered.

Colt: Hey, Allie. I miss you, and I'm really sorry. Love you.

Colt: Still not talking to me? Wow, I never thought I'd witness the day when Alexis Mack had nothing to say.

—

Colt: It's been two weeks, Al. I'm dying here.

Colt: I'm fucking sorry, okay? I miss you so much. Don't do this to us, Al...

Colt: I'm leaving in the morning, Allie...

Allie: It hurts, Colton.

Colt: I know. Believe me, I know.

Allie: Why?

Colt: I just have to.

Allie: This sucks.

Colt: I miss you. Can I come over?

Allie: It's 2 in the morning.

Colt: So?

Allie: Guess so.

I didn't bother getting out of bed to let him in. Colt had had a key to the house for as long as I had. I lay awake in bed staring at the door, just waiting for him to walk in. It hurt to breathe, I missed him so much.

Just when I'd started to think that he'd changed his mind,

—

the knob turned, and the door creaked open. He walked in with his head hung, and his shoulders slumped in defeat. And as he got closer to the bed, I saw on his face that this separation had been just as hard on him.

"Colt," I whispered tearfully.

"Can I?" he asked, waving his hand over the bed. He'd never asked permission before. That he wasn't sure whether or not he was welcome tore me apart inside.

I nodded. "Of course," I rasped.

He crawled in from the foot of the bed, and when his head reached the pillow, Colton hugged me from behind, burying his face in the crook of my neck. He feathered light kisses along my collarbone, up the curve of my neck, and the side of my face, until he reached my ear. "I'm sorry, Allie. I'm so, so sorry." I felt the wetness of his tears on my cheek, and the warmth of his breath on my ear caused a shiver to move through my body. I began to shake as my emotions took over.

"Colton," I cried. "Don't...go..."

"Come here, Al." He grabbed my chin, turning my face until my eyes met his. "I'll miss you every day. Every. Single. Day."

My head shook as tears blinded my vision.

"God, I want to kiss you so bad," he groaned through clenched teeth.

And I wanted it too, more than I'd ever wanted anything else in my life. "Then kiss me, Colton."

He bent his head until his lips hovered just above mine. "You sure, Al?"

I nodded—just barely—then felt his lips brush against my own. It was soft and slow, and blew every other kiss I'd ever had out of the stratosphere. When his tongue entered my mouth, it was more intimate, more meaningful than any sexual encounter I'd ever experienced. I couldn't even fathom what sex with Colton Fowler would be like if kissing him was this good.

We kissed ourselves to sleep and morning came far too

—

early for either of our liking. We'd finally got it right, and he was leaving. Life was a bitch that way.

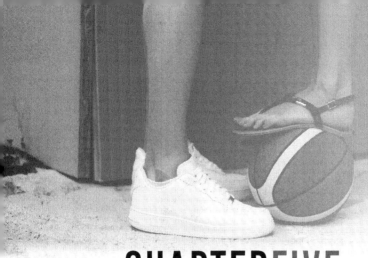

CHAPTER FIVE

Colton - Age 20

"GREAT GAME TONIGHT, FOWLS," MY TEAMMATE FINN congratulated as I stripped off my sweat-soaked jersey.

"Thanks, man."

I downed two bottles of water then grabbed my phone from out of my bag to check for any missed calls or texts from Alex. The locker room was alive with amped-up, testosterone-filled guys over our latest win. But my mind could focus on only one thing...Alexis. I glanced at our messages and re-read our exchange from earlier that day.

> **Alex:** Hey, Colt! It's me...Of course, you know that already. I just wanted to wish you luck at your game tonight!

> **Colt:** Hey, Al. Thanks. How's it going?

> **Alex:** Good...Really good, actually. I think tonight's the night!

> **Colt:** The night for what?

Alex: I think Dean's going to ask me to move in, Colton! I'm so nervous! He's been acting so strange lately... Anyway, he asked me to meet him at his apartment tonight...that he wanted to cook for me and that it was important. I just really got the feeling that this is it, you know?

Colt: That's great, Allie. I can't believe he's waited this long. Miss you!

Alex: Miss you too, bud. Kick ass tonight. I'll call you. Love you! XOXO

Colt: Love you too, Al. xoxo

No new messages...I couldn't shake the feeling that he was going to propose to her. Fuck! He'd be an idiot not to. I blew out a long breath and slammed my head against the locker door, forgetting myself for a moment.

"Dude, something wrong?" my buddy Blex asked from a few lockers down. "What'd that poor locker do to you?" he laughed.

"It's nothin'...You played a good game tonight," I answered while grabbing my things so I could hit the showers.

"Hey, you dropped this," Stephan jeered from behind me. "Who's Alex? Didn't know you had a boyfriend, Fowls. You been holdin' out on us?"

I rolled my eyes, snatching the phone from his hand. "Shut the fuck up and don't touch my shit."

He backed away with his palms out. "Wouldn't dream of it. Your shit's safe with me. I don't swing that way, homie."

Stephan had been a pain in the ass since joining our team in the beginning of this year. Most of us just let him roll off our backs, but I wasn't in the mood for his crap tonight. The adrenaline was already flowing from the game we'd just played, and now with the anticipation of Allie's call on my mind, I was wound so tight, I was ready to explode.

—

"I get it, man. It's hard when they don't feel the same way. That's why I don't do feelings. I let one girl fuck me up in high school and swore never again. That dude's obviously in love with another man, Fowls. Find a new ass to stick it in."

He snickered, and I lost it. I turned on Stephan, pinning him to the lockers behind me. "I'm not in the mood for your shit today. Stay the fuck outta my business." He started to buck up, and I was ready to pound his face in before I was jerked away.

"Fowls, cut the shit. We just made the tournament. The last thing you need is to get benched for fighting with that asshole," Blex warned. "Let it go. He's not worth your career."

Since moving to California, my life had revolved around ball. I had always been good, but now I was unstoppable. I rarely made trips back home anymore, using my grueling practice schedule as the excuse. But, honestly, I just couldn't fucking take seeing Allie with Dean.

I shot Stephan a final warning glare then made my way to the showers to cool down. The hard spray of cold water was refreshing. I placed my palm on the tile and let it roll off my back. When I turned to grab my towel, I found Stephan waiting for me.

"The fuck do you want?" I asked, pushing past him.

He followed closely behind. "Look, I'm sorry. I was just messin' around."

I ground my jaw side to side. "That's fine. Alexis is off limits. Got it?"

He nodded. "Alexis, that makes more sense. You got it bad, huh?"

"Off. Limits," I stressed, stepping into my mesh shorts.

I jogged through the crowded parking lot to my car, a black Mustang GT I'd received as a graduation present from my grandfather, to find Lyla Green perched on the hood. Just when I stopped believing, God went and answered my prayers. She was still dressed in her tiny cheerleader outfit, her tits on full display. Lyla and I had hooked up from time to time, and just then I needed a distraction like never before...

She hopped off the car as I approached, trailing a long, manicured finger down the front of my T-shirt. "Good game tonight, Colton...Wanna take me back to your place and celebrate?"

My cock was already starting to rise to the occasion, so I dropped my bag, backing her up against the car. "What'd you have in mind, doll?" I asked, tracing the low neckline of her top. I felt a chill ripple through her body as she reached down and fondled me through the thin fabric of my shorts.

She smirked, squeezing my shaft. "I think we're on the same page, don't you, big boy?"

"Get in the car," I told her, smacking her ass.

I unlocked the door to the apartment that I shared with Blex and my other buddy Finn and ushered her inside. The apartment was dark. They must've gone out to celebrate our win. I didn't need to tell Lyla where to go. She'd been here for this very reason countless times before. I dropped my keys on the side table and followed her up to my room, where she immediately pounced.

"God, I love your hair, Colton," she said as she jumped me against the door, wrapping her legs around my waist. She fisted a hand in my hair, tugging gently while she licked my neck. When she made her way to my mouth, I turned my head, deciding I wasn't in the mood for kissing tonight.

I carried her over to my bed and sat with her still wrapped around my waist. I didn't need to tell her what I wanted. Girls like her...ones with...*experience*...they just knew.

She giggled, sliding down to the floor to kneel between my legs. She looked up at me with her seductive blue eyes and gripped the band of my shorts. I lifted my hips, allowing her to pull them down, and my cock sprang free, standing tall and proud.

"You have the most perfect dick, Colton," she said, licking from base to tip. I loved how filthy she was. Such a stark contrast to Allie. She'd never speak that way.

Why was I thinking of her? I tried to concentrate. "Do I?"

"Mmmm," she said, swirling her tongue around the tip. "You're perfect."

"Explain," I said with a low, throaty chuckle.

"Well," she answered, replacing her mouth with her hand. "You got the best features from each side...Soft, curly hair and those gorgeous green eyes from your momma...Your skin is the perfect mix of light and dark..."

"And from my dad?" I asked, curious to see where she was going with this.

"From your dad, you got your incredible height and build... and this...this..."

My phone started ringing. "Hold that thought, beautiful," I said, placing my finger on her plump lips as I reached over to the table for my phone.

Lyla raised her brows in annoyance, and I shrugged my apology as I swiped my finger across the screen. "Hello."

"Colton?"

"Who else would it be, Al? You called my phone, remember?"

"Right. Are you busy?"

I looked down at the blonde who was growing very impatient. "Never too busy for you. Lyla here was just explaining to me how gifted I am." I winked.

"She's right. You're amazing. I tell you that all the time," Allie mumbled through the phone. Her tone was off, and I almost felt bad for how much it excited me to think that things hadn't gone quite the way she'd planned tonight.

"Hold on, Allie." I covered the speaker with my finger so I could deal with the beautiful blonde in my room.

"Rain check?" I asked, sliding back into my shorts.

—

Her mouth fell open. "Are you serious, Colton? You're going to pass on sex with me for a phone call?"

I sucked my bottom lip between my teeth and cocked my head to the side with a shrug. "It's important."

Lyla shook her head in disbelief. "She must be," she said, righting her clothes. "How am I gonna get home?"

Fuck. "Just go wait for me downstairs, and I'll take you when I've finished."

"Forget it. I'll call a Lyft. Call me if you change your mind."

After the door clicked shut, I lifted the phone back to my ear. "Sorry 'bout that. You okay, Al?"

"Colton Fowler! Are you with someone?" she asked, aghast.

I laughed. "Not anymore."

The line went quiet. "You got rid of your date to talk to me?"

"It wasn't a date."

I heard the cluck of her tongue. "It sure sounded like a date to me."

Ever the busybody. "It was an almost blowjob and maybe some casual sex. It wasn't a date. I don't date."

Alex gasped. "Oh my God. Oh my God, Colt. That's what you meant by gifted." She giggled. "Was she stroking your ego?"

"Among other things."

There was another quiet pause, and I thought I heard her crying. "Allie, are you all right?"

"He asked me to marry him," she offered quietly.

Fuck! Son of a bitch. It was one of those times I really hated being right.

"And what'd you say?"

CHAPTER SIX

Alexis–Age 20

AS I WAITED TO BOARD MY FLIGHT TO LOS ANGELES, I'D NEVER wished I was old enough to drink more. It was my first time flying, and I was a bundle of nerves. The acid in my stomach churned, and I felt like I was going to vomit.

My phone dinged. I slid my trembling finger across the screen and couldn't help but smile.

Colt: Hey, Allie. I can't believe you're really coming to spend the summer with me. I can't wait to see you. You're doing the right thing. Love you. Xoxo

Colt: P.S. Stop freaking out. You're not getting in my car if you smell like puke.

I laughed aloud as I typed out my reply.

Alex: If I die, you'll regret your last words, ass.

Colt: You're not going to die. But just in case...fine, you can ride in my car...but you'll have to ride naked.

Alex: I have extra clothes, idiot.

Colt: Why do you always have to take the fun out of everything?

Alex: We're boarding. See you soon.

Colt: Love ya, Al!

I filed into the plane, and after putting my carry-on in the cubby, I curled into my window seat. I put my earbuds in and shut my eyes, attempting to relax.

The plane jerked and started taxiing, and I squeezed my eyes tighter together, praying for God to just let me live through this.

A hand squeezed my knee, and I jumped. I opened my eyes to find the once empty seat beside me now occupied by an older woman. She must've been at least seventy years old. Her dark brown skin was wrinkled, and her long hair was solid white. "Virgin?" she croaked.

"I'm sorry, what?"

"You're a virgin, dearie. I can tell."

Was this woman serious? "Not that it's any of your business, but I am *not* a virgin. I haven't been for a very long time now."

She laughed 'til tears dripped from her weary eyes. "Oh, child. I meant that it's your first time flying. I couldn't care less who's been between those legs." She shook her head. "You're cute."

My cheeks flamed. "Oh." Now that I'd just made a complete idiot of myself, I didn't know what to say. I turned to stare out of the window and watched the city getting smaller and smaller beneath us.

"I'm off to spend the summer with my son and grandbabies. You?"

"That's nice," I said, smiling sweetly. "I'm spending the summer with my best friend. He goes to UCLA. A basketball player. He's really good. We haven't seen each other much in the last few years because he's always practicing."

"Ah," she said, giving me a knowing smile. "Don't waste this chance."

"Chance?"

"That's what this is, right? A chance to make him fall in love with you? To choose you?"

I shook my head. "Nah. You're wrong about this one. We're just friends...have been our entire lives. I actually have a boyfriend...well, had. I don't know what we are now."

She nodded. "What happened with the boyfriend?"

"He, ummm. He proposed, and I'm just not sure I'm ready for that, you know?"

"Have you been dating a long time?" she asked.

"A few years. I thought it was what I wanted...but when he asked, I just...I don't know. I just couldn't say yes. I told him to give me the summer to think about it."

"Can I be frank with you...?" she hesitated, waiting for my name.

"Alexis."

"Don't marry that boy, Alexis. If he were the one, you wouldn't have hesitated. A few years is enough time to know how you feel about a person. Trust me, he's not the one."

I laughed nervously. "And you can come to this conclusion after spending only a few minutes in my company?"

"Darlin' I've lived a long life. Take it from a woman who's been in your shoes. Marry the one you're running toward...not the one you're running from."

Her words struck a chord because I knew that she was right. I'd loved Colton for all of my life; I just never knew what to do about it.

"Thank you...?" I looked at her expectantly.

"Gertie. Name's Gertrude, but muh friends call me Gertie."

She showed me pictures of her grandchildren, and we talked like we'd known each other our whole lives. Gertie was an insightful woman, and I think I'd finally met my match. She barely stopped to catch her breath between stories.

—

Before long, the plane was taxiing, and I'd been so absorbed in her world that I hadn't even realized when the sick feeling in my stomach left. I thanked her for distracting me then we exchanged numbers. And as I drew closer to seeing my best friend, that awful nausea was replaced by a fluttering of butterflies. I was nervous and excited.

And I was on a mission.

When I reached the baggage claim, Colt was already there. My God, he was the most beautiful man I'd ever seen. Tears pricked my eyes as I ran into his waiting arms. Colton lifted me a good foot off the ground, swinging me from side to side as he hugged me close.

I reached up and ran my fingers through those golden brown curls I'd missed so much, and he leaned down, placing a kiss at my temple.

Tears poured from my eyes. I felt so at home for the first time in so long. Colton's arms, his smell, his curls, dimples, and those eyes...*dear God, those eyes.*

"Welcome home, Allie," he whispered, setting me on my feet. And he couldn't have spoken more perfect words.

"He's a cutie, Alex," Gertie said, appearing out of nowhere.

I laughed, and Colton gave me a confused smile. "This is my new friend, Gertie. Gertie, this is my *friend*, Colton."

Gertrude reached out her frail hand, which looked even smaller in Colton's ginormous one. "Nice to meet you, young man."

Colton smiled, revealing those panty-melting dimples. "Pleasure's all mine, ma'am. Thanks for keeping my girl company on the flight."

Gertie gave me a pair of knowing eyes, no doubt picking up on the possessive way that Colt referred to me, but it was nothing new. We'd always belonged to each other. It didn't mean anything significant.

I shook my head and hugged my new friend goodbye. Before releasing me, she whispered, "I know love when I see it. Don't let that boy go," then she kissed my cheek and swatted my behind, sending me on my way.

"So, Gertie was a character," Colt chuckled.

"Yeah." I smiled. "She's something."

I stared at him the whole drive to his house. It was surreal being there with him. We'd spoken daily, but we hadn't been alone together for so long. Even when he'd come home, Dean was always around.

We pulled up to a townhouse, and Colton turned off the car. "Before we walk into that house, I'm going to apologize in advance for my roommates. They have no manners. Al, they'll probably hit on you, but they do that to anyone with a hole between their legs. Just shrug 'em off, okay?"

Wow. I swallowed the lump in my throat. "Noted. I will not allow myself to believe that your hot college roommates could possibly find me attractive," I said, sticking my tongue out. This would be high school all over again. Only this time, I was ready to play.

"That's not what I meant, Al."

"I know. Let's go."

The rickety wood steps creaked beneath our feet as we climbed the front porch. Colton looked at me nervously before turning the key in the lock. "Don't say I didn't warn ya," he said, pushing the door open.

He moved to the side, and when I stepped into the small living room, there were two guys seated on the couch in basketball shorts. I could get used to this.

"Alex, this is Finn," Colt said, pointing to the blond, shirtless hunk on the right. "And that's Blex." He motioned to the left at the black, muscled giant with the remote in his hand.

"Nice to meet y'all," I said, grinning from ear to ear.

—

41

"Damn, bro, you didn't tell us little Alex was hot," Finn said to Colt as he stood from the couch and reached out his hand for mine. Instead of shaking it like I expected, he lifted my fingers to his lips and placed a kiss on my knuckles. "Pleasure's all mine, Lexi."

"It's Alex, asshole," Colt said, thumping him on the chest. "And remember what I said."

"What exactly did you say?" I asked, side-eyeing Colt.

He ignored that question as Blex walked over to greet me. He was a good foot and a half taller than my five feet two, and I had to crane my neck to meet his eyes. "Ignore those two idiots," he offered in a deep baritone voice that suited his large frame perfectly. "I'm Blex," he said, leaning in for a hug. Then he whispered into my ear, "And Colton is an idiot for not snatching you up when he had the chance."

I coughed to clear my throat. "Thanks," I whispered back. "I think so too."

"All right, Blex. Don't scare her off already," Colton said, walking over to grab my hand and pull me from his friend's embrace. "Let's go get you settled."

I turned back as Colt practically dragged me up the narrow, twisty stairs in the corner of the room. "So nice meeting you both!"

When I stepped into his room, a feeling of nostalgia hit me. It'd been so long since I'd shared his old bedroom with him, and although this room was different...it had that same smell that uniquely belonged to Colt. His room was much cleaner than the rest of the house, and I smiled remembering the way it used to drive him insane when I'd leave my things lying around his room.

Colt ran a hand through his hair and exhaled nervously. "We can share my bed...if that's okay, or I'll take the couch."

That we'd sleep anywhere but together had never entered my mind, but it was cute the way he tried to respect my personal space. It also made me a little sad because personal space had never existed between us before. "Together's fine,

Colt." I walked over to his dresser and found the framed photo of us from graduation, and it made me tear up. "God, we were inseparable. I miss us." My eyes welled with tears as I ran a finger over our smiling faces.

Colton walked up, wrapping his arms around my waist from behind and resting his chin on the top of my head. "We're still us, Allie." I could feel his heart beating hard against my back as I rested my head on his chest and tried to savor the moment. Now that I was there, I already dreaded the day I'd have to leave.

We stood there for a few minutes before Blex barged into the room. "Hey, guys, pizza's here!"

I was glad for the interruption. We were getting a little too close too fast. I didn't want Colt thinking that he could treat me like his girlfriend whenever he felt like it. I had to remember to distance myself. The night before he left for California was the best of my life before it became the worst. I'd sworn that it changed things. That he must've felt everything I did. I'd have left Dean in a heartbeat if Colt had given any inclination that he'd wanted me to. But he never said a word. Nothing. He left, and our roles never changed. I was a mess for weeks, and then I'd decided to make the most of what I'd had with Dean, and I had...until he proposed. Gertie was right. I realized the moment he pulled that ring out of his pocket and dropped to his knee that all I'd been doing was distracting myself from my true feelings. When I pictured my future, it wasn't with him.

"Great," I said, pulling out of Colton's arms. "I'm starved!"

"I'll be down in a sec, Al. Gonna use the restroom."

I followed Blex down the stairs to the kitchen and took a seat at the table.

"We only have a few minutes alone here, so I'll make this quick. That boy has been in love with you his entire life, Alexis Mack, and the fact that you're here and not wearing that frat boy's ring suggests to me that you feel the same. Am I right?"

My eyes widened. "Well, I...It's not that. Colt is," I sputtered.

"Exactly. I can help you get Fowls...if that's what you want.

—

So, Miss Alex, the question is…do you want Colton Fowler?"

Did I want Colton Fowler? More than anything else in this world. Could I admit that to this guy that I'd only just met? I guess I didn't have much choice. I bobbed my head up and down slowly. "More than anything," I whispered.

His smile was warm and his bright white teeth a striking contrast to his dark chocolate skin. "Then follow my lead," he said just as I heard Colt's footsteps descending the stairs.

CHAPTERSEVEN

Colton

WHEN I STEPPED OUT OF MY ROOM, FINN CORNERED ME IN THE hall. "You are so fucking in love with that girl, it's sickening."

"Whatever, dude, get outta my way."

"Fowls, you've been screwing this up for years, and if you don't fix it this summer, you might never get the chance."

"You don't think I fucking know that, Finn?" I asked, irritated as shit. If this fool could see how much I cared for Alex, why couldn't she?

"You need to make her jealous, Colton. Stop following her around like a lovesick puppy and treat her like one of your bros. Business as usual. We'll go out to the club. Have girls over to the house. Let her get a taste of what it feels like to see what she's missing. That's my advice."

For an idiot, he was making a lot of sense. I'd worn my heart on my sleeve for years, and if she couldn't see it, then what did I have to lose? I'd already lost the girl.

"All right, man. I'll give it a shot."

When I walked into the kitchen, Al was already sitting at the table with Blex, deep in conversation. "Hey, guys," I said, taking the seat beside her.

"Oh, there you are," Allie chimed with a mouth full of pizza. I laughed. "That's really hot, Alex." I dabbed the sauce dripping from the corner of her mouth with my thumb, and her face turned red. "You in the mood to go dancing?" I asked, reaching into the box for a slice of pizza.

"Really? I'd love to. I mean, I need a few hours to get dressed, but yeah!"

"A few hours? Allie, you look fine in what you have on." And she did. She was wearing a pair of jeans with a black flowy top. I saw no reason she'd need to change.

She scoffed. "I'm not going out in Los Angeles dressed like I just got off a plane, Colton Fowler. It's still early. We have time, right?" Her face was beaming. I couldn't wait to get her on the dance floor.

"Yeah, you have time, Al."

Alex wasn't exaggerating. Almost three hours after she'd gone upstairs to get ready, I finally heard her footfalls on the stairs. I turned my body on the sofa to get a good look at her, and my jaw damned near fell through the floor. *What the hell?*

Finn whistled. "Hot damn, Lexi. Those legs!"

She walked around the couch and into the living room, and I still couldn't find my voice. "Y'all ready?"

I shook my head.

"Do you need more time to get ready, Colt?" she asked innocently. Like she didn't know what her body in that tiny black dress and fuck me heels did to a man. A woman knew what she was doing when she put on a dress like that.

"Explain," I rasped.

"Huh?" She looked at me like I'd lost my mind.

"Explain what? Colt, are you okay? Are you sick?" she asked, leaning over to press the back of her hand to my forehead.

"Those," I said, staring at the cleavage that was very much on display. "Explain those."

Finn sucked in his lips, trying to hide his laughter, as Allie stood up straight, crossing her arms over her chest.

"The boobs, Alex. Explain the fucking boobs. Where'd they come from?" Those were a new development.

"Fuck, Fowler, are you trying to embarrass the girl?" Blex gritted out.

Alex shook her head. "No, it's fine. Colt's always had something to say about the size of my breasts, haven't you? First, they were too small...Now what? Too big? Too fake?"

I shook my head. "I never said your boobs were too small Alex. Why? Why'd you do that? You were perfect. Now every guy in the club's gonna be looking at you like you're trash."

The look on her face told me that was the wrong thing to say. She laughed a humorless laugh. "Now I look like trash. Please, Colton, keep going. Destroy what's left of my self-esteem while you're at it."

This was getting out of hand. "That's not what I meant."

"I didn't get boobs for you, or Dean, or anyone other than myself. I got them because they make me feel sexy. Thank you for taking that confidence away from me, Colton Fowler."

My friends both glared at me. She'd won their allegiance already. Traitors. "Take 'em back," I growled.

Finn cracked up laughing on the sofa beside me. I was gonna deck someone before we'd even left the house.

She leveled me with a murderous stare. "Fuck. You."

I wasn't done digging myself into a hole just yet. "I'll pay for it. There has to be a place somewhere around here that can remove those things and put you back to normal. It's fucking LA for God's sake...There's a plastic surgeon on every corner."

"I don't want to take them out," she gritted. "I think they look great. I could have never filled out a dress like this before.

—

What do you think, Blex?" She cupped her breasts, rotating from side to side the way girls do when they're trying on a new outfit, to give him a good look.

He choked. "Uh, I think they are some very nice breasts, Alex."

I was going to kill him. "Well, at least go change."

"I will not."

"Fucking, hell..." I said, standing from the couch. I walked over to Alex, which was mighty brave on my part, I must say because she was seconds away from castrating me. "Will you at least wear a jacket?"

"It's ninety degrees, Colton."

"I liked you better in your T-shirt and jeans," I groaned.

She shook her head, revealing the tiniest of smirks. "I didn't ask."

"Right. Let's go, then."

We took her to Night Caps, where a buddy of ours worked the door. None of us were twenty-one yet, but he always hooked us up.

While he was checking her I.D., I yelled over the music, "She's with me." Randy smiled, handing back her license and slapping a yellow bracelet on her arm.

Al looked at me hesitantly, and I nodded, ushering her inside. "Does that mean...?"

"You can buy alcohol. Just don't go crazy." I laughed, all of a sudden wondering how great of an idea this was.

Alex went directly to the bar to order her first drink. I came up behind her, handing the bartender my card. "She's with me. Put her on my tab."

"You don't have to do that, Colt." She looked back at me over her shoulder. Her lips were so close I could almost taste them. I could barely hear the bass over my own heart hammering in my chest.

I brushed a strand of hair out of her face, needing an acceptable reason to put my hands on her. "I know. I want to. Sorry 'bout earlier."

She shrugged. "It's fine. I just thought if anyone could appreciate a nice pair of tits, it'd be you," she teased, elbowing me in the stomach.

I groaned. She'd be the death of me.

We grabbed our usual table near the dance floor, and as expected, it didn't take long for the girls to begin flocking around us. Candy, a tall, lanky blonde I'd hooked up with a few times before, walked over, grinding her barely covered ass in my lap. I started to push her away and then remembered the game plan. "Let's dance?" I whispered into her ear.

Candy worked my body like a stripper on that dance floor, shaking her ass like her next meal depended on it, yet I couldn't take my eyes off of the couple dancing beside us. Alex's moves made Candy look like she was two-stepping at a country club. She and Blex commanded the attention of everyone in the room. It was scandalous and hot, and I wanted to wrap a blanket around my girl and beat the fuck out of my boy. This was not going according to plan.

I tried not to let my annoyance show...but when I glanced over to find him with his tongue down her throat, practically fucking my Allie on the dance floor, I lost it. I moved Candy aside and stalked over like a jealous boyfriend I had no right to be. I grabbed Allie's arm, yanking her out of Blex's grip. I'd deal with him later. "What the fuck, Al? You buy a pair of tits, and suddenly you're a slut? Did you sell your self-respect to pay for 'em?"

The slap that followed nearly brought me to my knees, and I knew I deserved it, but I was never one to give up while I was ahead. I traced the edge of the thin scrap of fabric that did little to hide her quivering breasts. She stood there staring at me with hurt and disdain, but she didn't move my hand, and she didn't walk away. "You like that, Allie?" I asked, dipping my finger just inside. "If you wanted to be touched, all you had

—

49

to do was ask. Wanna see what it's like to be with a real man before you decide if married life's for you?"

"All right, man. That's enough," Blex said, stepping up beside Alex.

With both hands, I shoved at Blex's chest. He barely budged. I wanted to hurt him, to take every ounce of frustration I felt out on him, but it would have to wait because when I heard her scream and saw the look of fear that crossed her face just before she turned and ran off, nothing else mattered.

I chased after Alex and finally caught up to her in the parking lot. "Come back, Allie. I'm sorry."

She kept walking quickly. "This was a mistake. I-I shouldn't have come here."

"Don't say that, Al. I'm a jerk and I'm sorry, but I'm still so happy you're here. Please don't go. I'll be better."

Alex stopped walking but kept her back to me. "I don't know where to go," she whispered.

"With me, Al. Just come home with me."

"I don't like you right now," she cried, rubbing her nose with the back of her hand.

I walked up behind her and wrapped my arms around her waist, and her body tensed. "I don't like me either," I agreed.

We stood there in silence for a few minutes before she finally gave in. "Let's go home."

When we arrived back at the house, much to my surprise, Allie went right up to my room. I moved to follow her, and Blex darted his arm out in front of me. "You need to give her some space, man. What was that? I thought you were friends?"

I whirled around to face him. "I thought *we* were friends, man," I said, shoving him. "What the hell was that?"

Blex leaned in close. "I don't know what that was, Colt, but you better get your shit together before you scare Alex off. That big brother shit isn't going to fly anymore."

"Leave Alex alone."

"You staking your claim?" Blex asked, and I started to tell him that hell yeah, I was...but I looked up and found Allie peeking out of my bedroom door and decided to stick to the plan. I couldn't risk her overhearing, and Blex would never understand the game I was playing with Alex. He'd already attached himself to her, and having three sisters of his own, I knew there was no way he'd approve. Besides, laying my heart at her feet for her to trample on hadn't worked out so well for me in the past, and I needed this to work.

"Nah, man. Just protective of her is all."

Blex sucked his teeth and nodded. "No worries. I won't disrespect her. I'm not looking to get into her panties. We're just having a little fun, but if you don't want to send her right back to Texas, then you better go do some groveling."

He was right. I really fucked up tonight. I nodded my head and pushed past him. "See you tomorrow. I've got an ass to go kiss," I called out as I made my way up to my room.

I pretended not to notice Al when she pulled her head inside and even walked a little slower to allow time for her to get away. Shaking my head to myself, I pushed the door open and found her perched on the end of my bed, still seething, acting as if she'd been there the whole time.

I'd had only seconds to brace myself for the tongue lashing that was about to ensue. Alex flew off of my bed as soon as the door clicked shut, her mouth running a mile a minute, and all I could think about was getting that little black dress off and having a good look at those man-made tatas.

"Are you even listening to me?" she shrieked, jabbing her finger into my chest.

I shook my head and lifted my gaze from her cleavage. "I'm sorry, what?"

"Were you just staring at my boobs, Colton Fowler?" She was incredulous.

I chewed on my bottom lip nervously. "I'm sorry. They're, uh. Well...they're distracting, Al." I shrugged.

—

She rolled her eyes. "They're just boobs, Colt. I'm still just Allie."

"You were never *just* anything," I answered a little too honestly. *How much had I drunk?* I was screwing the plan up before it ever even got started.

"I really want to be mad at you right now...but I think I'm gonna—"

Before I had time to move away, Allie gripped the front of my shirt and puked all over us both. Then she covered her mouth and took off running to my bathroom, leaving a trail of vomit the whole way. *Lovely.*

I followed behind her to make sure that she was okay, but ended up slipping in a puddle of slime. I'm sure to anyone watching, the scene would have been comedic, but it was pretty high up there on the worst moments of my life. My clothes...my hands...everything was coated in pink puke. The smell, oh dear God, the smell. I started to gag as I pushed myself up and got to the bathroom just in time to empty my stomach into the sink.

What a sight the two of us must've been.

After we'd both emptied the contents of our stomachs, we took turns showering, cleaned up, and fell into bed. I was just starting to doze off when I heard Allie whimpering beside me. "What's wrong, Al?" God, I'd always hated to see my girl cry.

She shook her head, sniveling.

"Are you still mad at me?"

"Yes, but that's not why I'm crying."

Ouch. "Okay, then why are you crying?"

"I think I cheated on Dean tonight...I haven't kissed anyone else since the summer we got together. That's not what I came here for."

"Was it that forgettable? Jesus, Allie." How could she forget the night before California? She had kissed someone else. She'd kissed me. That night...it meant everything, and apparently, it also meant nothing.

She gasped. "No, I...I don't know. I try not to think about

that night, to be honest."

Was she trying to gut me? "No?" I cleared my throat. "Did you feel guilty then?"

"No," she whispered. "No, I didn't..."

I didn't know how to respond to that. We laid in silence for a few minutes before I could hear her softly snoring. What a disaster our first day together had been.

CHAPTEREIGHT

Alexis

I FELT A HAND ON MY SHOULDER SHAKING ME AWAKE. "STOP IT, Dean," I mumbled, swatting it way.

"Sorry to disappoint...it's just me," Colton replied.

It took a moment in my sleepy state to remember where I was, and when I did, I wanted to die of mortification at the huge puddle of drool that I was laying in. I sat up quickly, wiping my mouth with the back of my hand. "Hey, you, time for practice already?" I asked, rubbing the sleep from my eyes. It couldn't have been much past 6:00 a.m.

Colt smiled at my disheveled state. "Yeah. I just wanted to tell you bye before I left. Didn't want to sleep with you and run," he joked.

"Ha-ha. What time will you be home?" I asked, missing him already.

Colton reached out, tucking a strand of hair behind my ear. "A little after noon. You wanna go out for lunch when I get back? I can show you around a little if you're up for it."

God, he was beautiful as ever in his muscle shirt and mesh

shorts. I had a strong urge to push him down on the bed and—

I heard a low, throaty chuckle at the same time that I felt his finger tipping my chin up. "Do I have something on my shorts? You're, uh...staring pretty hard there, Allie..."

Shit. "No..." I said, feeling myself blush from the top of my head to the tips of my toes. "Just spaced out for a sec. I think maybe I'm still drunk." The drunken part wasn't a lie. I felt like death, and I didn't even want to know what I looked like at that moment.

"Uh-huh, sure," he said with a wink as he rose to his feet and retrieved his keys and phone from the nightstand.

"Ugh," I groaned when my stomach revolted with the shifting of the mattress. I couldn't believe they'd let me get so drunk on my first night in LA. "Food isn't sounding so great at the moment," I said, clutching my abdomen and rolling over.

"You need to eat. Trust me, you'll feel so much better. I'll see you in a couple hours."

I groaned my approval, giving him the thumbs up as I shoved my face down into his pillow. I heard the sound of his laughter followed by the door opening and closing. Why'd it feel like he was *leaving* me all over again? I mean, he was going to practice, but that didn't account for the level of sadness I felt. It was like I'd been swallowed by a black cloud the moment he exited the room.

As soon as I'd finally fallen back asleep, my phone started to ring. Without checking the name, I grabbed it from the bedside table and answered.

"Alexis?" *Dean.* "Are you okay, baby? You sound sick."

A pit formed in my stomach at the concern in his voice. Dean was the perfect guy. I knew that I didn't deserve him, and he certainly didn't deserve what I was doing to him. "Hey, yeah...rough night," I croaked, feeling tears pool in my eyes.

The warm sound of his laugh made my throat burn with guilt. "Party girl," he teased. And the worst part was that it was genuine. There wasn't an ounce of jealousy or judgment.

I *had* to tell him what happened. We'd left things so up in

—

the air, but there wasn't a clear break up. I wasn't sure where we stood anymore, but it felt wrong. I let out a loud sob as I tried to find the words to tell him.

"Shit. Are you okay? I was just teasing. Where's Fowls?" I didn't cry often, and the sound of my hysterical sobbing was really freaking him out.

"Dean," I crooned. "I, umm. I did something last night."

The other side of the line went quiet as he waited for me to finish. I heard his throat clear, but I guessed he wasn't going to say anything, so I continued. "I-I kissed someone."

"Fuck. I fucking knew it!" he shouted. I heard a loud thumping like he was kicking or punching something.

"Huh? You knew what?"

The sound of his angry breathing was scaring me. Dean didn't get mad...maybe a little annoyed from time to time, but he'd never lost his cool with me. Not that I didn't expect him to be upset, but I guess I just really didn't understand his reaction. "I need to know one thing..." There was a desperation in his tone that made me feel sick to my stomach. "Was it him? Was it Fowler?"

I wanted to be angry that he automatically assumed it was Colt, but what a hypocrite that would have made me. I had kissed Colton while we were together, and without a doubt, I'd do it again. Still, I was unjustly perturbed. "What fucking difference does it make who it was, Dean?"

"I just...I need to know. Please answer the question. It matters." His voice broke, causing my heart to tighten in my chest. "It fucking matters to me."

"No," I whispered. "No...it wasn't Colton."

Dean released a loud sigh of relief, followed by a terse laugh. "Okay. Okay. That's good."

"What's good, Dean? You aren't making any sense. You think it's good that I kissed someone else?" What was even happening?

"You're confused..." he started in a much calmer voice. "You need to be sure. I get that. It's okay. We can...we can work

—

57

through this."

"And what if I'd told you it was Colton? What then?"

"Then..." He let out a humorless laugh. "Well, then I'd know I didn't stand a chance." It felt like someone had just knocked the wind from my sails as my traitorous heart crumbled into a million tiny pieces.

"Dean...I'm so sorry," I muttered through a steady stream of tears because I was. I didn't know what else to say. I couldn't sit there and deny my feelings for Colton, knowing full and well that he was the reason I couldn't say yes. That if I was honest with myself, I needed this summer, not to see how I felt about Dean, but to find out once and for all how Colton felt about me. Because, in all actuality, Dean would always be the consolation prize. I just never knew that he'd realized it too.

"Don't cry, baby. It's going to be okay." How'd we get from me cheating on him to him consoling me?

"Dean, I think we need a break..." I blurted out, feeling overwhelmed by his willingness to forgive so easily. I didn't deserve his forgiveness, and selfishly I didn't want it. This would all be so much easier if he were anything but absolutely perfect.

His nervous laughter filled the line. "I thought that's what this was?"

"Not just time apart...I think we need to break up."

"What are you saying?" The fear in his voice about did me in. "Is this...are you saying your answer is no?"

"I'm saying I don't know, Dean," I cried. "I'm saying that I can't have a boyfriend and kiss other guys. I can't stand knowing that I'm even capable of doing that to you and that you're just there waiting around for me."

"Whether we're broken up or not, I'll be waiting. You're it for me, baby." Another jab at my heart. When did I become such an awful person?

"I want the summer off...I need time to figure out what I want, and you should do the same. At the end of the summer, if you still want to be with me, I'll give you my answer."

"Do you still love me, Alexis?" he asked in a broken whisper.

"Yes," I answered truthfully and without hesitation. Whether I loved Dean or not wasn't in question. I'd just always loved Colton more.

"Then, I'll wait."

"What the? Why aren't you dressed?"

"Huh?" I asked, disoriented as I came out of a deep sleep. I peeled my tear-swollen eyes open to find Colton towering over me at the foot of the bed with the comforter clutched in his hands. "Don't you da—"

Before I could finish my sentence, he'd already yanked the blanket off and tossed it to the floor. "Get up, Al." I wanted to curse him from here to China, but he looked so excited, practically bouncing in his shoes.

"Colton..." I whined. "It's cold." His room always felt like a meat cooler, and this one was no different. With the thermostat set on sixty-five, ceiling fan on full blast, and a box fan on high in the corner, my teeth were actually chattering.

"Don't make me do it," he warned, smiling at me with the devil in his emerald eyes. He placed both hands on the mattress, crouching over like he was getting ready to pounce.

My heart started to race. "You wouldn't..."

"One," he started, lifting one knee onto the foot of the bed and moving forward just a smidge. "Two," he continued, raising his brows in a challenge.

"I'm not feeling well, Colt." I hugged my knees to my chest, which I realized was suddenly feeling lighter in his presence. My entire body tensed in anticipation of the attack I knew was coming.

"Three," he finished, reaching for one of my feet and pulling it to him, where he began his favorite method of torture.

"Stop!" I shrieked, flopping around the bed like a fish out

of water. "We're too old for this," I screamed, kicking and thrashing as I tried to relinquish my foot from his hold. It was a wasted effort. Colton was so much bigger than me. "I'm gonna pee!" I yelled, trying to hold it in.

Colton finally released my foot, and I came up swinging. He grabbed my fists in his hands, easily stopping my assault, and brought them down to my sides. We were on our knees in the middle of his bed, our faces red with laughter, our eyes glistening with mirth. Our chests heaving with exhaustion, our bodies less than a foot apart.

Electricity buzzed between us, and for a moment, I was sure that Colt was about to kiss me. I closed my eyes, leaning in closer. And then as if a switch had been flipped, he dropped my hands and hopped out of bed, leaving me dazed and feeling rejected.

Colt's eyes took in my sports bra and booty shorts. He cleared his throat, and his tongue darted out to wet his lip. "Put some clothes on, Allie, and meet me downstairs."

I stared after him without breathing a word as he headed for the door. "Colt," I squeaked just before it closed. Instantly, I regretted calling him back. Even I could hear the desperation in my voice.

Colton's head peered back in, regret clearly written in the dip of his brow and the downturn of his lips. "Get dressed," he practically begged. He stared at me a moment longer, my skin heating wherever his eyes passed. Then he schooled his features, seeming to get ahold of himself. "If you're not down in fifteen minutes, I'm going to drag you out in that."

I stared at the closed door for a minute or two after he left before scrambling to make myself presentable in the time I had remaining. I didn't doubt for a second that Colton Fowler had every intention to make good on his promise.

—

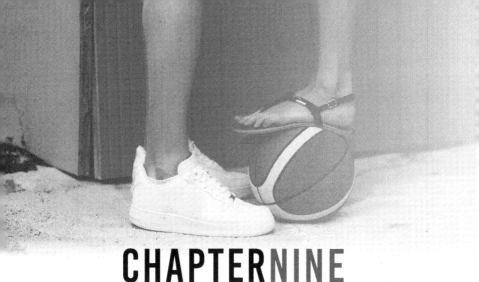

CHAPTERNINE

Colton

WITH LESS THAN A MINUTE TO SPARE, ALLIE CAME RUSHING DOWN the stairs dressed in a pair of cut-off jean shorts and the UCLA tank I sent to her for her birthday. Her hair was in a knot on the top of her head, and she wore large sunglasses to cover her red-rimmed eyes.

I pretended not to notice that she'd been crying when I woke her, mostly because I'd already ruined her first night and just wanted to see her smile. Also, because I was afraid that she was truly having regrets about coming here and I needed to change her mind before she up and left.

"Is this okay?" she asked, glancing down at her outfit while smoothing out the invisible creases in her shirt. "I have no idea where you're taking me...I can go and ch—"

"You look fine," I answered, trying not to go overboard. Alex was beautiful in anything. Feigning indifference with her would not be easy. Not when she made my heart race like this. Not when the mere sight of her made breathing nearly impossible.

"You sure? I didn't even have time to put on any makeup...

Can I have just a few more minutes?" She puckered out her bottom lip, sliding the glasses down the bridge of her nose while giving me the most pitiful puppy dog eyes. Red-hot lava coursed through my veins. I wanted so badly to suck that lip into my mouth. Shaking my head, I walked over to grab her arm. "Put those weapons away." I pushed her glasses up with my index finger. "They won't work today. It's already after one, and I'm starving." I rubbed my stomach. "You know how hungry I get after playing ball."

When we got on the road, I put into motion operation *Cheer Allie Up* with a song I'd downloaded while waiting for her to get dressed. I knew it would bring up a slew of memories for her, just as it always had for me. "Sha la la la la la la la la la la ti da," I sang, tapping my thumbs to the beat against the steering wheel while watching her face light up from the corner of my eye.

Alex kicked off her flip-flops, curling her legs up in her seat, smiling and blushing while I sang along to her song— our song. It was the song I'd been singing to my brown-eyed girl for as long as I could remember. Often times belting it out when we passed each other in the halls of Mercer High. She'd turn bright red, pretending to be pissed, but I knew deep down that she loved it. It was us, Allie and Colt.

"Every time I hear this song, I think of you," she said, beaming as the last chords played. "Nothing's the same when you're not around."

My heart clenched at her admission. "What? Are you telling me Dean doesn't serenade you in the grocery store?" I teased, remembering a time when her song came on at the Piggly Wiggly, and I just couldn't help myself. Her dad joined in, and we sang at the top of our lungs, drawing the attention of everyone around. We didn't care that they stared or whispered. Getting a reaction out of Allie was more than worth it.

She scoffed. "Um...no."

"No worries, Al. If embarrassment is what you seek, you've come to the right place." I winked as I flipped on the blinker,

—

turning in to the parking lot of Moe's.

"What is this place?" Her nose was scrunched as she looked around in disgust.

"It's not much to look at, but trust me, the food is fantastic. This is just what you need to cure that hangover."

Moe's was a hole in the wall located off a back road just outside of campus. The building was small and old. There was probably more paint chipped off the wood exterior than not. But, the inside was clean and the service top notch. It was the best place I'd found since moving to LA for when I was in the mood for some good southern cooking.

I glanced over to Alex as we approached the sagging steps and had to laugh at her upturned nose and pinched lips. "This place is really old, Colt...You sure it's sanitary?"

"Think of it as vintage, like a fine wine, aged to perfection."

She rolled her eyes as I opened the door, and with a hand on her lower back, ushered her inside. "After you."

"*Colton*...it's been a few days," Sally, our waitress, purred before realizing Alex was with me. "And you brought a friend." She eyed her up and down, giving Alexis an obviously fake smile. *This would be fun.*

"Hey, Sal," I said, wrapping my arm around Allie's shoulders and pulling her close. "This is my best friend, Alexis. She's staying with me for the summer."

"Oh, how nice..."

I fought hard not to laugh at the pained expressions on both girls' faces as they shook hands. At the way Allie rubbed hers against the side of her shirt like she was wiping off something dirty afterward.

There was an awkward moment of silence before Sally remembered herself, grabbed our menus, and began leading us to a table. While taking our drink orders, she kept a hand on my shoulder, clearly trying to send Alex a message. By the tight lips and narrowed eyes homed in on me from across the table, I'd say that it was being received. Loud and clear.

"You had sex with her, didn't you?" Alex leaned across the

table and hissed as soon as we were left alone.

I bit back a smile as I set my menu on the table. "No," I answered briefly and truthfully. I hadn't realized Sally was working today, or most likely I wouldn't have brought Allie here. She's usually off on Saturdays and Sundays, and I really was trying to make up for last night. But luck must've been on my side because the venom in Alex's tone just confirmed that Finn was right. She was jealous. I just had to feed that jealousy enough to make her as desperate for me as I was for her.

Alexis scoffed. "Yeah, okay," she muttered.

"I didn't."

"I don't believe you."

Reaching out across the table, I took her hand, relishing in the slight flush of her cheeks at the contact. "I've never lied to you before, Alexis Mack. Why would I lie about this? I have no reason to…"

She shrugged, pulling her hand away and lowering her shades to cover her eyes, which were beginning to water. "You did something…"

I nodded just as Sally walked up behind Alex. She licked her lips, drinking me in. Clearly, she'd heard the end of that conversation and was doing all she could to confirm that suspicion. "What can I get for you, Colton?"

"Ladies first," I answered, directing her attention to the woman seething across from me. I wanted to make her jealous. I didn't, however, have any desire to make her hate me.

Sally nodded, reluctantly turning to face Alex. "Do you know what you want?" She wasn't exactly rude, but her tone lacked any warmth.

My girl cleared her throat. "Bring us a few hamburger steaks and mashed potatoes with gravy." Allie reached out, snatching the menu from my hand and shoving them both toward Sally, effectively dismissing her.

I felt my eyes widen as our waitress stormed off. This time, I couldn't help but laugh at the pissing match before me.

"What's so funny, Colt?" She was *pissed*.

—

I shook my head, still laughing. "Nothing, Al."

"I don't like her."

"I can see that. Any particular reason?"

She leaned back in her chair, crossing her arms over her ample chest. "I just think she's rude, don't you?"

Pressing my lips together, I shook my head slightly. "She's not usually, no."

Allie shrugged. "It's a girl thing, Colt. You wouldn't understand..." She turned her head to glare in the direction Sally just went. "She was doing it on the sly."

I had to bite the insides of my cheeks to keep from laughing again because nothing that just went down with these two women was anything but blatantly obvious. I nodded my head in agreement, realizing the need to tread lightly. I wasn't about to risk turning that anger in my direction with words. My mouth had a way of getting me into trouble.

"*So...*" Allie drew out after a quiet moment, drumming her nails on the wood table.

"Yes?"

"You were saying?"

My brow quirked in question. "About?" I knew exactly what she was fishing for, but to be honest, it felt really fucking good to watch her squirm a little.

Alexis sighed. "Finish telling me what happened with waitress girl back there." She tilted her head back, waving her hand in the air toward the kitchen area.

"Does it matter?"

"Call me curious."

Shit. This felt like a trap. "She, uh..." Al looked at me expectantly as I glanced around the room to be sure that Sally was nowhere in sight and that the handful of other customers weren't listening in. "She suckedmydick," I mumbled.

I watched her throat move as she swallowed hard, nodding her head. "You seem to really like blowjobs..." she observed loudly.

"Show me a man who doesn't," I challenged.

—

65

Alex cleared her throat, shifting in her seat. "Did you two date?"

"I don't date."

"Like at all?" Alexis asked, bewildered as if she didn't already know. As if I hadn't told her this countless times before.

"Like at all," I echoed.

Alex huffed, looking simultaneously confused and impressed. "So, girls just suck your dick expecting nothing in return?" she asked at the exact moment that Sally approached our table to deliver our lunch.

Our plates were set down in front of us with a little more force than necessary. Sally moved to walk off but thought better of it. Placing both hands on the table in front of Alex, she leaned in close. "Some girls simply enjoy pleasing a man. It doesn't always have to be about getting something in return."

"Oh, I'm aware...Where I'm from, we call those girls sluts."

CHAPTER TEN

Alexis

THINGS WERE BEGINNING TO GET ROWDY DOWNSTAIRS AS I RIFLED through my side of the closet, trying to figure out what I was going to wear. I needed to make Colton notice me, but I also didn't want to look out of place.

When we'd returned from lunch, Finn had informed us that he'd invited everyone over for a kegger tonight. By the sounds of it, "everyone" was a lot of fucking people, and I was more than a little nervous. I had no clue what to wear to a college party. Dean and I didn't go to those things, at least not to any that sounded like whatever was taking place beneath me.

As I was stripping out of my purple dress for the third time, Colt's message alert sounded.

Colton: Where are you? Get down here!

Me: I don't know what to wear.

Colton: Something baggy. Really fucking baggy.

Rolling my eyes, I slipped the plum dress back over my

head. It was short, ending mid-thigh, with a scandalously low V-neck, held up by thin spaghetti straps. What I loved most about the new girls was that they were always perky with or without a bra. Colton's message was exactly the push I needed to forgo the strapless booby trap that I'd just be adjusting all night anyway. He'd notice all right...Hopefully, I wouldn't piss him off too much.

I slipped my feet into a pair of strappy silver gladiator sandals then sprayed a little perfume on my neck before inhaling a few deep breaths and heading down to join the party.

My heart raced as I gripped the banister tightly in my sweaty hand, feeling a little disoriented as I descended the twisty stairs. The music was so loud that I couldn't hear my own thoughts above the bass pounding in my head. During the few hours I'd spent getting ready, the living room had been transformed into a dance floor, complete with strobe lights and a fog machine. There was a DJ set up in the corner and a handful of girls on the dance floor, grinding all over one another. The furniture had been pushed up against the far wall where there were already couples getting hot and heavy with their tongues down each other's throats and hands pawing away beneath their clothes.

"There you are," Blex said, intercepting me at the bottom of the steps. *Instant relief.* The guy was a saint.

"Hey, you." I beamed, taking his hand as he led me to the kitchen. "You guys work fast."

"Yeah," he agreed, smiling back at me over his shoulder while filling a Solo cup from one of the kegs that were now taking up the space where the kitchen table sat just a few hours earlier. As he handed me the cup, Blex's eyes gave me a once-over. He sucked in a deep breath, scrubbing his jaw in his hand. "Very nice, Miss Alexis." He nodded with an appreciative smile. "Fowls is going to shit when he sees you."

I gave him an exaggerated wink. "That's the plan."

"Brace yourself," Blex warned, placing a warm hand on my lower back as Colton strode over with yet *another* blond bimbo on his arm. *So, apparently, blondes and blowjobs were his thing.*

I fought hard to keep my emotions from showing on my face as I smiled at my best friend and his latest Hoover. "Hey, Colt!"

His eyes were scathing as they scanned my body. Colt cleared his throat, opening his mouth to say something before quickly clamping it shut. From the corner of my eye, I saw Blex shaking his head slightly.

"You look nice," I said, running a hand down the front of his white button down. I swallowed the saliva pooling in my mouth. He didn't just look nice. He looked...*delicious.* Colt had traded his signature mesh shorts for khaki cargos and his Jordans for Sperrys. His white shirt was cuffed at the elbows, and his hair was a fluff of wild, tousled curls. I fought the urge to lick his jaw—the desire to feel the day-old scruff growing on his face against my tongue. He looked like summer. Momentarily, I was taken back to weeks spent at the beach. Memories of the two of us lounging in the sand for days on end flooded my head. Catching starfish and hermit crabs and storing them in buckets as temporary pets for the duration of our stay.

The rough sound of Blex clearing his throat brought me back to reality, making me realize I'd been standing there with my hand on Colton's chest far longer than anyone would deem appropriate. His heart was thundering against my fingers, matching the erratic rhythm of my own. "Sorry," I whispered, snatching my hand away.

"You're fine...It's fine, Allie," he rasped, clearing a ball of emotion from his throat. The way he looked at me at times— the way he was looking at me right in that very moment—had me questioning how it could even be possible that he didn't feel what I felt. But if he felt this too, why the games? Why the girls?

"I'm Lyla," the blonde on Colton's arm announced, extending her hand in my direction, breaking the trance I'd obviously needed help getting out of. If she'd noticed that I'd

—

been fawning over her—*whatever Colt was to her*—she didn't let it show.

The kind smile on her face and the softness of her voice had my stomach churning with guilt. "Nice to meet you, Lyla." I reached back, shaking her hand. "I'm Alex."

Recognition dawned on her face, and she burst out laughing.

Colton's head hung, his hand lifting to pinch the bridge of his nose, and I swear I heard the word "shit" groaned in his voice despite the music and conversations taking place all around us.

I looked over to Blex, who shrugged his shoulders. Apparently, he wasn't in on the joke either.

"What's so funny?" I asked, feeling less guilty and more annoyed.

"It was you." She shook her head with a resigned smile. "I was the one with Colton..."

"Umm, okay." Did she think she was special or something? From what I could tell, Colt was *with* a lot of girls.

Colt looked up at me beneath his thick dark lashes, nibbling on his bottom lip.

"I was about to suck his dick when he got your call and sent my ass packin'." She elbowed Colton. "It was her, right?"

He mouthed the words, "I'm sorry," as he bobbed his head slowly.

"Dayum, girl. Is your pussy made of gold or something? I must say, I've never had a man snatch his dick out of my hand and shove it back in his pants like that."

Heat filled my cheeks...my neck...I felt it radiating in my ears. "We're not...Colt and I aren't like that. We're just friends." I felt like I would faint on the spot, but Blex's hand reached out for mine, steadying me.

Lyla eyed me suspiciously. "You sure, honey?"

I raised the cup in my hand to my lips, downing its contents. "Yup...*Best* friends. Right, Colt?"

For a moment, he had this blank stare, and I didn't know how to read it. "The best," he finally agreed with a smile that didn't reach his eyes.

"Dance with me?" Blex asked, presenting me with a fresh beer. I hadn't even noticed when he'd left my side to grab it. He was like my guardian angel sent to look out for me. I was so grateful for his presence.

"Thank you." I smiled up at my new friend, taking the drink from his hand. He was offering me an escape, and at that moment, I needed one desperately. "I'd love to."

Blex was an incredible dancer, and the more I drank, the more I began to enjoy the feel of his hard body rubbing up against mine. I wanted him to touch me. To kiss me. But Blex was the perfect gentleman, thwarting all my advances, which would have been a good thing...If only I wasn't totally shit faced. If I hadn't got an eye full of Lyla straddling my best friend on the couch. If her tongue weren't down his throat. If that bitch wasn't dry humping my Colton right in front of my fucking face. If my heart hadn't damn near stopped beating in my chest.

"Blex," I whimpered, squeezing his arm.

"It's okay, Alex...Don't look." He shook his head, disappointment written in every crease on his face. "He's a fucking idiot."

"Blex," I whimpered again. The alcohol, my emotions... everything was hitting me all at once. "I-I really need you to kiss me right now." Colton had reduced me to begging a man to kiss me. I'd never forgive him for this.

My new friend bit his bottom lip, shaking his head to himself. "I can't. I promised Fowls...he'd kill me." He started to move the thumb of the hand at my back in soothing strokes. Blex thought that he was comforting me, but he was only making things worse. I didn't want to be comforted. I wanted to retaliate. I wanted revenge. I wanted to gouge my eyes from my head because I couldn't *un-see* this. To cut my heart from my chest and stomp on it repeatedly 'til it was numb, because I couldn't *un-feel* this.

And then I sort of lost it. "Fuck. Him," I spat, backing away from Blex, my fists tightly clenched to my chest as if I could squeeze hard enough to stop the pain radiating deep within.

"Please don't be mad at me, Alex," Blex begged as I continued backing away with my eyes glued to the train wreck on the couch. What they say is true. I couldn't stop watching them no matter how much it was ripping me apart.

"I'm not. I just...I need to be alone. I need some air."

He nodded as I finally tore my eyes away and hauled ass, pushing through the crowds of people until I made it through the back door. It was the middle of the night, and I needed to talk to someone. Only one person knew how I felt about Colton, and she had told me to contact her if I needed anything. I was too drunk and desperate to care that it was far too late to be texting a woman of her age. Fishing my phone from my clutch, I pulled up Gertie's number. I sat on the edge of the cement patio and poured my drunken heart out to my eighty-year-old friend. *I was a loser.*

> **Me:** Hey. It's me, Alex. I know it's like after midnight, and you're old so you're probably sleeping and won't get this 'til morning, but there's this party at Colton's house, and he's practically having sex with this blond bitch right now in the living room. I just...I have no one to talk to. No one else knows about my feelings for Colton...I hope it's okay that I'm messaging you.

> **Me:** Shit. I just realized I called you old. Damnit. I didn't mean that. I'm sorry. You're so nice. I'm so drunk and sad. Let's have lunch soon. K?

I was about to send another drunk text when a red Solo cup appeared before my face. Wrapped around that Solo cup was a very sexy hand. One I didn't recognize. It was too white to be Colt or Blex and too thick to be Finn...I followed the arm it was attached to, finding an even more attractive man. Was Gertie a fairy godmother? Had she sent my prince to rescue me?

"You look like you could use a drink," Prince Charming said, squatting to sit beside me. He was really tall. His legs stuck out a good two feet past mine into the yard.

I cleared my throat, swatting away tears. "Th-thank you," I stammered, taking the drink from him.

"Rough night?" His brow dipped with the question, and I found myself staring at his chiseled jaw. His bright blue eyes. The spikey, cotton-blond hair that topped his head. I could certainly do worse. He was like a beefed-up version of Dean. *Dean.* What I wouldn't give to be in his arms right now. To have him ease this ache in my chest. Why couldn't I just be satisfied with what I knew was good for me?

I took a pull from my beer. "It was awful."

"I'm sorry to hear that. Anything I can do to help?"

Yes! My drunken mind was coming up with all sorts of wonderful ideas. Fucking my brains out in front of Colton being at the tippy-top of that list.

"Maybe..." I slurred. "Are you a prince?" I giggled to myself. I knew he wasn't. I was drunk, not insane, but I felt like indulging myself a little. Silly felt good, and I was grasping at straws.

A loud, boisterous laugh boomed from his chest. "Hardly."

"Are you a friend of Colton's?" Just saying his name caused a lump to form in my throat.

His lips puckered, turning to the side. "Meh. Not really. We do play ball together, though."

Even better. "What's your name?"

"I'm Stephan. Stephan Young. What's yours, pretty girl?" He thinks I'm pretty...I like him. I like him very much. He's cute and nice, and he seems to like me back...He also doesn't like Colt very much. We have so much in common already.

"I'm Alexis, or Alex, or Allie, and sometimes Colt calls me Al. But don't call me that. He's the only one that does, and I'm kind of mad at him right now."

Stephan huffed out a laugh. "Got it..." He tucked a finger under my chin, turning my face up to his. "Alexis," he rasped,

—

73

and oh my God, my name on his lips was an aphrodisiac. His face moved closer. I could smell the beer on his breath, and I wanted to taste it. "So, you and Fowler?"

"Are just friends...maybe not even that right now," I whispered as my eyes fluttered closed and my heart lurched.

Soft, pliant lips molded to mine as he dipped his tongue into my mouth and tangled it around my own. I felt so many things, and all of them were wrong, but it felt so good that I didn't even care. Stephan laid my body on the ground, cradling my head in his hand to keep it from resting on the cement. His other hand cupped my thigh, squeezing gently. Conflicting thoughts swirled in my mind. One moment I was afraid he'd take things too far, and in the next, I was bucking against him and practically begging him to do just that. Feelings of fullness and emptiness warred inside me. I wanted this. I wanted it so bad...but when I closed my eyes, the ones looking back at me were green, not blue. When I reached up to grip his hair, my heart plummeted in my chest. It's just fucking hair. Why were tears rolling down my cheeks? Why was I suddenly sniveling in the arms of the man who was to be my revenge? Why hadn't Colton walked outside yet? I needed him to see what I saw. To hurt like I hurt.

"Shhh," Stephan crooned, rubbing my back as he helped me to sit. My hands went to the sides of my head and squeezed in an attempt to keep the room from spinning. "It's okay. I think you might have had a little too much to drink tonight, Alexis. Let's get you on up to bed, huh?"

"You're really nice," I offered as he walked me through the crowd and helped to guide me up the treacherous stairs. "This one," I said, pointing to Colton's bedroom door.

"Fowler's room, huh?" He eyed me skeptically.

I shrugged, rolling my eyes. "It's nothing. Trust me. We've been sleeping together since we were babies."

Stephan's brows shot straight up, and he chuckled at my poor word choice.

I slapped my palm to my forehead. "Like in the same bed.

—

Not like...you know..."

He touched a finger to my lips. "I knew what you meant."

"I know." I paused to hiccup. "I know it seems weird to most people, but we're like brother and sister." I nodded, feeling bile rise in my throat. I didn't have any siblings, but I knew without a doubt that what I felt for Colton was anything but sisterly.

"Well, in that case..." His face lit up. Gosh, he was so handsome. "Can I take you out tomorrow night?"

"I'd love that," I said a little too eagerly as I sat on the bed to remove my shoes. Colton wouldn't be happy. That thought brought a smile to my lips.

"Great, I'll pick you up at five?"

"It's a date," I answered just as Colton came barreling through the door. His eyes went first to me, sitting on the bed. Seeming satisfied to find that I was still clothed, he turned his attention to Stephan. "What the fuck do you think you're doing with my girl in my fucking room?"

Stephan's lips curled into a smirk. "Your girl, huh? Funny, that's not the story I heard from Alexis here." His head tipped in my direction. "Tell me, Fowls, while she's been crying on my shoulder for the last hour...where were you?"

Colton's face fell.

"Yeah...How's Lyla?" Stephan snarled, shaking his head. Colton said nothing. What could he say? "That's what I thought...I'll see you tomorrow, pretty girl."

I nodded my head with new tears streaming down my cheeks as Stephan shouldered past Colton on his way out.

The room was quiet after Stephan left, aside from my sniveling and Colton's heavy breaths. He kept looking at me... *glaring at me.* What the fuck did he have any right to be angry over?

I got up from the bed, stumbling over to the dresser to grab a tank top and shorts to sleep in. Acting as if Colt was not even in the room, I went about my business, setting my clothes on the bed and fighting to free myself from the dress that I'd taken off and on so many times with ease just a few hours ago.

—

Stupid alcohol.

Warm fingers grazed my skin as Colton's hand appeared at my back, sliding the zipper down my dress. My whole body quaked at his touch, traitorous bitch that she was. I closed my eyes and visions of he and Lyla on the couch came back, making it easier to ignore his effect on me. I slipped the spaghetti straps down my arms, allowing the dress to pool at my feet.

Colt's breath hitched behind me, and I ignored that too, taking my time to cover the breasts I could feel him staring at. I was just drunk enough not to care that he was seeing me naked. After slipping the top over my head, I bent to step into my shorts and nearly fell on my face when there was a loud *thud*. My head jerked up at the sound, finding Colton kicking and punching the door.

Had I not been so inebriated, I probably would have gone to him and attempted to soothe his anger. As it was, I couldn't give two shits about his feelings. On second thought, maybe the alcohol wasn't so stupid after all. "You about done with your tantrum yet?" I snapped, climbing in between the cool sheets and resting my head on his feather pillow.

The noise stopped, probably due to his shock over the lack of fucks that I had to give. Maybe I should drink more often. I kinda liked me drunk.

Colton's face turned and his bloodshot eyes locked on mine.

"Get in bed or get the fuck out. I'm drunk; I'm tired; I'm horny, and I'm fucking done. Got it?" I was so proud of myself for not shedding a single tear.

His green eyes narrowed to slits, and his jaw ticked. Colt stared at me for a long moment before nodding his head, grabbing his clothes, and closing himself up in the bathroom.

I tried like hell to fall asleep before he returned, to no avail. When I heard the telltale clicking of the bathroom lock, I laid deathly still with my eyes shut tight. I didn't move a muscle as he entered at the foot of the bed and crawled up to lay beside me. I bit my lips to keep from crying with a broken heart when I felt him snuggle into my back and his arm snaked around my waist, pulling me closer to his chest. And I swear that I stopped breathing altogether when I felt his lips press a kiss on the back of my shoulder.

"I'm sorry, Allie," he whispered into the silence.

Sober Allie would have cracked. But drunk Allie...she had her fucks on lockdown tonight.

Long after Colton passed out, I laid awake in his arms with silent tears pooling beneath my face and the scent of Lyla's perfume lingering on his skin.

CHAPTERELEVEN

Colton

ALLIE...I'D SEEN HER CRY PLENTY OF TIMES THROUGHOUT OUR lives, but never like this. Not even the night before I left for California was it this brutal.

I knew that she thought I was asleep...But how could I sleep with her body shuddering against me? I'd gone too far, barging in here like I had any right to dictate what she did or whom she did it with. I'd humiliated her. This had to stop. I was so fucking in love with her that it was making me crazy. The one thing I knew without hesitation was that I didn't want to ever hurt Alex, yet somehow that's all I'd been doing since she arrived.

"Morning, Al," I greeted when her eyes finally fluttered open.

"Hey," she said, stretching her arms and legs. "What time is it?"

"A little after ten."

She rose up onto an elbow, reaching to the side table for her phone. I watched as her eyes scanned over her messages, widening before she threw herself back onto the bed with a dramatic groan.

"Um...everything all right there?" I asked, curious.

"I'm never drinking again," she whined, swinging her forearm to cover her eyes. The stretching motion caused the bottom of her shirt to rise up, exposing her flat stomach.

That little glimpse had memories of Alex's strip tease the night before racing through my head. My heart was pounding. I moved the blanket to cover the tent in my boxers before licking the pad of a finger and wet-willying her bellybutton.

"Colton!" she shrieked, tugging her shirt down and squinting her eyes at me.

"Sorry, I couldn't resist." I shrugged, laughing into my hand. I *had* to do something. If she'd only known how close I was to running my tongue over her body instead.

Her tiny fist connected with my bare chest, and I grabbed her wrist, the way I always did when she got violent with me. Alex's breathing changed. Her eyes became hooded. There were sparks shooting off from every direction, and still, we both ignored them. Eyes locked, chests heaving, each waiting for the other to make a move. Finally, Allie pulled her hand away and the moment was lost.

"I, uh..." She shook her head, laughing. "I drunk messaged Gertie last night." She sucked her bottom lip between her teeth, chewing it nervously.

Shit. She must've really liked Stephan if she didn't even wait 'til morning to start blabbing about him. "It couldn't have been all that bad."

Alex snorted. "I called her old..."

"Ouch..."

"Awful, right?"

"What'd she say?"

"She laughed it off. We're gonna meet for lunch tomorrow."

My throat thickened. The thought of her getting together to gush over her date with Stephan was making me nauseous. "Al?"

"Yeah?" she asked, sitting up in the bed.

Absentmindedly, I grabbed the end of the lock of hair that was hanging over her bare shoulder and twirled it in my fingers. "I just wanted to say that I'm sorry for barging in here and freaking out like that last night. I had no right. I just..." Fuck. I couldn't tell her why it upset me so much. Not yet. I had to stick to the plan. It was working. It had to work. "You were just so upset after kissing Blex, and I didn't want you to do anything you'd regret in the morning," I lied.

She narrowed her eyes at me, seeing right through my bullshit.

"Okay, fine...I can't stand the fucker." I let out a noncommittal laugh. "But I am sorry for going all caveman and embarrassing you like that. I was out of line."

Allie nodded and smirked. "Dean and I broke up yesterday," she whispered, looking up at me beneath her long dark lashes while fiddling with the hem of her top. She'd die if she saw the mascara smeared below her eyes and streaked down her cheeks. My heart reached for her. I'd always loved these moments with Alex. The intimacy of having her in my bed first thing in the morning. Being able to look at her like this... raw and unpolished.

It took a minute for her words to register. Dean was finally out of the picture. "Are you serious?" My heart was racing. I'd spent years just waiting for the day I'd hear her say those very words. "So, you're not going to marry him?"

Allie shrugged. "That depends."

"On what?"

She gave me a flirty little wink. "On what happens this summer."

"You really like him, don't you?" *Fucking Stephan.* Well, I had news for him, I was not losing my girl again.

"He *was* really sweet." Her face lit up. "I think he likes me." *It was fucking Dean all over again.*

"Of course he does, Al. What's not to like?"

"You're right. I'm pretty awesome." The sound of her giggle

—

was music to my ears, but I was curious about something.

"So, you're just what? Keeping him on the backburner?" I asked when I'd had a minute to digest her words. "And he's okay with this?" None of this sounded like anything Alex would do.

She frowned. "Well, shit. It sounds awful when you put it that way."

"I'm just trying to understand, Al."

Her eyes welled up. "I love Dean," she started, twisting the knife in an old wound. "But, I just am not sure I'm *in love* with him."

"Okay..."

"When he asked me to marry him, I wanted to say yes. I want a husband, Colt." I nodded. "I want children and the white picket fence. All of it. We've been together for so long, it's only logical that I would want that with him..." she trailed off.

My heart was lodged in my throat. "And you don't?"

A tear dripped down her cheek as she shrugged. She looked so small. So fragile. "I don't know...I wanted to say yes and I couldn't. I started hyperventilating, and I just wanted to get away. Far, far away. I don't know if that's because I'm just scared or a huge red flag that he's not the one."

You ran to me, my brain was screaming. That should have told her everything. "And here you are," I rasped.

"Here I am." She gave me a half smile.

"And Dean?"

"He won't let go." Her lips quivered. "After kissing Blex, I knew that I couldn't be *that* girl. I told him what happened and that I thought we needed to break up and explore this summer...that he should do the same...Colton, we've been together since we were just kids."

I nodded. She didn't need to defend herself to me. "I get it, Allie. Don't do anything you aren't one hundred percent sure of. Marriage is a really big step." *And he's the wrong guy*, I thought.

—

"Anyway, he said that I was it for him and he'd be waiting for my answer." She shrugged, tipping her head to one side, indicating that was it.

"You won't be an easy girl to get over, Allie," I whispered, knowing full and well just how impossible that feat would be.

"Okay, what about this one?" Allie called as she began to make her way down the narrow stairs for what felt like the hundredth time that day. I swear that girl was getting a kick out of modeling everything in the closet.

Finn was catcalling from his vantage point across the room before I'd even got a look at her. My buddies were enjoying this entirely too much.

"Well? What do you guys think?" Alex spun around slowly in the center of the room to give us a good look at her latest outfit.

"Hot damn, Lexi," Finn purred. "You sure you wanna waste all that—" his eyes roamed up and down her tight body "—on Stephan?"

Alex glared at him, crossing her arms over her chest.

"I'm just saying, I would be more than happy to take his place."

"Like hell," I growled and then flinched when I felt Blex's shoe make contact with my shin.

"You look beautiful, Alex," Blex said, jabbing me with his elbow. When I didn't say anything, he gave me another jab. "Doesn't she look nice, Fowls?" His tone was that of a mother trying to coerce the proper response from her child.

"Colt?" Allie asked nervously, her cheeks growing rosier by the second.

I cleared my throat, adjusting my position on the couch. I couldn't even find words. That little black dress was hugging all her curves. I had the strongest urge to scoop her into my arms and carry her right back up those stairs. I wanted to rip her clothes off and to finally claim her as mine. I wasn't sure how much longer I could do this. "You look..." I paused, swallowing hard, as I looked her up and down, my heart pulsing.

Alex's brows rose.

"You look," I repeated, rising from my seat before I walked over to join her. I felt the charge in the air between us. Noticed the hitch in her breath. The goose bumps that lined her arm as I ran a finger from her wrist to elbow.

"Yeah?" she whispered, her voice heady.

Lowering my head to the bend of her neck, I inhaled the scent of her flowery perfume. "You look," I rasped, allowing my lips to brush her throat, "like...I need another drink," I whispered in her ear.

"What's the matter with you?" she asked with a nervous laugh as she playfully shoved my chest.

I started for the kitchen, calling back over my shoulder, "Nothin', Al. I'm empty." I shook my can in the air as proof. "You want one?"

"No, I...I'm fine, Colt." The disappointment in her voice pierced my chest, but I had to get away for a few minutes to clear my head. I stood in the open fridge and downed half a beer before looking up to find Blex standing in the doorway.

"You need to figure this shit out, man," he warned, walking over to grab another beer for himself. "You can't keep sending her all these mixed signals." He locked eyes with mine on his way back out to the living room. "Shit or get off the fucking pot, Fowls."

I finished off that beer and grabbed one more before making my way back out there. Alex sat slumped over on the armchair with her head in her hands. Her earlier excitement had been washed away with my inability to give her a simple compliment. I was such a dick.

"Hey, Allie," I said, crouching before her. At the sound of my voice, she looked up. Her brown eyes wet with unshed tears. "You look really, really nice."

She nodded in agreement, but I could tell she didn't believe me.

Pulling her head to my shoulder, I eyed my roommates over her back as I began to massage the nape of Alex's neck. I motioned to the stairs, and they followed my cue, leaving us alone in the living room.

Allie's breath was warm on my skin, and she smelled so fucking good. I wished I could just sit there and hold her forever, but dickhead would be arriving soon and I couldn't let her leave like this. "Hey," I husked into her hair.

She sat up, rubbing her nose with the back of her hand.

"I'm sorry, Al. I'm the world's biggest asshole. You look *amazing,* and I guess...Well, it just sort of shocked me...how beautiful you are." *Someone fucking shoot me and put me out of my misery.*

Her lips began to tremble as she searched my face, trying to decide whether or not to believe me.

"It's hard for me to see you with guys," I continued, revealing how truly pathetic I was. "You mean a lot to me."

She nodded. "You mean a lot to me too, Colt—"

Just then the doorbell rang. *Of course it did.*

Alex stood, adjusting her dress. "Will you get it?"

"Yeah," I rasped, pushing up from the floor. My lips pressed into a line as I gave her a final once-over before answering the door.

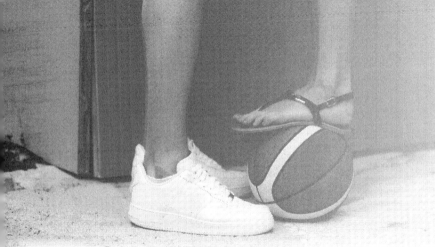

CHAPTERTWELVE

Alexis

MY HEART RACED AS COLTON'S EYES LICKED EVERY INCH OF MY body and liquid heat began to pool between my legs. I squeezed them together, trying to calm the swarm of butterflies that had suddenly taken up residence in my vagina.

As Colt pulled the door open to Stephan's gorgeous face, I forced what I hoped to be a genuine-looking smile...Suddenly, this date was feeling like a really bad idea. *What was I doing?*

"Alexis," Stephan purred in appreciation as he too undressed me with his eyes. The fluttering vanished. Those fucking butterflies had always been loyal to that clueless son of a bitch who was all but glaring at my date, and apparently, they'd decided it'd be a great idea to migrate south for the summer.

"Stephan," I squeaked, trying to get a grip on myself. "You look nice." And he did. He had on a pair of charcoal gray Dickies that hugged his ass to perfection with a red washed out button down cuffed at his elbows. His hair was spiked up in a messy, styled but not too put together look. *Sex hair.* He had *sex* hair!

"Thanks," he said, stepping inside when it was made evident that Colton was not going to extend the invitation. "You are stunning, Alexis."

I could feel my best friend's eyes rolling without even looking at him. Who said things like *stunning* anymore? "Thanks." I grabbed my purse from the coat rack next to the door, and before walking out, turned to press a kiss to Colton's cheek. "I'll see you later. Love ya."

He sounded like he had a ten-pound bolder sitting in the back of his throat when he answered. "Have fun, Allie. I love you too."

"I hope you like to dance," Stephan said with a huge smile as he pulled up to a swanky little place called Bailando.

"I love to dance!" I answered excitedly. He couldn't have chosen a better place to get me out of the doldrums. The thought of tearing up that dance floor had me bouncing where I sat.

Stephan opened my door and helped me out of the car. Such a gentleman. It was easier to appreciate him without my body going haywire over he who shall not be named or even a thought for the remainder of the evening.

"Reservation for two, under Stephan Young," he announced when we approached the podium in the very festive foyer. The walls were lined with photos of various celebrities dancing or posing for photos at the bar. There were lights strung around the entryway and a huge pink neon sign that said, "Salsa." It was bordering on tacky, but somehow it all worked together with the atmosphere.

"Marie here will be your waitress, enjoy." She was short and curvy with big curly hair and wore the same black pencil skirt and white button down as the rest of the staff. Her smile was warm and welcoming. Marie grabbed a couple of menus from the side of the podium and led the way to our table.

Stephan pulled out my chair before taking the one across from me.

"What can I get the two of you to drink?"

The margaritas looked fantastic, but being that neither Stephan nor myself were twenty-one, I went with a strawberry lemonade and him with a water.

"Chips and *salsa*?" she asked, shimmying on the word salsa and waggling her brows animatedly.

"Yes, please," Stephan answered.

"Great. I'll be right back with your drinks."

As I watched her walk off, I found myself distracted by the couples dancing around us. There was a permanent smile fixed on my face as I watched men and women alike swinging their hips with so much confidence. I'd never been in a real salsa club before. The atmosphere was unlike any place I'd ever seen. So fun and sexy. I couldn't find a single face that wasn't just exuberant.

"This okay?" Stephan asked, looking around the restaurant and back at me.

My answering smile visibly set him at ease. "It's amazing. Do you know how to dance like that?" *Please say yes. Please say yes.* I wanted to be touched the way the men were touching those women. And I really wanted to see Stephan move the way they moved.

Stephan bit into his bottom lip as a shy, almost embarrassed smile appeared on his face. "Yeah...My mother owns a dance studio...She, uh, made me take classes." He turned bright red as he playfully lifted both hands to cover his face, peeking at me through the cracks in his fingers.

Thank you, God. "That could be the cutest thing I've ever heard."

Stephan and I both ordered beef fajitas. I made it a point not to overeat. One, I didn't want to look like a heifer, and two, I didn't want to puke when we finally made it onto the dance floor.

"You ready, pretty girl?" Stephan asked, standing and

holding his large hand out for mine.

For the first few songs, I felt a little out of my league. Stephan was a natural, and a great teacher. I don't know how I looked to everyone else, but it felt like I was doing a pretty good job of keeping up, and I hadn't consumed any alcohol, so I knew it wasn't that.

Stephan's hands were all over me, his moves so sensual. It should have felt wrong. I was just coming out of a three-year relationship. No other man had ever touched me so intimately and to tell you the truth, after all of the sex I'd had with Dean over the years, even he hadn't made me feel this kind of heat.

The rhythm of the music had my blood pumping, and Stephan played my body like the most skilled musician. If I thought I had some pent up sexual energy before, it was nothing compared to what I felt at that moment. The problem was...the person I wanted to expend it on wasn't here.

Thoughts of Colton were killing my mood, and of course, my date could sense the change in me. "Hey, everything all right?"

"Yeah, I'm just really tired." I placed a hand on my chest trying to catch my breath.

"Why don't we go sit for a few minutes and recharge?" Stephan was adorable. I hated that I was too hung up on my best friend to give him the attention he deserved. Any other woman would have given their left tit to be with a man like him. Smart, athletic, sensitive, sweet, hot, and he could fucking dance like those guys in the movies. He was almost too good to be real, and I was about to push him away for a guy I wasn't sure would ever even give me the time of day. I needed my head examined...and probably my heart as well.

"Actually, can you just take me home? I'm not feeling well."

Stephan's face fell with disappointment, but ever the gentleman, he recovered quickly. "Sure." He flagged down our waitress, paid the bill, and then took me back to Colton's house. When he threw the car into park, the mood suddenly became tense. To kiss or not to kiss. The dreaded first date

—

question. "Can I kiss you good night?" he asked.

He asked. Who does that? For all the shit Colton talked about what an asshole Stephan was, I'd never met a more considerate or well-mannered man. And that says a lot because I didn't know they came sweeter than Dean.

I nodded my head, leaned over, and met him halfway across the center console. His lips were soft and skilled. I tried to get into it. I really did, but in the back of my mind, I kept thinking of Colton on the other side of that door, and it was a serious mood killer.

Sensing my discomfort, Stephan pulled away. "I had a really nice time with you tonight, Alexis." His lips curled into a resigned half smile. "I can tell you really aren't feeling well. Why don't we try again soon when you're up to it?"

"I'd love that."

Stephan moved to get out to walk me to the door, but I told him to stay. There was no need. Honestly, I was afraid he'd try to kiss me again, and I just wasn't up for it tonight. He idled in the parking lot while I fished the key Colt had given me out of my clutch and unlocked the door. I heard the engine rev and turned to watch him back out of the lot, then I pushed the door the rest of the way open and stepped inside.

The house was dark. It was still relatively early, being only a little past nine, so I figured the guys had probably gone out. After sticking the key back into my purse, I set it down on the table near the door. My feet were really starting to cramp up from dancing all night in four-inch heels. They had to come off. I braced myself against the wall for balance and started to remove my shoes. But I was stopped dead in my tracks when I heard moaning coming from the couch to my right.

Whoever was hooking up on that couch was so engrossed in their sexcapade that they hadn't heard me come into the house. I felt guilty for standing there in silence like some creeper, but I was frozen in place. There was a tightening in my core as the decidedly male moans became louder. Slurping and heavy breathing filled the quiet space.

—

As my eyes began to adjust to the lack of light, I could see a woman's head bobbing up and down an enormous...Oh dear God in heaven, please no...

"Just like that, baby..." *Colton.* My eyes adjusted further and I could see that his hands were fisted in the girl's hair, guiding her mouth up and down. His head was thrown back. His lips parted. The golden curls I'd loved for as long as I could remember bounced with each shift of his hips. My whole body went tingly and numb.

Pain unlike anything I'd ever felt shot through every cell of my body instantly as if I'd been struck by a lightning bolt. My heart...I wasn't sure it would ever beat again. With each thrust, it shriveled up and died a little more. I felt tears pouring down my cheeks as I reached for something—anything to grab hold of to keep my balance. My hand gripped the edge of the little table, but instead of holding me up, it went down with me.

There was a loud crash. A scream that could only have come from me. The light came on just as Colton was tucking his dick back into his pants and my fucking mouth had the nerve to water. Why was my body such a fucking whore for this man?

I couldn't breathe. I wanted to disappear. I wanted...I wanted to stop loving Colton Fowler because loving him was slowly killing me.

"Allie?" Colton slurred, dropping to his knees beside me on the floor. Great. He was fucking drunk.

"What the hell?" the blonde bitch on the couch screeched as she pulled her tank top back over her head. I recognized her as the girl he was with at the bar on my first day here...Candy. Another day. Another blonde. Another blowjob.

Colton ignored her, running his sloppy hands all over my body to make sure I wasn't hurt. "Are you okay? What happened?"

I tried to answer, but couldn't speak past the sobs that had stolen my breath. So, I shook my head, nodded, and then shrugged.

Candy rolled her eyes as she approached. She too must've

recognized me from the bar. "Seriously? Girl, you need to get a fucking life and stop cock-blocking. It ain't cool." Her too-long manicured finger pointed in my direction before she stormed out, slamming the front door behind her.

Colton lifted me into his lap, holding me close. He pressed wet, smelly beer kisses all over my forehead and down the side of my face. I was disgusted, but I craved his attention more. So, I laid there in his arms, wrapped my trembling limbs around his chest, and let the source of my pain comfort me while simultaneously gutting me.

My eyes were heavy, and I was beginning to doze off when, in a shaky voice, he asked, "So...did you have a good time?"

"Mmhmm," I answered, looking up just in time to catch the broken expression on his face before he was able to school his features.

Colton cleared his throat and ran a hand through his mop of curls, a move of his I'd always found incredibly sexy. "Where'd you go?"

He looked as broken as I felt, and his pain, believe it or not, cut deeper than my own. "Do you really want to hear about this?"

His Adam's apple bobbed with a hard swallow, and he nodded.

"He took me salsa dancing."

Colton's head hung. I felt his body shake with a humorless laugh. "Damn, he's better than I thought."

"It was fun."

"You always did love to dance..."

Reaching up, I cupped the side of his forlorn face. His skin was rough with day-old stubble. I realized I was absentmindedly rubbing his cheek and quickly pulled my hand away. "You're still my favorite partner."

Colton's hooded eyes locked with mine. As he continued to stare, my heart began to race. "Dance with me?" His tone was pleading, bordering on desperate.

"Now?" I asked, taking in the mess we were still sitting in.

—

My obsession cleared his throat. He looked almost nervous like he actually thought there was a possibility I'd ever have told him no. "Now," he affirmed.

I shifted to my knees, between Colt's legs, positioning myself with my face toward his. "I'd love to."

Colt took my hand into his own, practically dragging me up the stairs to his bedroom. He powered up his laptop, and within minutes, I heard the opening chords to "Despacito."

I was staring out of his bedroom window when I felt his presence behind me. He didn't breathe a word, and I didn't dare move. My body temperature rose by at least ten degrees before he even touched me. I could feel my heart pulsing in the back of my throat. Colton closed the space between us, pressing his erection into my ass, as he grabbed my waist with both hands and molded his body to mine. And I swear to baby Jesus, I nearly orgasmed on the spot.

Colton started out slowly, undulating our hips in time to the beat. His lips were on my neck. His hands exploring my body in ways they never had—in ways I'd only ever imagined in my dreams. They brushed over my breasts, traveled down the outside of my legs, and crept up the sensitive skin of my inner thighs. I was a puppet, putty in his hands.

I tried to reason with my overzealous body. Colton was drunk. We were just dancing. Only dancing. It didn't mean anything. The hard length pressing into my back wasn't any indication of how he felt for me. I bit my lip to keep from crying out at the all too recent memory of Candy's lips wrapped around that very erection.

I was in heaven and my own personal hell. It was the closest I'd ever got to everything I'd ever wanted, and at the same time eons away. Because while he may have been igniting a fire in my body, I'd just witnessed him doing so much more with another woman mere minutes before. That hard-on, now pressing into my most intimate places, wasn't for me. As much as I wanted to believe differently, I knew that it belonged to *her*. I was a convenient body to rub up against, to work out the sexual frustration I'd caused with my interruption.

With every breath against my neck, I smelled the alcohol, reminding me of how drunk he was. My nipples grew hard despite the pain I felt inside. My panties were soaked. Physically, I was aroused. Emotionally, I'd never been more damaged.

Just when I felt like I would crumble in his hold, I heard my best friend singing softly into my ear. He was completely oblivious to my feelings in his drunken state. "Desperito, this is how we do it in Puerto Rico. Do you wanna play with my big burrito?" His face landed on my shoulder, and his arms tightened around my middle in a bear hug as Colton's body began to shake with the force of his laughter.

Amid the tears and heartbreak, I was reminded of why I loved him so much. Of why no matter how much it hurt, I would love him always.

When I awoke the next morning, Colton had already left for practice. The only indication that I hadn't imagined the entire ordeal was the faint sound of "Despacito" playing on loop coming from the direction of his laptop, which was still open on the desk. My life was such a fucking mess.

I glanced at the glowing red numbers on Colton's alarm clock, noting that it was already after ten. I was meeting Gertie in an hour and was a hot mess in every way imaginable.

After a quick shower, I blew my hair out, applied minimal makeup, and threw on a sundress and flip-flops. Then I headed downstairs.

As I retrieved my purse on the way out, I noticed that someone had cleaned up my mess from last night. My eyes wandered to the couch and began to sting. I shook my head to myself as I pulled the door shut. *Not today, Satan.* I had to get a grip. Colton was free to put his dick wherever he wanted. Apparently, he wanted to put it in the mouth of every blonde hoochie in LA. But that was not my business.

My Uber arrived within two minutes. It seemed like there were always five cars lurking around any given corner in LA. The level of convenience was out of control. I was becoming spoiled.

Less than ten minutes from the time I walked out of the door, my driver was dropping me off in front of Sammy's Café. Gertie said they had the best French onion soup and grilled cheese she'd ever tasted. Apparently, her son lived just down the road, and she ate there often.

Sammy's was small, located on the corner of a shopping center. The entire front and left side of the restaurant were floor to ceiling windows. I spotted my friend right away seated at a booth with her wrinkly little arm flailing in the air to get my attention. My heart warmed at the sight of her. I loved that she seemed just as excited to see me as I was to see her.

A huge smile split my face as I yanked the heavy door open and rushed over to join her. Gertie stood, wrapping me in a tight hug. I squeezed her back. I didn't want to ever let go. I knew no one apart from Colt and his friends in the city...But with Gertie, I could finally let my guard down a little. I knew she was on my side.

"All right. All right, child," she said, patting the back of my head affectionately. "Have a seat and tell me alllllll about this blonde bitch." Her lips curled into a smirk when my mouth fell open. "Oh, don't look at me like that. Those were your words." Gertie winked, slipping back into the booth.

"Well..." I laughed, taking a seat across from her. "There are two now. Actually, three altogether, but two since I messaged you."

Her eyes narrowed as she sat back in her seat, crossing her arms over her chest. "What kind of shady shit are you kids doing in that house?"

Water sprayed from my nose as I choked mid-swallow. "Gertie!"

"Honey, I thought we decided you came to get the guy. So,

explain to this old woman how you're off dating his friends, and he's having whores over to the house." Her brows rose, and her eyes homed in on my face. Well, when she put it like that...

I felt my face heat with mortification. "Well, I...Blex said we should make him jealous..." Good *one, Alexis. Blame Blex.* "Blex is...?"

I squirmed a little in my seat. The condescending look she gave me made me all kinds of nervous. "Colt's roommate."

Gertrude steepled her hands together, resting them beneath her chin. Her lips puckered in thought, twitching side to side. "How old are you, Alexis?"

A ball of nerves lodged in my throat. Why'd I suddenly feel like an errant child being chastised by a parent? "Twenty..."

"Mmhmm..."

Mmhmm...*What did that even mean?* "So..."

"So, don't you think you're a little too old for games, darlin'?"

Blood rushed to my cheeks. I could feel how red they were as I sputtered a bunch of nonsense...She was right. We weren't children anymore. This wasn't a game. This was my *life.* "I just thought that if I could make him jealous..."

Gertie's head nodded slowly. "You thought you'd make him realize what he was missing..."

"Exactly! Except he's just going about his business...Maybe he doesn't have those kind of feelings for me, Gertie." I felt tears burn the backs of my eyes. "What if it's all one-sided?"

Gertie rolled her eyes, waving a hand in dismissal. "A blind man could see the love that boy feels for you. I saw it, Alexis. I felt it." She thumped a hand on her chest. "Right here...You feel it too." Her eyes met mine, daring me to deny it. "Tell me you don't honestly believe that boy is crazy about you."

My heart tightened in my chest. "I think...maybe...I mean, I guess. Yeah. I feel it. There are times I'm sure of it. But then I walk in and he's getting a blowjob in the living room of the house we're sharing, and I just don't know how he could possibly feel the way I feel for him." Tears lined my cheeks. I

—

97

swatted them away.

"You don't?"

"No! Who does that, Gertie? I mean, if he loved me...why? Why would he do that?"

Gertie covered her face with both hands, blowing out a long and frustrated breath. Her head finally came back up, and there was a sad smile on her face. "You, Alex...You have been doing that for three years. You're the one here under the guise of trying to decide whether or not you want to marry another man. A man you've been dating for three long years. You're flirting with his friends. Dating his friends."

My jaw dropped as I was stunned into silence.

"Honey, when was that boy supposed to tell you he was in love with you?" Her warm hand reached out, rubbing the tops of mine, which were laced on the table in front of me. "You think you're hurt, and you're confused. Put yourself in that boy's shoes for two minutes. What have you done to show him how you feel? Have you given him any reason to be confident enough in his feelings to think that you might actually return them?"

CHAPTER THIRTEEN

Colton

I HAD MY FEET KICKED UP ON THE COUCH, WATCHING TOP GUN while stuffing my face with a bag of popcorn when I heard the front door knob rattle. Instantly, my heart rate sped up in anticipation of seeing her face. It was a physical reaction I'd been having for so long that you'd think I'd have gotten used to it by now. But I guess they wouldn't call it addiction if people ever become numb to the high. Alexis Mack was like a drug to me.

"Hey," she called out, rushing into the room with a smile that stretched from one ear to the other. Alex joined me by the couch, dropping a to-go bag from Sammy's onto the coffee table. Then, she leaned over and pressed a kiss to my forehead. "Brought you some lunch."

"Ahhh," I moaned, patting my stomach. "You know the way to my heart."

"Your dick?" she quipped.

I winked, sitting up on the couch to give her room to join me. "How was your visit with Gertie?" I asked, digging into the doggie bag as she sat to my left. Her leg pressed up against mine.

"Insightful."

"How so?" I asked with a mouth full of club sandwich. I moaned my appreciation, giving Allie the old thumbs up.

Alex chewed on her lip, a nervous habit of hers. "She just made me realize some things." *Being evasive, were we?*

I swallowed the food in my mouth, licking a bit of mayo from my bottom lip. "Such as?" I asked, deciding not to call her out on how hard she was staring at my mouth.

"Hmm?" Allie asked, looking up to meet my eyes.

Chuckling to myself, I repeated the question. "What kind of things did Gertie make you realize...Stay with me here." I winked and she smiled.

"Well, the most important thing is that I shouldn't be wasting my time going out on dates when I came here to spend the summer with my best friend." She blushed, nudging my arm with her shoulder.

"Have I told you yet how much I like Gertie?" I took another bite of my sandwich. "Wise, wise woman, that one."

Her laughter hit me right in the feels. She sounded like my Allie again. Somehow, I knew everything was about to get better between us. It's crazy how much I still missed her, even with her right here. We hadn't been ourselves. We weren't usually so tense with one another.

"I'm glad you feel that way...because she also said that you shouldn't be having whores over to the house."

I choked.

"Shit." Alex was laughing so hard as she pounded on my back. "Dramatic much? Damn, Colton. I mean, if it's going to kill you, you can keep the blonde Hoovers." She rolled her eyes deliberately.

It took me a couple of minutes to dislodge the food that got caught in my windpipe. Allie sat there in hysterics throughout the ordeal. I cleared my throat a couple of times before responding to her last remark. "I'll ditch the blondes, but I can't promise I won't need some mouth to cock resuscitation. He may go into shock without any attention." I winked, tucking a finger beneath her jaw to push her mouth closed. "Know of any brunettes that want to attempt such an arduous task?"

Alex's face turned beet red as she began sputtering all sorts of nonsense. "I can't believe you just said that to me!" she finally got out.

"I can't believe you aren't willing to compromise here. Meet me halfway, baby." I gave her my best hubba hubba eyebrows.

That little poke earned me a punch to the ribs. "You're such a pig, Colton Fowler."

I was having way too much fun with her, and I wasn't ready to quit yet. "You remember that deal we made when we were kids?"

"Which one?" she asked, giving me a little side eye. She knew me well enough to know that I was up to something.

"Veda and Thomas," I rasped, licking my lips to see how she'd respond.

Alex's breathing quickened. "Mmhmm." She nodded, looking around the room, refusing to make eye contact. As an unspoken rule, we'd never discussed that kiss.

"I thought we could maybe try something similar, for old time's sake..."

She ran her tongue over her top teeth, glaring at me. "What'd you have in mind?"

This was going to be good. I wished I would have had a video camera to record her reaction. It was going to be epic. "Okay, so...hear me out before you go all batshit crazy on me, okay?"

"Just spit it out already!" She looked ready to strangle me and finish off the job I'd started with the sandwich.

"That is *not* what he said," I quipped, earning myself a giggle.

"Colton..." She tried for a serious look, but there was no hiding that Cheshire cat grin she was wearing.

"So, it appears we could have a mutually beneficial

—

arrangement here." I moved my finger back and forth in the space between us. "It has recently come to my attention that you've got some horniness that needs tending to, and, well, my dick ain't gonna suck itself, so..."

Alex jumped off the couch like her ass was on fire. Her skin was red from the tops of her ears to the tips of her toes. I couldn't stop laughing as she just stood there, unable to form words.

"Cat got your tongue, Allie?"

"I'm not sucking your dick, Colton..." she warned, staring at my crotch.

I got up from the couch and walked over to stand in front of her. "It's intimidating to most girls at first. I'll ease you into it. Just think about it and let me know when you change your mind."

Alex coughed, biting the sides of her cheeks in an attempt not to smile. "You said when not if," she pointed out.

"I know what I said."

"You're awful." She dug her finger into my chest.

"We're a forgone conclusion, Allie...our parents would be so proud."

Alexis shrugged, unable to argue that point. "Touché."

"What're you kids up to tonight?" Mom asked. Our weekly Skype sessions helped to shorten the distance between us.

"Alex is forcing me to take her to watch some new chick flick that just came out."

Momma smiled big. "That sounds awful date-ish, Colton." Her brows rose as she shimmied in her seat.

"Stop," I deadpanned just as Alexis came out of the bathroom.

My heart skipped a beat at the sight of her. She was dressed simply in a flowered tank and wearing those damn short cut-off shorts again. Her hair was left loose in big waves. She wore makeup, but it wasn't overdone. I couldn't point out what it was about her that was rendering me speechless. I guess it was just her.

She rushed over, placing her hands on my shoulders and greeting my mother. "Hey, Mrs. Fowler," she chirped like she was speaking to her long lost friend.

"Hey, baby. We miss you out here in the country. My boy treatin' you okay?" It's like I wasn't even in the room any longer, and that was just fine by me. I was more than content to sit there with Allie's tits pressed against my back and her breath hot in my ear.

"I miss y'all too. Colton is great." She squeezed my neck in a hug, pressing a kiss to my cheek, right there in front of my mother. Was she trying to fuel the mother hens?

My mom was giddy as we said our goodbyes. We had to get moving if we were going to get decent seats.

"Did you see her face when I kissed you?" Alex asked as I laced her hand in mine and led her down the stairs. I knew she did that shit on purpose.

"You're gonna get their hopes up, Allie." I shook my head, and she let go of my hand to retrieve her purse from where she left it on the table near the door.

"Oh, relax. They've had their hopes up since we were in utero."

She was still smiling at her own comment when I clutched her chin in my hand and turned her face up to mine. Confusion was written all over her face at the intimate gesture. I gulped, working up the nerve to say what was on the tip of my tongue. This time, I didn't choke. "Okay, fine," I said, rubbing my thumb back and forth over her bottom lip. "You're going to get my hopes up."

Alexis stared back at me. "You have hopes for us?" she asked, her voice so low and shaky that it was almost inaudible. But I was staring so hard, there was no way I'd have missed it even if the sound hadn't accompanied the movement of her lips. Lips that I had been dying to kiss since she'd arrived, and even more so since we'd started our incessant flirting.

"So many," I rasped. My heart was beating impossibly fast.

Her big brown eyes shone with barely contained emotion. She nodded, lifting her hands to caress the sides of my face, and then she breathed out a long sigh of relief. "Me too, Colton," she stammered. "So many."

I moved my hand around to cup the back of her neck and pulled her closer as I dipped my head and brought my lips to hers. And it was everything. Every single thing I'd remembered and more. I kept my hand on her chin, guiding her mouth as we licked and nipped. As our tongues battled out all of the suppressed emotions and a lifetime of regret. I ate up every whimper and moan until we became completely lost in each other. Losing myself in Allie felt a whole lot like being found. I knew without a doubt that this was where the two of us belonged.

"It's about fucking time," Finn called from the kitchen, causing Alex to pull away. She held onto my upper arms, resting her head on my chest. I could feel her entire body shaking against me. "You two were giving me blue balls."

I chuckled into Allie's hair. "Later, Finn," I called, dismissing him. Trailing my fingers down the back of her arm, I clutched Alex's hand in mine. "Ready?" I asked, dipping my head toward the door.

Her answering smile was all I needed to know that she didn't regret the kiss we'd just shared. "Let's go."

"Later, lovebirds."

I held Allie's hand throughout the ten-minute drive to the cinema, feeling a lot like a fifteen-year-old on his first date. Such a simple gesture was a huge step for the two of us. We may have dipped a toe over the friendship line a time or two, but we made it our life's mission to tread that line carefully. Sure, we'd held hands before, but that was as friends, and this was as...something more.

After purchasing tickets and snacks, we found seats in the back row of the nearly empty theater. It was still a little early,

—

but we never were ones to risk being stuck in the front row.

"Colton?"

"Yeah, Al?"

She nibbled on that bottom lip for a moment. "Why is this weird?"

"Because we're so used to hiding." I brushed her hair from her eyes with the back of my hand. "It's just different."

"I'm all nervous and jittery. Like I have to keep reminding myself that it's just you."

"Hey," I said, squeezing her hand. "It's just going to take some time. We'll take things slow. I'm not expecting anything more than you're ready to give."

Alex squeezed my hand, smiling up at me. "Thanks, Colt."

I hated that she felt the tension too. We were so close that at times it felt like we were the same person, and yet here we were feeling like virtual strangers. Allie and I had reached a crossroads. It was time for the two of us to either go all in and make it work or cut our losses. We couldn't continue with things the way they'd been. Neither of us would ever be able to give our hearts fully when half was already taken. It was time to double down. And if I had my way, we were going to come out on top.

"So," I whispered after another long period of silence. I couldn't take it anymore. I had to do something to lighten the mood.

"Yeah?"

"How do you feel about theater head?" Her tiny fist connected with my thigh. "That good, huh?"

CHAPTER FOURTEEN

Alexis

"YOU ABOUT DONE IN THERE?" COLTON ASKED, POUNDING A FIST against the bathroom door.

Lathering up my loofa for the second time, I began scrubbing over my skin again. "Be out soon," I shouted back, making sure to scrub extra hard in all the important parts...under my arms, my breasts, between my legs, you know...just in case. A girl had to be prepared. Finally satisfied that I was not going to get any cleaner, I dried off and sat on the edge of the tub, where I smoothed on some of my favorite lotion: Be Enchanted from Bath and Body Works.

"Come on, Al," Colton griped through the door as I was finishing up with my teeth.

After running a quick comb through my tangled hair, I turned the knob and was nearly knocked on my ass when Colton came tumbling toward me. He must've had his head resting on the outside of the door.

Colt, who was always quick on his feet, managed to grab hold of the counter to stop his fall. His other arm wrapped around my waist, effectively stopping mine as well. Instinctively, my hands latched around his neck. Colton held me at an awkward angle. His face mere inches from my own. He smelled of man soap and mouthwash. I felt each heavy breath he released ghost across the side of my face. Our eyes were fixed on each other, swirling with a mixture of relief and lust. My heart was close to leaping out of my chest with desire.

"Fancy meeting you here," Colt teased. He lifted my body, as if I weighed no more than a ragdoll, and sat me on the counter while positioning himself between my parted legs. I felt the rough pads of his fingers trace a path from my ankles to the sensitive skin behind my knees. At the same time, Colton trailed his nose over one of my shoulders, up the curve of my neck, and along the shell of my ear, sniffing lightly. Goosebumps broke out over every inch of my skin. "That smell," he groaned. "It's been taunting me since the day you got here."

"C-Colton," I mewled. My head rolled back as my hips began rocking into his waist. It felt like I would explode with how badly I wanted him. It was as if the oxygen had all been sucked from the room and I needed him just to breathe air into my lungs.

Colt squeezed both of my thighs, resting his forehead against mine. Letting out a frustrated sigh, he gripped my hips, stilling my movement.

I buried a hand into his hair, tugging until his eyes were on mine. The pained expression he wore seared my heart. Colt swallowed, then his tongue darted out to wet his lips. "I'm overwhelmed," he admitted, breathing heavily. There was a steady tick in his jaw.

I understood his hesitation because I felt it too. Desire was like a wildfire rushing through my veins, but along with it was an almost crippling fear. There was a line that we'd drawn so long ago and that line we were now on the verge of crossing served to protect a friendship we valued above all else. I'd always known that if I'd ever allowed myself to become

—

intimate with Colton Fowler, there would be no going back. I could see it in his eyes that he knew it too.

"Just kiss me," I whispered, running my hand through his hair and trailing it down to the middle of his back. "We're going slow, remember?" I smiled at my boy, nipping at his chin playfully.

Colt nodded, nudging my nose with his to position my face just the way he wanted it. His mouth hovered above mine, and I could hardly breathe. As my lips parted, he dove inside, slowly mating his tongue with mine. The sensation was nearly too much. But then every experience with Colton had always been *more*. Every glance, every word, every touch. In the back of my mind, I knew that whatever he and I were doing with each other would either be the best thing to ever happen in our lives or the catalyst that would finally destroy us.

Just as things started to get a little heated, Colt pulled away, resting his hands on the counter on either side of my body. His green eyes bore deep into mine, his chest rising and falling rapidly with exertion. "Go wait for me in bed?" he rasped. I fell in love with the rough, gravelly tone of his voice. The helplessness in the way he was looking at me at that moment. It felt amazing to finally hold some power over this man who'd somehow always been right by my side yet so far out of reach.

"Okay," I whispered. My head was spinning so fast that I had to grip the edge of the counter to keep from falling over.

Colton shifted, adjusting himself. The movement drew my eyes to the massive bulge in his shorts. *Holy shit.* I knew that I was staring, but couldn't seem to look away. I heard a low throaty chuckle...felt his finger once again, lifting my jaw closed, and turning my face to meet his.

"Just say when," he taunted, waggling his brows.

"Are you fucking kidding me?" I shot back as my head moved slowly from side to side. It was no surprise that he was big. After all, I'd been feeling that monster poking me in the back for as long as I could remember, and even got a glimpse or two the other night. But to be that close, beneath

—

109

the fluorescent lights and not having to avert my eyes, I was completely in awe of just how big. Without thought, I reached out and began feeling him up. It had to be at least ten inches in length, I mentally calculated, and thick as a fucking tree trunk. It was hard. So fucking hard. The butterflies were back, and it seemed they'd decided to set up permanent residence in my vag.

Colton hissed, and his hand came down on top of mine, effectively trapping it against the steel rod in his shorts. It was then that it dawned on me...what I was doing, and I felt my face flush with embarrassment. I swear I must've been in a trance. "When?" he asked, toying with the band of his shorts.

"Nuh uh." My eyes widened as I began shaking my head back and forth, swallowing down the huge lump that had formed in my throat.

Colton bit down on his bottom lip, dipping his eyes toward the bathroom door. "Go to bed, Allie," he rasped before clearing his throat. "I need a cold shower." Colt released the hold he still had on my hand and scrubbed at his jaw. I yanked mine back, nodding as I began walking backward, my eyes trained on Colton's dick the entire way.

Collapsing on the bed, I ran a hand lightly over the peaks of my breasts and slid the other into my panties. My neglected body spasmed on contact. *Colton. Colton. Colton.* I moaned his name over and over in my mind as I attempted to relieve the arousal that had me on the verge of tears. My body shook, exploding almost instantaneously. As I came down from the last wave of pleasure, my eyes fluttered open to find Colt lurking in the doorway, paralyzing me with the heat in his stare.

I tried distracting myself by staring at the shadows dancing on the wall above his head. But they disappeared, and the room was bathed in complete darkness as Colton's hand reached behind him into the bathroom, flipping the switch. Tears sprang to my eyes. I couldn't believe he just saw that. Seconds later, the bed dipped with his weight as Colton climbed in

—

beside me. My heart pounded against my ribcage at a furious pace. My throat went dry. I was on my back, gazing up at the ceiling, fighting back the urge to cry, and he on his side with his head propped on a hand, staring down at me. Our eyes locked and my pulse sped up. I would have absolutely died of mortification if he so much as smiled.

"Colton," I whispered, my voice shaking with want. Could he hear the desperation? Did he have any idea how badly I needed for him to put his hands on me? God, I hoped so, because I didn't think I had it in me to say the words.

"Allie," he answered, trailing the back of his hand along the side of my face. I felt the hairs on the nape of my neck rise as Colton traced a thumb over my lips, down my neck, along the V-neck of my shirt. Goosebumps broke out across my skin as he then took the hand that I'd just used to get myself off and lifted it to his mouth, sucking the tips of each of my fingers individually. I'm fairly certain I came again. "So good," he moaned before feathering kisses along my collarbone.

Colton moved lower, skimming his thumbs lightly across my breasts, sending a jolt of electricity straight to my core. His full lips brushed mine in a whispered kiss. White hot need heated my blood. His warm tongue touched mine, and I dissolved into a puddle beneath him. Colton groaned into my mouth, deep and throaty.

His kiss was mint flavored. Delicious. I wanted to eat him. To drink him. To lose myself in that moment, never to be found.

"Shhh." Colt licked his lips, and I felt a hand slip beneath the hem of my shirt. My body jerked in surprise as his fingers splayed across my middle. His skin was so warm against my own. When Colton brought his lips back to mine, it was with renewed hunger. The scruff on his chin scratched my skin as he devoured my mouth. I couldn't have cared less if he rubbed me raw, just so long as he never stopped kissing me.

"Wake up, Al." I felt his fingers dancing across my back before a gentle tug on my ponytail whipped my head back. I tried to open my eyes, but the light was blinding. Squeezing them shut tight, I grabbed the pillow from beneath my head, pulling it over my face.

"Go away." His laughter was infuriating...and also wonderful. Oh, how I missed being woken up by this frustrating boy. He always was an early riser. I, on the other hand...not so much. "Too early, Colt," I grumbled, curling up tighter into the blankets.

Before I knew what was happening, the comforter and pillow were lifted off my body and thrown across the room. "Get up," he instructed, walking over to the closet and pulling one of my Texas State tees from a hanger and tossing it to me on the bed. Then he moved over to his dresser, opening the drawer, which housed my shorts and lounge pants. He hummed as he rifled through my belongings as if he did this every day.

"What are you doing?"

A pair of black running shorts flew over his shoulder, landing on the bed beside me. "Get dressed...and hurry...I wanna take you somewhere." I started to protest but forgot everything, including how to breathe, when he flashed his pearly whites my way. It was unfair how gorgeous he was, and boy did he wield it like a weapon.

I brought both fists to my eyes, rubbing the sleep away. After a yawn that could have woke the dead and a good long stretch, I gave him my full attention. "Why are you picking my clothes? And where are we going that has us dressed for the gym?" Honestly, I didn't care where we were going because Colt looked amazing in his dry-fit Under Armour top and matching shorts. He had a sweatband around his head with his curls flopped over in the most adorable way. Even his tennis shoes coordinated with his outfit. I swear he had fifty pairs. I'm not even exaggerating. I'd never known another man with as many shoes as Colton Fowler.

—

Colt flopped down onto his stomach beside me on the bed, propping his chin in both hands. "We're going on an adventure."

"Where to?"

"It's a surprise." I felt the sting of his hand as it connected with my ass. "Put your hair up. Don't waste time with makeup." Colt glared at me as I tried to refrain from rolling my eyes. "I mean it, Al. We have to get moving." His nose scrunched. "Do spend a few minutes with the toothbrush, though." His fingers pinched his nose, and he cringed.

"Dick," I mumbled, my ass still burning a little where he'd just slapped it. Oddly enough, I wanted him to do it again. *What the hell was wrong with me?* I cupped a hand over my mouth, huffed into my palm, and then cringed. Morning breath to the tenth power. Snatching up the clothes, I scrambled out of bed and made a run for the bathroom.

"It's three in the morning!" I screeched, finally noticing the time on the bathroom clock. *Was he insane?*

His answer came from just outside the door. "It'll be worth it. Trust me."

"You know how grouchy I get without my sleep," I warned, pinning my hair up in a knot on the top of my head. I'd only got three hours, and it showed in the bags under my eyes and the paleness of my skin.

"I've got a cup of coffee waiting for you, princess."

"Thanks," I answered, pulling out my Caboodle from beneath the sink. I knew he said no makeup, but I couldn't leave the house in this condition. Ignoring his huffing and puffing, I worked at lightning speed, applying a quick layer of concealer, powder, and mascara.

Colton gave me "the look" as I came out of the bathroom, clearly unimpressed. "Can't you ever just do what you're told?"

I grabbed the Yeti cup from his hand, taking a long swig then moaning with satisfaction. *Perfect.* "Is that a serious question?" I asked, setting the coffee on the dresser behind him and using his shoulders to balance myself as I hopped

—

around, sliding my feet into my Nikes.

"Guess not," he answered upon seeing the daggers I was shooting his way. "Let's go."

"This better be good, Colton."

"You woke me up in the dead of night to go traipsing in the woods?" By that point it was 4:30. I'd been awake for over an hour and was only giving him a hard time.

Colt shrugged his broad shoulders, giving me a sexy little smirk. "Unless you're too scared…"

He knew I couldn't refuse a dare. "Never," I growled, running ahead of him. "Eat my dust." Colt stayed a step behind, allowing me to lead the way. It was eerily dark, and to tell the truth, I was a little afraid. I'd never have admitted that to Colton, however. I had a reputation as a badass to uphold. But then something howled in the distance, and every hair on my body stood on end. Stopping abruptly, Colt slammed into my back, but unlike the last time, there was nothing within reach to stop our fall. "Shit! Are you okay?" Colton lifted onto his knees, rolling me over to my back.

I nodded, my heart racing. There were rocks digging into my back and twigs sticking out of my hair. As uncomfortable as it was, I never wanted to move from that spot. With Colton hunched over, running his hands over my body. Looking at me like I was the most precious thing in the world to him. His concern made my heart dip.

"Yeah," I breathed heavily. "I, ummm…I heard something."

The left side of his mouth curled. "Did you?"

"Are you sure we're allowed out here right now, Colton? Are you going to get me arrested?"

His tongue darted out, rolling over his top teeth. "Technically…no. But—"

I felt my eyes widen. "So, we're trespassing?"

His hand rubbed across my forehead, moving the hair from

—

my eyes. "No, Bonnie, I"

Lifting a hand to his face, I traced his bottom lip, cutting him off. "Cuz, that's kinda hot, Clyde," I rasped, chewing my lower lip.

"What is? Breaking the law?" A laugh rumbled from deep in his chest, echoing through the Hollywood hills.

"Mmmhmm," I moaned, gazing up into his smoldering stare.

Colt went quiet, dipping his head to brush his thick lips over mine. His nose bumped my nose and then his mouth was back on mine, his hands were cradling the sides of my face. His fingers massaged my scalp while his thumbs softly rubbed over my jaw.

A knot formed in my stomach. My hips lifted from the ground, rocking into his. I could feel him hardening with every thrust, and I was so hot. Panting into his mouth, I gripped two hands full of his hair and pulled. I wanted him. All of him. I was desperate for him to ease the throbbing between my legs. To feel how wet I was for him. To see how crazy he made me.

Something about being out there in the open. The fear of being caught...it had turned me into a wanton hussy. Fuck taking it slow. I wanted him to rip my clothes off and make love to me right now.

"Allie," Colt moaned against my lips. His hands tensed in my hair, pulling. It's like there was a direct connection from my roots to my sex because that little move had me trembling with need.

"Colton...don't stop...Please."

His brows dipped. I could see him wrestling with something in his mind, so I reached between us, palming his erection. Trailing my hand up and down softly, loving the feel of him twitching in my palm in response.

His hands went to his waist and victory was within my grasp. Colton gripped the band of his shorts, and just as he was about to free his brilliant cock, a bright spotlight shone down right on us.

—

"What the?" Colton jumped up, grabbing my hands and pulling me to standing. I had no clue what was happening. Desire muddied every one of my thoughts. Had we been caught? Where was that light coming from?

Both of Colton's hands went into the air with his middle fingers extended, and then he folded in half, laughing.

What was happening? "Are we going to jail?"

Colton's laughter only intensified, so I kicked him in the shin, because desperate times, right?

"Ouch, Alex!"

"What's so funny?" I demanded, crossing my hands over my chest.

He cleared his throat. "What I was saying before you *distracted* me being all sexy and shit..." He raised his right brow. "Is that my buddy, Wyatt, works here and let us in thirty minutes before they usually open so we could make it up the hill in time for the sunrise."

Poking my bottom lip out, I frowned. "So, we're not outlaws?"

He snorted. "Not hardly."

"Some friend." I harrumphed, turning to head back up the winding path. "Cock-block," I muttered under my breath. Colton must've heard because his maniacal laughter followed behind me. I'm glad he found this funny because I was going to die of blue *clit*.

"You wouldn't happen to have a cigarette?" I asked, peering at my best friend over my shoulder.

"You don't smoke, Al."

I let out a loud sigh. "I know." But fuck if I didn't need that cigarette something fierce.

The hike was steep and rocky. Thankfully, Colt and I were both in pretty good shape and made it without any issues, but we were both panting by the time we reached the top.

"Just there to the left," Colt instructed, placing a hand on the small of my back as he guided me to the right spot. "There," he said, shining his flashlight into a small clearing. Right near

—

the edge of a cliff was a pine tree sitting all alone. It felt like we were cut off from the rest of the world. The feeling was so out of place in the middle of such a busy city.

"It's beautiful. What is this?" The sky was just beginning to lighten to a deep purple. From here we could see out over the Hollywood hills. It was breathtaking.

"Come on." His knuckles rubbed up and down my back a few times before he took my hand. I followed him to the tree where he pulled out a tin box. It was army green and inside were a couple of notebooks, various trinkets, and a shit ton of business cards. We sat side by side on a large boulder and Colt pulled out one of the books, opening to a page in the middle. The entries were dated from 2007 all the way to the present.

"Is it a journal?"

"Yeah, sort of. There was a fire in the hills back in 2007. This tree was the only survivor. People started hiking up here to visit the tree as sort of a good luck omen. Someone along the way nicknamed it The Wisdom Tree, and it stuck. This tree even has its own Instagram page."

Colt held the flashlight over the book as we read through page after page of entries. Some visitors simply recorded the date of their visit. There were lots of short poems and some very profound words of advice. It was especially neat to see the ones who came back multiple times. We even found a few suicide notes that were obviously jokes. One was signed Pauly Shore. It was one of the coolest places I'd ever been. I felt like we were part of some secret club. "This is amazing." I looked over to my best friend with his big goofy smile and fell a little more in love with him. "We have to write something..."

Colt took the book and pen from my hand. I watched over his shoulder as he wrote. "I'm here today with my best friend, Allie, and it's really sort of perfect. This tree has withstood the unimaginable, and like this tree, I know that no matter what figurative fires life throws our way, we'll come out standing. July 14th, 2017. Colton Fowler."

I nudged him with my shoulder. "Well, aren't you a surprise."

—

"Hey. I can be a fart smella when I wanna be." He was a smart fella all right. "Here," he said, passing the journal. "Your turn."

"Go away," I said, shooing him with my hand.

Colt glared at me. "You read mine."

Shrugging, I gave him a little shove. "You let me."

"Do I get to read it when you're done?"

I thought for a brief moment on how long would be a reasonable amount of time for us to figure things out. "Nope... six months." By then if we hadn't got our shit together, we were never going to.

Colt stood, dusting off his butt, right into my face. "Fine," he said, laughing as I wiped dirt from my face. He walked around to sit on a rock on the opposite side of the tree, facing out over the hills. "Don't take too long. You don't wanna miss this."

After packing the journal back into the metal lockbox, I crept over to where Colt sat. "Rahh!" I shouted, clawing his sides with both hands from behind.

"What the fu—" He shot a foot up into the air and immediately I realized what a bad idea that was. Visions of Colton tumbling to his death flashed in my mind.

"Sorry," I screeched, grabbing the back of his shirt. He was in no danger of falling. Thank God, he jumped up rather than forward.

"Damnit, woman. You tryin' to kill me?" he teased, pulling me around to sit beside him, with his arm wrapped around my shoulders.

I shrugged, snuggling into his chest. We were both quiet for a few minutes, taking in the scenery, when my body began to tremble with laughter.

"You okay, Allie?" Colt asked, moving to see my face. "Are you laughing or crying? I can't tell."

"You sh-should have seen your face," I choked out between guffaws. "I got you so good."

The next thing I knew, I was being lifted into Colton's lap, and his lips were on mine, properly silencing me. My body was a livewire any time we touched, and this time was no exception. I wasn't sure I'd ever get used to the intensity, or that I even wanted to.

Long minutes passed before Colton pulled his lips from mine. "Look, Al," he whispered, pointing toward the horizon where the sun was just beginning to peek over. Orange beams kissed the treetops, and instantly a chorus of birds started to sing. Nature's alarm clock was truly majestic.

"Wow. It's so beautiful, Colt."

Colt's lips pressed a kiss to the bend of my neck, and his arms tightened around my middle. "*You* are beautiful. I love you, Alexis Mack..."

CHAPTER FIFTEEN

Colton

"SO, YOU AND ALEXIS HAVE BEEN ACTING LIKE AN OLD MARRIED couple lately," Blex mused, depositing a huge bowl of Coco Puffs on the table and pulling out the chair across from mine. "You two official yet?" my nosy friend asked before shoveling a bite of cereal into his mouth.

"We haven't put a label on it or anything. We're having a good time. Taking things slow." I couldn't help but smile at the mention of Alex as I stared down into my cup of coffee. The past few days had been almost too good to be true. We were slowly becoming more comfortable with the physical side of our relationship, and I couldn't get enough of her.

Blex eyed me as he took his next bite and started humming the tune to that Beyoncé put a ring on it song. *Boy, was he being subtle this morning or what?*

"Oh, I love that song," Al said, seeming to have materialized out of nowhere. "Alexa, play 'Single Ladies' by Beyoncé."

"Morning, Allie," I greeted with a nervous smile over my shoulder. Why'd it feel like I'd just been busted? I had no qualms about marrying Alexis. In fact, there was nothing I wanted more, but it was way too soon to be talking about marriage. Especially after the way she reacted to Dean. *No thank you.* Slow and steady is what it would take to win the race, and I was damn tired of fouling out where she was concerned. "You're up early. It's not even two." I blocked my head with my hands and ducked, anticipating the blow, but she was too busy gyrating in the kitchen to that stupid song to come after me.

"Uh oh, oh oh oh oh, uh oh oh oh oh." Damn. My girl could move. She was sexy as hell in her tank top and my boxers rolled at least five times at the waist. Her hair. Well, I didn't even know what to think about that disaster. I was just glad not to be the one to have to tame that mess. How it went from that to the silky strands I loved running my fingers through was one of life's great mysteries.

Blex sang the chorus, holding his hand out and rubbing his ring finger in full Beyoncé fashion. He raised his brows, a not so subtle hint as to our earlier conversation, before joining my girl in the middle of the kitchen for a dance off.

"What the fuck?" Finn said, scrubbing at his eyes with his fists. "There's no partying without Finn." His eyes darted around the room, glaring at each of us individually. "Alexa, play 'Call Me Maybe.'"

I was beginning to think I'd somehow woken up in some alternate universe where I lived with a bunch of drag queens before the lyrics started, and I got where he was going with his song choice.

Finn lip sang, all dramatic. The very first line about the party not starting 'til she walks in.

"Come dance with me," Allie pouted, grabbing my hands and pulling just as the beginning chords to "Pour Some Sugar on Me" drifted through the speaker. I felt a little ridiculous dancing sober in the kitchen with my roommates around, but there was no way I'd ever pass on having Allie rubbing up against me.

It didn't take long to get over my hesitation. Alex was

—

insanely hot, and my dick was giving her a standing ovation. We'd yet to get past second base, and I found myself in a constant state of...*hard*. Still, I was reluctant to go any further. The last thing I wanted was her to feel cheated out of the whole dating phase just because we'd known each other forever. All jokes aside, Alex was not and would never be a forgone conclusion. I wouldn't cheapen her by treating her that way. I didn't want to take it. I wanted to deserve it.

Alex was busy using my body as a pole—such a hard life—and I was on the verge of nutting in my shorts when I felt something wet on my face. Then Allie started to squeal, and I turned to find Finn and Blex shaking bottles of beer and spraying it into the air.

Never. A. Dull. Moment.

"So, Remy's having a pool party at his parents' house tonight. You two coming or veggin'...again?"

Alex turned her head, which had been resting in my lap, up toward my face, awaiting my answer. I laced my fingers with hers and squeezed. "Nah, man. You and Blex have a good time. We're gonna stick around here."

"Dude...you haven't hung out with us for almost two weeks. Are we breaking up?" Finn was apparently still channeling his inner Beyoncé from this morning.

"I'm just not in th—"

Alex pushed up from my lap, cutting me off. "Let's go."

"It's fine, Al. I really," I stressed, narrowing my eyes at Finn, "really don't think it's a great idea." Things had been going so well since we cut the parties. It was always the same people at these things, and that meant Candy, Lyla, maybe Sally, and a slew of girls I'd hooked up with would be there. Not to mention Stephan. Yeah, no thanks. "It's a disaster waiting to happen."

Finn rolled his eyes and waved his hand in dismissal. "It'll be fine, Fowls. You're worrying over nothing."

By that time Allie had completely removed herself from my lap and was sitting up on her knees beside me on the couch. "Is it because of the Hoovers?"

I cleared my throat. "Uh..."

"What is it you think I'm gonna do? I *can* control myself, Colton Fowler...I mean, unless you give me a reason not to..." Alex trailed off, her left brow darting up in a challenge.

A nervous pit began to form in my stomach. This was a bad idea. "I'm not worried about you doing anything, Al."

Her face softened. "Are you worried about my feelings?"

"I just don't see any reason to go anywhere that you'll feel uncomfortable."

She scoffed. "Dude, if I'd worried about girls snubbing me, I'd have spent my entire teenage life hiding."

Huh? "What're you talking about?"

"I'm just saying...girls have always been jealous of our friendship. It's nothing I can't handle. Besides...I'm kinda looking forward to taking a victory lap." Alex winked, pressing a kiss to my cheek. She held an imaginary spoon in her hand and moved it in a stirring motion.

Fucking wonderful. "We're staying home, Finn."

Alex gave me a hefty dose of side eye. "I'm going to get dressed. This is gonna be so much fun," she squealed before hopping off the couch and bounding up the stairs.

"You're about to make my life really fucking difficult, Finley."

He twisted his lips to the side and shrugged a half-hearted apology. "Whoops."

Two hours had passed when Alex finally came back down. Jesus, Mary, and Joseph. She was going to get me killed tonight looking like that. What was she thinking? Her hair was flat-ironed, long, and straight down to the middle of her back. She had a full face of makeup. And she was practically naked.

"Bald as a hairless cat!" she chimed, twirling before me.

"*Badow!*" Finn walked in from the kitchen, not even attempting to hide the way he was admiring my girl. "When you decide to make a statement, you go all out, Lexi girl."

Alex's face pinkened. "Yeah?" she asked, nibbling on that damn lower lip.

"Hell yeah!" my roommate shouted, walking around to see the back. "Need someone to inspect for stray hairs? I'd love to see your bald kitty."

I lowered my head into my hand, shaking it from side to side. "Too far, Finn," I muttered.

"I'm good, Finley."

"Hell yeah you are." Finn nodded, scouring his eyes over her body again.

"Out," I growled, moving my eyes toward the back of the house.

Finn held his hands up, palms out. "Chill. I'm goin'. I'm goin'." He walked a few paces, before turning back in our direction and giving one last poke. "*Meeeow,*" he purred then disappeared up the stairs to get ready.

"I live with a child," I muttered as Allie walked over to sit in my lap.

"He's harmless," she whispered, running her manicured nails through my hair. The sweet smell of her perfume invaded my senses. She had her tits on display in a red bikini top, and they were right under my nose.

"Which is the only reason he's still alive," I agreed, darting my tongue out to lick the creamy white skin spilling over the top of her suit.

"Watch it, mister." Her eyes narrowed as she squirmed in my lap. "You'll get my cover-up wet."

I snorted. "Is that what this is?" I asked, fingering the see-through mesh she was wearing.

Alex nodded, adjusting the useless scrap of barely-there fabric.

—

125

"Shouldn't a cover-up...I dunno...cover something up? Like maybe these?" I cupped a hand over her breast. "Or this," I added, running a finger up her thigh and tracing it along the top of her bathing suit bottom. My heart was beating a mile a minute. I could feel her pulse racing.

"Colton," she moaned, squirming in my hold.

"Yeah?"

"Don't start unless you plan to finish." She lifted a hand, squeezing both of my cheeks together, causing my lips to pucker. Then planted a kiss on my mouth before hopping out of my lap.

"You look beautiful, Allie."

"Thank you, Colton," she answered wearily, waiting for the but.

"Please go put some clothes on."

Alex did not go put any clothes on.

Surprised? Yeah, me neither.

Walking into that house with Allie looking like she'd just stepped off the pages of *Sports Illustrated* was no easy feat. The thought of other guys ogling her body had me on edge. That Stephan would see it...Well, that just made me murderous.

"Colton! My man," Remy called, greeting us at the door. "So glad you ended up being able to make it after all."

"Hey, Rem. Thanks for the invite." He and I did the obligatory handshake/backslap.

"Hi, I'm Alexis." Allie snaked her hand around my back, introducing herself before I could.

"*Hellooo*, Alexis. Nice to meet you, babe. You here with Fowls?" Remy was a good guy. I couldn't fault him for being interested in Allie, but at least he'd had the decency to check before making a move.

In true caveman fashion, I wrapped my arm around Alex's shoulders, pulling her to my side. "Remy, this is Allie. Allie,

—

Remy," I offered, a little too late. "And, yeah, she's with me."

Remy's eyes got big in mock surprise. "But...she's so... brunette."

Alex giggled, burying her face into my chest.

"I don't think she's your type, Colton..." he teased. "Lemme take her off your hands," he added with a wink.

Rubbing a hand up and down her arm, I placed a kiss on Alex's forehead possessively. "Allie's everyone's type."

"Touché." Remy laughed, ushering us inside. "Grab a few drinks from the kitchen and head out back, guys. I'll see you in a few."

"He was nice," Allie offered, squeezing my side tighter as we walked through the throng of people to get to the kitchen.

I'd decided before leaving the house that I wouldn't be drinking tonight. I needed a level head to get through this. Plus, Allie and I blitzed...together. That scenario hadn't worked out for us so well thus far. "Beer?" I offered, opening the fridge.

"Yeah. I'll have one of those Mike's Hard Strawberry Lemonades," she said, pointing to the pink, girly drinks on the third shelf. "You aren't drinking?" she asked with a hint of surprise in her voice when I handed her the drink and pushed the door shut.

"Nah. I'm good."

When we stepped through the sliding doors leading out to the pool area, we ran right into Candy, who was on her way into the house, presumably for another drink. By the looks of it, she was already well on her way to drunk.

"Colton." Candy perked up, poking her tits out. Her finger lifted to twirl the lock of blond hair that had been resting on her shoulder. Her tongue darted out, wetting her collagen-filled lips. "Where ya been? I haven't seen you around." She stepped forward, running a hand down the front of my shirt. I felt Alex's grip tighten on my arm, her nails nearly piercing my skin as Candy leaned forward, speaking right into my ear. "And trust me, I've been lookin'."

As I was clearing my throat, I felt Allie's tiny foot stomp

down on my own and whipped my head in her direction. It took every ounce of restraint I could muster not to laugh at the pinched expression on her face. By the grace of God, I held it together. "I've been busy," I responded without looking up from the murderous eyes of the only girl I had any interest in. I lowered my head at the same time that I lifted Alex's and gently pressed my lips to hers. Her breath hitched as I traced the tip of my tongue along the seam of her mouth. Before I knew it, we were full on making out, and Candy was nowhere in sight.

"That went better than expected," Alexis said, swiping her fingers over her kiss-swollen lips as we walked hand in hand to an empty table at the far end of the pool area.

Remy's parents' house looked like something taken straight from an episode of *MTV Cribs*. The pool alone had to have cost a small fortune. It was a freeform, natural design with a few rock waterfalls and grottos placed around the edges. There had to be at least fifty people hanging out in and around the pool, and it didn't feel crowded at all. It was completely dark out and the pool lighting made for a very intimate atmosphere.

Alexis set her huge Coach beach bag on the table and pulled her useless "cover-up" over her head, shoving it inside. Great, now she was even more naked.

Goddamnit, she was too beautiful for my own damn good.

"What're you scowling at?" she asked, reaching her hands around to her back, adjusting her top.

"Huh? Nothing," I said, directing my answer to the beautiful mounds of flesh that were just begging for my attention.

"Colton!" Her foot connected with my shin. "Stop staring," she gritted out, glancing around for onlookers. "It's just a bathing suit."

"Oh, don't 'It's just a bathing suit' me. You've got those boobs on display for a reason...and it better be me," I warned playfully as I reached out, pinching the nipple that was straining against the flimsy material.

"You son of a—" she screamed, cupping her tits in her hands.

—

"There you guys are," Blex called as he and Finn walked up, drinks in hand. "Thought you could hide from us?" He harrumphed, frowning at the dense landscaping helping to seclude us from the rest of the party.

"Need some help holdin' them titties up, Alex?" Finn offered, waggling his brows.

Allie's hands dropped to her sides, and her angry eyes settled on mine. "I hate you so much right now."

"Don't be so dramatic, Al." I gripped her tiny waist in both hands, bringing her to my lap and nuzzling my nose into the bend of her neck.

Finley snapped his fingers a couple times, drawing our attention. "I'm not gonna stand here all night waiting for your answer, Alex. I'm sure I can find someone around here in need of my services."

Dude was a fucking idiot.

"Candy was looking a little trashed when we met up with her a few minutes ago," Allie offered. "Maybe you could go help her out."

Finn's face fell. "Bro code, Alex."

"Huh?"

"Don't go fishin' where your brother's been dickin'." He pumped his fist in front of his mouth, rubbing his tongue along the inside of his cheek to fully paint the picture for her.

Allie's jaw started to tremble. I made a cut it out gesture to Finn. But it was either too dark for him to see or he was too stupid to listen because his mouth just kept running, mistaking Allie's silence for confusion.

"She's Colton's chick."

Blex got ahold of Finn before I could. "Learn when to shut the fuck up, Finn." His head dipped toward Allie, who practically had smoke coming from her ears.

It was that exact moment when Lyla decided to make her presence known. Of course it was. "Well, well, well, look what the cat dragged in," she teased, walking over to where I sat with Alex in my lap and planting a kiss on my cheek. "Alex, right?" she questioned, knowing damn well she knew her name. "Good seein' ya again." Her comment dripped sarcasm. "I see you're still making it your life's mission to suppress Colton's cock."

Alex shifted in my lap, turning to face our unwelcome guest, and I braced myself for the impending explosion. "You know...I feel really, really sorry for you, Lyla." Allie's voice was eerily calm.

Lyla's lip curled into a snarl. "What for?"

"Didn't your momma ever teach you not to chase a man?" she asked with a sympathetic smile. "It's just...Well, it makes you look kinda *desperate*." She whispered the last word, patting the top of Lyla's hand, which was resting on the table in front of us.

Lyla's head tipped back and she cackled. It wasn't attractive at all. "You feel sorry for me?" Her hand went to her chest. "You're like Colton's fag-hag...and he's not even gay."

Holy fuck. I tried to speak up to put an end to this before it got out of hand, but as soon as Allie felt my movement, I was shushed. I looked to Blex and Finn for help, but they both just stood there with their arms crossed, watching the show.

"Lyla, honey. You can be friends with a guy and not suck his dick..." Alex was killing her with kindness, and for some reason, it was really turning me on.

Lyla narrowed her eyes. "Oh, I heard what happened when you walked in on Candy sucking him off. Don't even try to pretend you aren't jealous, little miss high and mighty."

Alex tensed in my arms. "You and Candy are friends?" She didn't even try to hide the judgment in her tone.

Lyla shrugged.

Allie's mouth hung in the air for a minute. "Wow," she said, shaking her head. "Y'all must just do things differently around here. Go deep throat a cactus, Lyla. This dick's going through a *suppression*." She winked, making a shooing motion with her hand. Then she turned to Blex and Finn, who were still standing there, mouths agape. "Apparently, y'all need to teach these bitches some sister code."

"*Alex*," I groaned, shaking with laughter as Lyla stormed off.

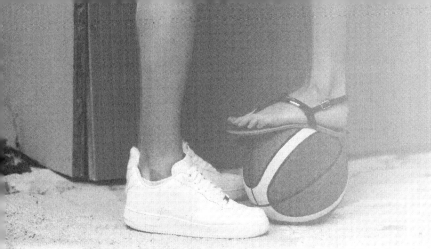

CHAPTERSIXTEEN

Alexis

THAT LITTLE ENCOUNTER WITH LYLA HAD ME ALL ON EDGE. THE B.J.
twins were friends? If that's what having girlfriends was about,
I was happy I didn't really have any. Thank you very much.
Imagining the two of them swapping stories about Colton was
making me sick to my stomach.

"Grab me another drink, Finn?" I asked when he walked off
to replenish his beer.

A crowd had assembled in the open area behind our table,
turning it into a dance floor, and that's where we'd been for the
past couple of hours.

"Allie, I think maybe you should slow down," Colt suggested,
pulling me into his chest. "You're going to make yourself sick."

Nope. No way. I was not going to survive this night without
lots of liquor. "You're so sweet," I slurred, running my hands
over his shoulders. "I'm fine, Colt, really," I insisted, trying to
look very, very sober.

Colton rolled his eyes and huffed in frustration. God, he was
so cute. "Will you at least eat something?" he begged.

I always did love the way he looked out for me. "Okay," I agreed. "Feed me."

A slow smile moved across his face. "All right. I'll be right back. Don't go anywhere."

I must've been drunker than I thought because it seemed like almost no time had passed before I felt Colton grinding his body against mine. And did he ever come back recharged. The way he was moving felt almost indecent, but I was too turned on to care.

"Goddamnit, Alexis," Blex growled, stalking off.

What the hell? I followed his movement with my eyes and could have sworn I saw Colton tear through the back door into the house. But, how could he, if he was—

"We move well together," Stephan said, spinning me in his arms.

My heart started to beat like a bass drum. Loud. Hard.

The air left my lungs. *Oh, Colton.*

"Something wrong?" That no good motherfucker.

I shoved at Stephan's chest as tears poured down my face. "Why? Why would you do that?" My hands were on my chest. I felt like everyone was watching me. Laughing at me. Like they were all in cahoots with the universe to spoil any chance I had of finding happiness.

"Come on, Lexi," Finn said, shielding me in his arms. "You'll get yours later, asshole," he shot at Stephan before guiding me around the pool, through the house, and into the back seat of Colton's car.

Colton's anguished eyes met mine in the rearview, revealing his every emotion, and it cut me like a knife. I mouthed the words "I'm sorry," but he just turned away, twisted the key into the ignition, and headed for home.

Finn kept whispering that it was okay. That everything would be okay, but how could it? The car was deathly quiet, apart from the sound of my cries and the occasional pounding of Colton's fist into the steering wheel.

When we arrived at the house, he had barely taken the time

to throw the car into park before he was slamming the driver side door and storming off into the house.

"I didn't know," I cried to both Blex and Finn. I could feel them judging me. "I th-thought it was h-him."

"Give him a few minutes to calm down, Alex," Blex suggested, his face softening.

Walking into the house was like stepping into a war zone. It sounded like bombs were going off upstairs with all of the banging.

"Don't go up there right now, Lexi," Finn warned as I began making my way toward the stairs. "I've never seen him like this."

Nausea churned in my stomach as I continued the twisty climb. "I'll be f-fine, Finley. Colt would n-never hurt me." *Not physically anyway*, I thought.

"Let me go talk to him first to try to explain, Alexis." Blex was approaching the steps when I shooed him away.

"You guys, he's not going to do anything. Ch-chill."

When I got to the room, I hesitated for a minute, afraid of what I would find when I opened that door. Slowly, I twisted the knob, peering my head inside. He was right there, standing so close, I would have hit him had I swung it all the way. His hands were fisted at his sides. His breathing labored. His nostrils flared as he stood there staring back at me, unmoving.

"C-Colt," I whimpered. Squeezing inside, I shut the door, and on shaky legs, took a few steps to stand before him. I wanted to reach out and hold him but was too afraid of being rejected. A river of regret streamed down my cheeks. "I th-thought he was you," I explained. The back of my throat burned as I continued. "I swear. I never would have—I'm sorry," I cried. "I'm so sorry, Colton."

He swallowed. Every line of his face was hard.

"I want to touch you," I whispered, taking a step closer. Looking up into his pained eyes, I waited for permission. Just when I was about to give up and walk away, his hand lifted to cup my cheek, and I started to tremble with relief. Colton's

—

thumb swiped across my lips. I thought that I might die from feeling so much. He gripped the back of my head, pulling me into his chest. He'd never held me so tight.

Colton's chin rested on the top of my head. "I can't lose you again, Al." I felt his body shake as the anger began to dissipate. "Not again," he whispered, pressing a kiss to my temple.

The fear in his voice was breaking my already shattered heart. I wanted to give him everything—all of me. To show him how much I loved him in the only way I never could. "Make love to me, Colton." I sounded weak and needy but was too drunk and emotional to care at that moment.

He stared at me in a stupor. Like he wasn't sure if he'd heard me correctly. I was filled with enough pent up sexual tension and liquid courage that I was desperate enough to beg for it. "Please, Colt. I need you." My hands twisted into the front of his shirt.

All of the hard lines of his face softened. His eyes glistened, and his head shook. "No."

No? No? Did he just say no?

"Not that I don't want to," he groaned. "I want to." His head hung as he blew out a frustrated breath. With a sad smile, he continued, "More than you know. Just, not tonight, babe. You've been drinking, and we're...emotional. It wouldn't be right."

"I'm not even drunk anymore," I insisted.

He quirked a brow. "I'm pretty sure you out drank most of the guys, Alex."

I frowned. That fag-hag comment from earlier was at the forefront of my mind, taunting me. Why was he so quick to drop his pants for those bitches but kept telling me no? Didn't he want me? Feeling desperate for his attention, I fell to my knees and began fooling with the buckle of his belt. I was going to show him that I could suck a dick as good as any of his blond Hoovers.

Colton's hips jerked, and suddenly his hands were fighting with mine, trying to stop me. *Why was he always stopping me?*

"Allie, what are you doing?" he groaned. "Please get up."

"What's it look like?" I forced a giggle to keep from crying at the sting of being rejected by him yet again. "I'm saying *when*."

The next thing I knew, Colt had me cradled in his arms, and we were halfway to the bed. His chest vibrated as he released a resigned laugh. "Alexis Mack, what am I going to do with you?"

I kept quiet because I couldn't have made it any clearer what I wanted him to do with me, and apparently, he wasn't interested.

Colt deposited me on the center of the bed. He removed his T-shirt before climbing in beside me. "Here, put this over that bathing suit so I'll remember to control myself."

I touched a hand to his bare chest, sliding it over the dips and ridges that lined his muscles. I bit my trembling lip, looking into his eyes, his shirt still balled in my hand. "What if I don't want you to control yourself?" I asked in a broken whisper. "I'm not made of glass, Colton...I won't break."

"Listen to me, Alex," he said, his voice low and full of emotion. "I have spent years dreaming of being inside of you." His hand lifted to his chest, covering mine in his warmth. "This isn't me not wanting you. I want you so bad that I can hardly see straight, but I love you enough to wait until it's right." He squeezed my hand then kissed the tears from my cheeks. "This isn't right, Al."

His words were beautiful. But, God, I wanted him beyond reason. "When," I cried, pounding my little fists into his chest. "When, when, when," I repeated as he grabbed my arms and held me down beneath him. I lifted my hips, wrapping my legs around his waist. Feeling his hard length right where I needed him. "Touch me. You're killing me, Colt."

His jaw was clamped shut. He looked so defeated but held on to his damn moral compass, clinging to it like a lifeline. With a deep sigh, he rested his forehead on mine. "Show me, Allie."

—

Finally. If this was an audition, I was going to give him the best damn blowjob of his life. Reaching between our bodies, I started to dip my hand into his boxers, and again he stopped me. *What the fuck?*

His head shook. "No." Colton cleared his throat. "Show me how you like it. I want to watch you fall apart."

"Colt?" I called out with hesitation when I awoke to an empty bed.

The bathroom door opened and I could hear the water running. "In here, Al. Brushing my teeth," he garbled through a mouthful of toothpaste.

Flashes of the night before flooded my mind. A lot of which I hoped was only a dream. Did I? No. I wouldn't.

I rolled out of bed and went to join him in the bathroom, taking a seat on the lid of the toilet.

"Here," he said, holding out my pink toothbrush with a thick blob of toothpaste on top.

We stood side by side, just like when we were kids. I kept my face turned down, unable to meet his eyes in the mirror. After rinsing his mouth out, Colt sat on the counter, staring with an almost giddy smile. I knew without a doubt what that look meant. I was a whore.

The tips of my ears radiated as I rinsed out the sink, looking anywhere but at that infuriatingly sexy man.

"How are you feeling this morning?"

Finally, I worked up the nerve to turn his way. "Like I want to die."

He frowned. "I'm sorry. I told you not to drink so much. You wouldn't listen."

My hands crossed over my chest, and I glared at him. "Not because of that, idiot," I shot back. "I can't believe you made me do that."

A shit-eating grin spread clear across his face. "Do what?"

—

he teased.

"Show me," I answered in a mocking tone, making air quotes. The heat spread from my ears to my cheeks and neck.

Colton's eyes became hooded. "That was the hottest thing I've ever seen in my life."

"You took advantage of my drunkenness."

He coughed. "Took advantage? No, babe. Taking advantage would have been me having sex with you in that state. Taking advantage would have been me allowing you to try to prove yourself by shoving my dick in your mouth."

I gasped.

"You needed a release. You got one, and it was sexy as fuck." His eyes bore right into mine. "You shouldn't be ashamed of that."

"Well, I am!" I shouted, damn near hyperventilating. Then I got an idea. It was the only way. "Your turn," I said, moving to stand between his parted legs.

"Huh?"

"You heard me." I snapped my fingers. "Get krankin'," I ordered, eyeing his crotch.

Colt bit his bottom lip, staring at me for a moment to determine whether or not I was serious. "Take it out," he ordered.

Gulp. "Huh?"

"Touch me, Alexis, and then I will."

I shook my head. "That's not fair. You didn't touch me."

A cocky shrug. "You were drunk. I'm not. Baby steps," he hissed as I lowered the band of his boxers and his dick sprang free. With his hands braced on the counter, he lifted his bottom into the air, allowing me to slide the material off.

I was in a trancelike state as his hand fisted around his semi-hard cock and slowly began moving up and down. His eyes were fixed on my face as he stroked himself repeatedly, and I got it. Suddenly, I understood. My mouth salivated with how badly I wanted to wrap my lips around that beautiful appendage. It was textbook perfect.

—

"Colton," I whimpered, resting my palms on his thighs as I grew weak in the knees.

"Allie," he grunted, his fist pumping faster as he grew impossibly larger.

Before I realized what was happening, my hand had joined his. Almost instantly, his cock spasmed and warm cum shot out, landing on his lower stomach. With my thumb, I wiped what had leaked down his length and smoothed it over the head. Then I let go, and suddenly I didn't know how to act.

"Th-thank you," I muttered with a hard swallow.

Colt's breathing was labored. "No, Allie, thank you."

"Let's get out of here," Colt suggested, plopping down on his stomach beside me on the bed. He was fresh out of the shower, and the scent of his soap and shampoo was strong and doing delicious things to my insides.

"Where do you wanna go?" I asked, not looking up from the novel I was using to hide behind. The events of the past twelve hours had me all flustered.

The book was snatched out of my hand. "I was thinking of taking you to Santa Monica for the weekend." His eyes browsed over the page I'd been reading, and I fought not to laugh when his jaw dropped and the book snapped shut. Let's just say that I was at a really juicy part.

"What's in Santa Monica?" I sat up in the bed, crossing my legs Indian style and folding my hands in my lap, eager for his answer. A weekend getaway sounded amazing—so couple-y. I had no clue where this thing with Colton would lead. I was both anxious and afraid to find out.

"Well, there's the beach and then Santa Monica pier with the big Ferris wheel on the water." His wide grin made him look so boyish. "Shopping..."

"Sold!" I said, touching a finger to his lips. His mouth opened and he bit down gently, eliciting a moan from my lips.

—

Colt popped up to his knees, leaning in and pressing a chaste kiss to my lips. "Well then, pack a bag and let's get movin'."

"Colton," I screeched, squeezing his thigh as the Uber pulled up to a fucking beachfront mansion. I was having trouble catching my breath. "Is this a joke?" It had to be a joke. The house was *on* Santa Monica beach...like I could see the freaking Ferris wheel spinning from here.

My best friend grinned ear to ear, looking quite satisfied with himself. "Pays to be the star of the basketball team, Al." He shrugged, climbing out of the car. *How did I not know my best friend was living the life of a damn rock star?*

I was still sitting there gawking at the floor to ceiling windows and multi-level balconies when I heard his voice.

"You planning to get out today?" he chuckled, reaching inside to help me out. "I take it you approve?" He couldn't seem to wipe the amusement from his face at my reaction.

At a complete loss for words, I simply nodded my head and continued to stare at what was to be our home for the next few days while Colton tipped our driver and retrieved our bags.

"Come on, Al. I wanna show you the inside."

We stepped into an elaborate foyer, complete with marble floors and a chandelier fit for a palace. Colt dropped our bags at the door, taking my hand and tugging me through to the living room. Two of the walls were nothing but glass with the ocean as far as the eye could see. He gave me the tour going room to room. By the way, there were six bedrooms. Six.

"It's enormous," I said, regarding the pool sized Jacuzzi tub in the master bath.

"That's what she said," he teased.

"Whose house is this?"

Colt shrugged. "A family member of one of the coaches. I mentioned yesterday that I was thinking of taking you out

—

here sometime before you went back to Texas, and by the end of practice he had this all lined up." The mention of my departure gave me a sick feeling. I never wanted to leave.

"You talk about me with your coaches?" I don't know why that made me all warm and gooey inside, but there I was, turning to mush.

His hand cupped the back of my neck, pulling me toward him. "They're practically family, babe. Besides, I talk about you to everyone."

"Do you?" I asked, my voice low and gravelly as I lifted to my toes, lacing my fingers behind his neck.

"Mhmm," he moaned his agreement against my lips before molding his mouth to mine and kissing me long and slow. By the time he pulled away, we were both panting, and my panties were soaked.

Colt rubbed a hand over his swollen lips. "Where to first?"

"Is bed an acceptable answer?" I asked with a sideways smile.

His brows shot up. "A little foreplay first, hussy," he teased, grabbing two fists full of my ass.

Ohhh, foreplay. I liked the sound of that. "What'd you have in mind?" I asked, fluttering my lashes. I was pulling out all the stops.

His lips puckered in thought. "The pier is just down the road...Why don't we start there?"

"I didn't realize you were into exhibitionism..."

Colt tsked, rolling his eyes. "I didn't bring you here to have sex, Alex. We could have done that back at the apartment."

Oh, we were having sex all right. In every room and on every surface of this bajillion dollar house if I had anything to say about it. "Not in glass rooms and swimming pool sized tubs," I argued.

With both hands still on my ass, he pulled me tighter to his body. Whisper-soft kisses brushed my forehead, my nose, my lips, my chin...His lips traced a path from my mouth to my ear. "I have plans for you later," he growled, nibbling my lobe.

Tingles everywhere. "Now," I mewled, going limp in his

—

142

arms.

Colt bit down on my ear. "No."

He was getting a little too comfortable with that two-letter-word for my liking.

"You're mean."

"The worst," he agreed. "Now go get your purse."

The sun was hot on our necks as we carried our shoes in our hands, walking right along the water's edge to the pier. The wet sand was much more forgiving on our calves. I loved the way it felt, washing between my toes.

"Good Lord, there are a lot of people on this beach." The closer we got to the pier, the denser the crowd became. They were literally packed like sardines. I didn't understand how any of those parents were able to keep track of their children. It was giving me anxiety.

"Yeah," Colt agreed. "It's a lot different from Pensacola." His hand squeezed mine affectionately, and my heart did a flip. We had so many great memories at that beach house.

"I miss it," I whispered, squeezing his back. "Why'd we ever stop going?" I shielded my eyes with my hand so I could look at his face.

"You had Dean…" His lips pressed into a flat line. "And I had ball."

After the summer Dean and I got together, we just stopped going. Colt had taken off to California, and I didn't feel right going without him. Our parents still made their annual trip and begged us to come along. I'm so happy that I didn't taint the memories of that place by going with Dean. It wouldn't have been the same.

"Colton," I hissed, digging my nails into his forearm as I planted my feet to the ground.

"Ouch, Alex. What the he—" He stopped walking, staring in the direction I was looking while struck momentarily speechless. It was a lucky thing for those freaks too.

"Is he doing what I think he's—"

"Yeah," Colt answered, cutting me off. He tugged my arm

—

in the direction of the pier, hurriedly getting us out of earshot before I could make a scene. That boy always could anticipate my next move.

"There are kids all over this beach," I shrieked, my hands flailing around in the air.

Colt could not stop laughing at my mini tantrum. "It's California, baby," is all he said in response. Like that was all the explanation I needed. I didn't care if it was fucking Mars. It was disgusting.

"He was milking her, Colton. *Milking* her tit like it was a fucking udder!" The couple walking past us to get to the stairs were looking at me like I was insane. I felt close. I could not believe I just watched a grown ass man pull a woman's tit out of her bathing suit and suck it in broad daylight on a beach filled with children.

"I know, Al." He put his hand on the small of my back, ushering me up the wood steps. "Watch your step. It's wet."

"Like a dairy cow," I muttered under my breath, unable to shake the sight from my head. My nipples were sore just thinking about it.

We were on our way to the booth to buy bracelets for the rides when we came upon a young woman with a guitar singing a beautiful rendition of "I Never Told You" by Colbie Callait. For years that song had reminded me of him, of us, of what we could have been. "I never told you what I should have said...I just held it in." If ever there were lyrics that encompassed the regret I had where Colt and I were concerned, this was it.

"She's good," Colt noted, dropping a couple of dollars into her tips bucket, clueless to the way that song had twisted me up in knots for years over the feelings I harbored where he was concerned.

"Yeah," I agreed with a strained smile.

He came back to stand behind me, bending to rest his head on my shoulder. We swayed side to side to the music. His hands were around my waist and mine resting on his. The heaviness the song had brought to my chest started to dissipate. I didn't need to feel sad any longer. We were here together, and we were figuring this thing out. We were going to be okay.

From there we got our bracelets and went for a whirl on the world-famous waterfront Ferris wheel. The view over the ocean was just breathtaking. "Wow," I breathed out. My heartbeat quickened.

Colton's hand came to rest on my thigh and a lump lodged in my throat. He moved a little higher and my body tensed. *What was he doing?* "Colt," I rasped as my breath quickened and my head rolled back. "It, umm..." His hand went higher still, slipping beneath my skirt. *Oh, dear God, yes.* "Wh-what are you doing?" My head was swirling. I could hardly think straight.

"Foreplay," he rasped, brushing the tip of a finger along the fabric of my bikini bottom. *Could he feel how wet I was?* Colt began to hum to the tune of "Wild Horses." Reese Witherspoon's infamous rollercoaster scene from *Fear* played on a loop in my mind. He was trying to be funny. Watching that movie together was one of the most awkward preteen memories I had. But, it was really turning me on right now.

"Colt," I moaned as the video surveillance sign near the entrance came to mind.

"Mhmm?" His finger moved to the elastic at my bikini line, teasing, and I nearly came on contact. The rush of the ride, the thrill of his touch. I was a live wire ready to burst into flames.

"We're on v-video," I gasped as his finger dipped inside, grazing over my lips.

My purse landed on my lap. "There." A chill rippled through me as his tongue traced the shell of my ear. "All better."

The fact that whoever was watching these videos would have absolutely zero question as to what was going down in this car did cross my mind briefly, but in my pre-orgasmic state, his solution felt adequate—genius even.

"Do you want me to stop?" his raspy voice threatened, causing my anxiety to spike.

I slipped a hand beneath my skirt, curling my fingers around

—

145

his wrist in a death grip. "Don't you fucking dare."

There was a chuckle, then my world faded to black when Colton slid two fingers into my sex and leisurely began pumping them in and out. My body quaked with need as the pad of his thumb began to circle my swollen clit. Each stroke was measured, deliberate. This wasn't some inexperienced boy. Colton was a skilled lover. He knew *exactly* what he was doing to me.

"Oh, God," I moaned, my ass lifting off the seat. The pressure building inside of me was too much. *Air. I needed air.*

I felt the bite of his teeth on my earlobe, followed by the flick of his tongue. Thrashing in my seat, his mouth covered mine and he swallowed my screams. His other arm went around my waist, stilling my frantic movement and quite possibly saving my life. I was so far gone, there was no room for thought of trivial things like safety. Nothing else mattered but chasing that feeling.

Just as the car made its final descent, Colton pulled his lips away and his forehead came to rest on mine. Our eyes locked, the heat in his stare scorching my skin.

"The control booth is gonna thank you for that little performance." He smirked. "So fucking hot."

Shoot me.

My skin was on fire as we departed the ride, and it didn't have a thing to do with the sun.

Did that really just happen?

We walked for a minute or two in silence before I'd finally worked up the nerve to glance in his direction. Colt stared down at me with a cocky grin. I had an urge to smack him, but in all honesty, he had every right to be proud. If I could spend the rest of my life with his hand in my panties, there would be no hesitation.

"Can we go to bed now?" I whined, teasing-*ish*.

"How 'bout some lunch?" He rubbed his washboard abs, and as if on cue, it growled. They had a special relationship, those two. I felt my eyes roll.

—

"Fine," I grumbled, pouting as I trailed a step behind.

Colt led us over to Marisol, a Mexican restaurant at the edge of the pier. We were seated right away at an outdoor table with a great view of the ocean.

"Mmm," I moaned, breathing in the fresh, salty scent that hung in the air.

Colt bit his lower lip. "Still thinking about it?" he teased, pressing his first two fingers together while arching them back and forth. His other hand shot up in an attempt to block the chip I threw at his face, and he let out a deep belly laugh.

The sound of his hearty laughter gave me life. I felt the warmth deep in my chest and couldn't help the big grin that split my face as I stared at my beautiful boy, wondering if I'd ever become used to this. To the giddy elation at finally having his attention lavished on me. To the empty pit in my stomach that was a constant reminder that this could all be gone in the blink of an eye. And if that were to happen...a lifelong friendship would go right along with it.

Gah, I couldn't think of that right now.

"Maybe just a little," I teased back, caressing the side of his calf with my foot beneath the table.

Colton popped another chip into his mouth, chewed, and then swallowed. I was mesmerized.

When did swallowing become a sex move? Well, for straight men anyway.

His eyes grew serious. "I can't stop thinking about it either." Colton winked, giving me his signature lopsided grin, and the butterflies started up again. It was going to be a long fucking day.

After lunch, we went on to tour the little aquarium. We strolled up and down the boardwalk for hours, listening to various street musicians. Amid crowds of people, we danced and goofed off like teenagers without a care for what anyone thought of us. We were just two crazy kids who may have always loved each other but were finally allowing ourselves the chance to fall.

As we walked the last few paces to the beach house, my body began trembling with nerves. *This was it.* Tonight was the night, but in the back of my mind was a nagging fear: *What if I didn't live up to his expectations?*

"What's the matter, Al?" Colt asked, pulling me from my thoughts. He was standing in the open doorway, and apparently, I had stalled a good five feet back to stare off into space.

Smiling through my nerves, I shook it off and moved to join him. "Nothin'. I just got distracted, I guess," I answered, lacing my arm through his. I hoped he couldn't feel it shaking.

"It happens," Colt agreed, but his eyes told me he knew better. "Come on. Dinner should be ready." Colton's face glowed with excitement as he pulled me inside, shutting and locking the door behind us.

"I thought we were here alone..." *Please, please, please tell me we are alone.*

He looked back at me over his shoulder with a shit-eating grin. He knew exactly where my thoughts were. "We are *alone.* I had dinner delivered and set up while we were out."

"Well, look at you," I mused, locking my hands around his neck from behind and jumping up onto his back. "All grown up and adulting."

"I have my moments...Don't tell anyone."

Colt brought me up to a staircase on the third floor that led to a rooftop terrace that he'd neglected to show me earlier. "Holy shit." My eyes about bugged out of my head. It was... *everything.* I was having a hard time absorbing it all. Next to the pool. Yes, pool, was a table with fancy covered dishes. On the other end was a cabana with a bed, draped in layers of sheer white curtains. It was picturesque. "Can we, uh, skip dinner and do that?" I asked, gawking and pointing.

Colton choked on a laugh. "No worries, Allie. We'll get

there...eventually." My heart sped up at the gravel in his voice. His warm hand cupped my cheek as Colton lowered his lips to mine. The kiss that followed was soft and slow. All lips and breath and toe-curling wonderful.

"Let's eat before our food gets cold." I started to tell him that I couldn't care less about the damn food, but Colton had worked so hard to make this day perfect. I at least owed it to him to see it play out the way he'd imagined it in his head.

"Oh, thank God," I said when he began removing the silver dome lids.

Colt gave me a hefty dose of side eye. "Two minutes ago, you wanted to skip dinner altogether, and now you're thanking the man upstairs?" He laughed. "Clearly I'm missing something here."

"I'm just relieved that it's normal food." I waved my hand over the spread of filet, potatoes, and green beans.

"Mmhmm," he agreed with a nod of his head. "Did you expect play food?"

I spat out a laugh. "No. I did half expect caviar and octopus," I teased.

What I didn't expect was his face to fall. "Is this too much?" Doubt furrowed his brow.

Shit. "No. I was just teasing, Colt. Everything is perfect... This has been the best day of my life." I felt awful. Colt was always so upbeat and playful that I hadn't even considered that I may have hurt his feelings with my remark.

He perked up a little at that. "Seriously?" he asked, looking all boyish once again. I nodded my head, and I knew that he could see it in my eyes that I meant it. Colton blew out a sigh of relief. "Mine too."

The food was delicious and we both *stuffed* ourselves.

"Wanna go try out that cabana now?" Colton teased, waggling his brows as I moaned in discomfort.

"Sure, I could use a nap," I fired back, frowning.

We ended up in the pool. The sun was just beginning to set, casting an orange glow over the horizon, and I was in the arms

—

of the sexiest man alive. Life was feeling pretty damn good. So were his hands, which were cupping my breasts, and his lips that were kissing my neck.

Reaching between us, I slipped my hand into his trunks, palming the erection that had been poking my belly. An audible gasp slipped from between my lips when I felt how hard he was.

His hips jerked back at my touch. "Allie, you don't have to—"

"Colton Fowler," I growled, "if you deny me one more time, I will go straight up Lorena Bobbitt on your ass and feed this thing to the sharks."

His hands shot up, palms out. "Well then, by all means, have your way with me."

My heart raced as I slipped my thumbs into the band of his shorts, pushing them down until his hard cock jutted out into the water. Colton sucked in a sharp breath as I resumed stroking him in a slow and steady motion.

His eyes grew bedroom heavy as his cock began to throb in my palm. "Allie," he rasped, pulling my hand away and placing it on his chest. "Not like this," he growled, covering my mouth with his. Colton's hand dove into my bikini bottom, cupping my sex. With the butt of his palm, he applied pressure to my throbbing clit while sliding a finger along my opening. Then he pushed two fingers inside, pumping in and out while circling my nub with his thumb.

"Colton," I mewled into his mouth, my body already coming undone at his touch. "Stop...I'm gonna—Oh God," I moaned, digging my nails into his shoulders as I rode out my climax.

Colton's voice was gravel when he spoke. "So fucking beautiful, Allie." His hands moved to the ties on the side of my bikini bottom, tugging until they both came loose and the scrap of fabric floated on the water's surface. "I wanna feel you explode like that on my cock, baby."

Holy shit. That was so fucking hot. "Yes," I whispered as he pulled the string at my back, leaving me completely naked.

"God, yes."

Colt's hands cupped my bottom and lifted. Tangling my legs around his waist, I devoured his neck as he walked us out of the pool and over to the cabana, positioning me in the center of the bed. "Don't move."

Propped on my elbows, I watched the muscles of Colton's shoulders flex with his movement as he worked at the ties on the bedposts. One by one, the curtains came down, cocooning us in our own little slice of heaven. It felt like we were the only two people on earth. Like we'd been transported to an alternate universe.

Colton's hungry eyes locked with mine as he joined me, his body perfectly aligned with mine. We were all hands and tongues and teeth. Skin to skin. Heartbeat to heartbeat. With my fingers twisted in his hair, I began rocking myself onto his erection. Colton's hands gripped my hips, halting my movement. The head of his cock moved, sliding along my opening, causing me to let out a loud moan. My body tensed, pulsing with need as he held me still, sucking one of my nipples into his mouth.

It was the most exquisite form of torture. "Colt," I cried out. "Please..."

"I've got you, baby," he rasped. Positioning himself, he thrust forward, breaching my entrance in one fluid motion. "Are you okay?" he asked, stilling his movements. "I don't—" He groaned, his brow furrowed with concentration. "I don't want to hurt you."

"It's okay," I cried. "Hurt me, Colton...Just—just move," I begged. "Please move," I panted, rolling my hips into him, desperate for friction.

I felt a tear sneak down my cheek as Colton gripped my ass, thrusting forward again with a loud groan. *Holy shit.* Colt captured my cry with his mouth, kissing me long and hard. Stretching me. Filling me. *Owning me.*

With every thrust of his hips, we destroyed that invisible wall. There was no way we could ever go back now. The thought

—

both thrilled and frightened me.

CHAPTERSEVENTEEN

Colton

WAKING UP IN THE MORNING TO ALEX HOGGING THE COVERS WAS nothing new. Waking up to Alex sprawled naked across the bed, however, was, and I'd just decided it was the single most beautiful thing I'd ever seen. Her long, dark hair draped over her breasts like a curtain, pert, pink nipples peeking through, begging to be lavished with attention. And, I mean, who was I to deny them?

It was barely after seven in the morning, but the room was already bathed in sunlight. Thanks to the floor to ceiling windows, I couldn't sleep. Allie, however, would be in bed 'til three if I'd let her. I wondered briefly whether she'd be upset if I—

Well, there was only one way to find out. Bracing myself on one arm, I leaned in, running my tongue gently over the already erect bud. Alex stirred but quickly fell back into a deep sleep. I licked the pads of the index finger and thumb on my left hand and reached over to tweak the nipple farthest from my face. At the same time, I curled my tongue over the other.

She moaned softly, and I pressed on, lapping and nipping, tweaking and pulling until Alex was writhing beneath me. Until her hands were in my hair, pulling. Until my name fell from her lips repeatedly.

"Oh, God," she cried out when I slipped a finger between her folds. "Don't stop, Colt."

I didn't. Not until she was screaming my name and I'd milked the last tremor from her release. Until she was covered in a light sheen of sweat, lying limp in my arms.

"Is there anything about you that isn't high maintenance?" I asked, my chest vibrating with laughter.

Her sex-hooded eyes turned up to glare in my direction. "I'm afraid to even ask where you're going with this."

I tipped her head up further, pressing a kiss to her warm lips. "If I'd have realized orgasms made you so agreeable in the morning, I'd have started dishing 'em out a long time ago," I teased, earning myself a nip to the chest.

"Let's go make some breakfast," I suggested when I felt her cozying into the crook of my arm like she was about to fall asleep.

Lazy fingers thrummed on my chest. "You have fun with that."

When I rolled out from underneath her, she groaned, stretching out on her stomach.

"Come on, Al." As tempting as it was to stay in bed and fool around all day, I'd already made arrangements.

"It's so cold without you," she complained. "Come back." Her arm stretched out, fingers wiggling in my direction.

After stepping into my boxers, I tossed a shirt at her. "Put that on," I said, trying to maintain a straight face. "I have a busy day planned for us." She harrumphed, turning her head the opposite direction. "Don't make me do it," I added in a warning tone.

"You wouldn't."

"Try me," I deadpanned, quirking my brow.

Begrudgingly, she sat up, her eyes narrowed my way. "Stop

—

staring at my tits," she ordered, pulling the tank over her head. "You want to get rid of them, remember?"

"That was before I was allowed to play with them." I winked. "I've since had a change of heart. They can stay."

"You're too kind."

I bit my lip, watching and waiting for her to notice the T-shirt as she looked down, sliding both hands along her neck and lifting to pull her hair out from the back of her shirt. Alex's hands came around to the front, stretching the shirt out in front of her, and her mouth fell open with a gasp. "Colton!"

Finally! It was a black tank with a white screen-printed rooster beneath the word, "big." "I thought you'd never notice." I laughed.

"Is this yours? Do you actually wear this?" she asked, aghast.

"Come on now, I'm not that cocky," I quipped. "I ordered it just for you."

She smiled with her whole face, shaking a finger at me. "You're good, Colt."

I felt my chest swell with pride.

"Are you sure *you* don't wanna wear it?" she asked, staring up at me with those big doe eyes. "After all, you are a *big dick*."

Dang, Alex, I thought, laughing. "You keep it...Now that you've been inducted into the *big cock* society, you gotta represent," I said, pounding my hand against my chest twice.

Her jaw dropped, morphing into a huge grin. "I got nothin'."

"Come on," I ordered, grabbing her hands and pulling her from the bed. "Let's go eat."

I sent Allie out to the terrace while I whipped up some microwave pancakes and fresh fruit, strawberries, and pineapples—her favorites. Alex was quite impressed by my newfound ability to work a stove. I may have left out the fact that the pancakes came from the freezer. But, hey, a man's gotta do what he can to impress his woman.

After breakfast, we cleaned up and got dressed, then biked the seven miles to Marina Del Rey. It was still early enough that the trails weren't completely inundated with people and there was a nice breeze coming off the ocean. Best of all, Allie hadn't stopped smiling at me all morning.

"Are we going fishing?" she asked while I was locking up our bikes near the dock.

I glanced back at her over my shoulder. "Nope."

"Dolphin sighting?"

My lips puckered in thought. "You might get lucky and see some dolphins."

Alexis held up a fist, using her other hand to reel up her middle finger just as my buddy Ryker pulled up in his boat. His big, lime green boat with the word "Parasail" in huge white letters.

"Oh my God!" she screamed, jumping up and down. "I haven't been since we were teenagers."

I felt like the king of the world when she looked up at me with those big brown eyes bursting with excitement. "Good surprise?" I asked, watching as her whole face lit up.

She squeezed my hand hard enough to cut the circulation off. "Ahhhmazing surprise!"

Allie and I boarded the boat, fastening our life jackets and taking our seats in the back. She looked around in confusion when it took off with just Ryker, his helper, Jude, and the two of us.

"It's just you and me."

"How'd you pull this off?" Her finger came up, cutting me off before I could answer. "Lemme guess...another 'star of the basketball team' thing?"

I gave her a wink and shrugged. Wrapping my arm around her shoulders, I pulled her in closer, kissing the side of her head. I couldn't tell if this all really made her uncomfortable or if she was just bustin' my chops. Allie and I had always had a playful relationship, and I hoped that's all it was. I guess I didn't really see any of this as weird anymore. Although Allie and I were in constant contact with each other, there are some parts of my life she wasn't accustomed to. She'd better get used to it because if I ever made it pro, I had every intention of taking her with me.

Any awkwardness or reservations she may have had vanished when they strapped us in, and we went soaring five hundred feet into the air. Allie's face was exuberant. I couldn't stop myself from staring.

"What?" she asked, her face blushing.

"I just like looking at you."

Her foot reached to the side, hooking around my ankle. I was suddenly regretting the decision to trap us in harnesses for an hour because with the way she was looking at me...I wanted nothing more than to put my hands on her.

"I'm going to be a mess when I have to leave you." We still had two weeks, but that dreaded day was already looming over us.

My chest felt tight. "So, stay."

Allie let out a loud sigh, her head tipping to the side. "You know it's not that easy, Colt."

"It could be, Al. It could be that easy."

Allie's eyes drifted out over the water. I could tell she was deep in her thoughts.

"Hey," I called after she had been quiet for a few minutes. Alex turned back to look at me, her eyes a little glossy. "No pressure. I just want you to know that it's an option."

A slow smile moved across her face. "Thank you."

"Come here," I growled, moving both of my hands to the rope in the center so I could lean my body toward hers. Alex's face brightened, following my lead. Her mouth found mine in the space between us. Our teeth clashed amid lips that couldn't keep from smiling. It was such an adrenaline rush, our bodies firing on all synapses. I knew that nothing would ever compare to the taste of her laughter on my lips.

We were still kissing when Ryker dropped us down, allowing our feet to skim the water. Still kissing when he lifted us back into the air and began towing us in. Only when we landed on the boat's deck did our lips part, and instantly I wanted hers back.

—

"Thanks, man," I said to Ryker as he pulled up to drop us off at the dock.

"No problem," he answered with a knowing smile. "Hope you two had a good ride."

We left our bikes tied up there, walking a couple of blocks to Third Street Promenade, where we grabbed a bite to eat, and Allie shopped 'til she dropped.

"We're going to have to grab a Lyft to get this all back." I laughed. Alex and I had completely forgotten the fact that we'd biked out there. "We can swing back for the bikes with the car when we leave and drop them at the beach house."

"Do we have to go home?" Allie whined. "I love this place so much, Colt." Her eyes drifted around the outdoor courtyard lined with shops and street performers. "It feels like ours—like we belong here, doesn't it?"

"We'll come back again soon," I promised, not wanting to leave either.

"How soon?"

Biting my lower lip, I stared into her brown eyes. *As soon as you move in,* I thought, but I stopped myself from saying it aloud. I'd told her I wouldn't pressure her, but it wasn't easy. "Next visit," I answered, placing a kiss on her forehead.

When our car arrived, we loaded the bags into the back before climbing inside. Allie sat right beside me, her leg pressed against mine. She smelled like sunshine and coconut lotion. The apples of her cheeks were rosy, kissed by the sun. I spent the five-minute ride to the house memorizing every detail of the way she looked tonight. It had been the best weekend of my life, and I didn't want to forget a thing.

Before leaving the house, Allie and I paid one last visit to the rooftop cabana, making love by the ocean to the sound of the waves crashing against the shore.

—

CHAPTEREIGHTEEN

Alexis

RING. RING. RING.

Jeez. Whoever it was, was persistent. After the third call in a row, I'd decided it was probably important enough that I should answer. "Hello?" I groaned, my voice still drunk with sleep.

"Alexis," Dean breathed out, his voice cracking. "I'm so glad you picked up."

We hadn't spoken in weeks. Not since the morning I broke up with him. I couldn't tell for certain, but it sounded like he'd been crying. A huge knot formed in the pit of my stomach. Immediately, I started imagining all of the many horrible things that might have happened. "Hey, Dean," I cooed. "Is everything okay? You sound upset."

"Yeah, uhh. It's Dad...He was in an accident."

"Oh God, Dean. Is he—Is he going to be okay?" Memories of Mr. Ryan, who was like a second father to me, flashed in my mind.

A loud sob broke my thoughts, nearly ripping my heart in two. "They don't think he's going to—" He couldn't finish. My entire body began to shake as I broke out in a cold sweat, his words ringing in my ears. His cries suffocating my heart.

"Dean," I cried, clutching my hand to my chest as warm tears streamed down my cheeks. "No." I gasped for breath, but it was no use. It was as if the air had been sucked from the room. This couldn't be happening. This wasn't real.

Dean cleared his throat, taking a moment to compose himself. At his next three words, I began shoving my belongings into my suitcase. "I need you..." He *needed* me.

I jotted down the hospital information, promising him that I'd be there as soon as I could, and booked the next flight home. All I could think about at that moment was getting to the hospital as fast as possible. I needed to be there for Dean. I had to see Mr. Ryan before he— *No. I wouldn't even think that way.*

After packing the last of my things, I attempted to call Colt, but the sound of his ringtone came drifting through the bathroom door. He'd forgotten it on the counter. *Brilliant.* There was no time to wait. My plane would be departing in two hours. My only option was to leave a note.

Dear Colton,

I miss you already, and I haven't even left...

As soon as I finish writing this, I'll be on my way to the airport to catch the next flight home. Dean's dad was in a bad car accident this morning, and it doesn't look good. I know that you understand how much Mr. Ryan means to me, and why I need to be there right now. Still, I hate leaving without saying goodbye—truthfully, I hate leaving at all. The past few weeks, especially last weekend, were the happiest I've been in years.

This is a conversation I hoped we'd have in person, but I don't want you to come back, find me gone, and assume the worst. So, this letter will have to do. I've made my decision. Hell, if I'm honest, I made it the minute I hopped on that plane to come to LA—to come to you. You're the reason I couldn't say yes. I know that now, without a doubt. There's no way that I could ever marry Dean feeling the way I do for you. I'm in love with you, Colton Fowler. I think maybe I always have been.

Thank you so much for everything. The summer, this weekend, your big cock-the shirt, you perv. I'll call you later tonight when I get settled.

Love always,
Allie
xoxo

After folding the note in half, I wrote Colton's name really big on the outside, then set it on the nightstand, placing his cellphone on top. There was no way he'd miss it. Colt would come straight for his phone the minute he got home, and he'd find my letter.

The three-hour flight back to Texas felt more like three days. It was crazy how time always seemed to stop at the most inopportune times. I'd gotten myself so worked up by the time we landed that I was ready to bowl over the line of slow-moving passengers just to feel my feet on solid ground. God, I hated flying.

When I finally got off that plane, I hightailed it to the baggage area, locating my mother almost immediately. With her arms flailing above her head, she stood beaming up at me as I moved down the escalator at a snail's pace. When I got to the bottom, she was there, wrapping me in her familiar embrace. It was then when I finally felt safe enough to allow myself to fall apart. Right there. In the airport.

"Oh, honey," Momma crooned, finger combing my hair as she held me tightly to her chest. I didn't realize how much I'd missed her 'til she was holding me in her arms. Burrowing my nose into her neck, I breathed in a deep whiff of her perfume, holding it in and allowing it to sooth the hurt for just a moment.

—

161

I was afraid to ask, but I needed to know. A lot could happen in three hours. "Is he—?" I choked on a sob, unable to finish the question, but Momma knew what I was trying to ask.

"He's alive—" her face contorted into a frown "—but it's not looking good, baby."

I nodded, trying to swallow down my tears. I had to get my shit together before I saw Mr. Ryan and before I saw Dean.

On the way over to the hospital, I filled mom in on my summer with Colton, intentionally leaving out the parts where we'd been hooking up. Until I was certain of what would happen between the two of us, I was not getting our parents involved. But I had hopes that maybe soon...Just the mere mention of him had my heart clenching in my chest.

When she stopped at a red light, Momma's head turned in my direction. I could see a question brewing in her eyes and that she was trying to decide whether or not to ask it.

"What?"

Her throat cleared as she fidgeted a little in her seat. "Did you decide what to do about Dean?" My mother looked terrified of my answer.

"No," I answered quietly, clearing my throat. "I can't...I'm not ready."

"Oh, thank God," she let out a loud sigh, tossing her head back with relief.

Rolling my eyes, I swatted her arm gently. "Light's green."

My mother dabbed at the tears in her eyes as she pressed the accelerator. Ever the drama queen. "I'm proud of you, honey."

"For what?" I certainly wasn't feeling proud of myself for any of this.

Her eyes stayed fixed on the road as I felt her right hand patting my leg. "For being brave enough to put yourself first. I know how much you care about Dean, and it's never easy to hurt the people you love, even when you know in your heart that it's the right thing to do." Mom turned to look at me briefly with a sad smile. Too emotional to speak, I simply nodded my head. "I was so afraid you'd end up marrying the wrong guy for all the right reasons."

"I just can't...He deserves better, Mom," I croaked. "To think I let him waste so many years with me." A wave of nausea hit and my throat thickened.

"Don't be so hard on yourself, Allie. A broken heart is easy to fool...You fell in love with *being* loved, but you can't force your heart to love a person back...no matter how badly you may want to."

Tears pooled in my eyes. "I wanted to, Mom. I really thought I did."

"I know you did, baby."

"Alexis!" I heard my name bellow through the waiting room the instant I stepped through the emergency room doors. Spinning around to locate his voice, I was nearly knocked off my feet when Dean's body slammed into mine. I felt his arms snake around my waist as his lips landed on the bend of my neck, and my pulse started to race. I stood stalk still, holding my breath with tears pooling in my eyes as Dean's grip tightened. It felt as if he was afraid to let go. As if he thought I might disappear. *As if he already knew.*

Arms that for so long were my shelter suddenly felt all wrong. My body tensed as I laced my fingers behind his neck, hugging him back, sending up a silent prayer that he couldn't feel the strain. Internally, I warred with the desire to comfort him and not wanting to give him even an inkling of false hope. Dean loved me *so much*. It was in the way he looked at me, the way he touched me...It's no wonder his love was such an effective band-aid to my shattered heart. And here I was about to break his. *I hated myself.*

My eyes swam with tears as I untangled myself from his hold, backing away just a little. "How's he doing?" I rasped.

Dean shrugged, his eyes glossy as he fought back tears. "He's in surgery now to try to repair a lacerated lung."

—

"What happened?"

Dean's hand moved through his hair, pulling at the ends. "He, uh. He fell asleep after pulling an all-nighter at the plant...Went off the road and slammed into a tree at around five this morning."

My hand lifted to cover my mouth as I sucked in a sharp breath. I felt his knuckles trail up and down my spine in what was meant to be a comforting gesture and nearly jumped out of my skin. *What was the matter with me?*

"Alexis?" Mrs. Ryan asked, squinting her eyes as if she were seeing a ghost as she came around the corner. I was thankful for the interruption.

"Mrs. Ryan," I returned, meeting her halfway and wrapping her in a hug. She looked awful. Her usually impeccably styled hair looked like it hadn't seen a comb in days. The makeup on her face was smudged and her clothes rumpled. She'd been through hell today, and it showed. "I'm so sorry," I whispered, kissing the hair at the side of her head.

"I don't know what I'll do if he—" Her face contorted with pain, silent sobs wracking her tiny frame. Her fear was tangible, shaking me to the bone.

As her cries began to quiet, she went limp in my arms, nearly fainting from exhaustion. Dean stepped in, walking her over to a small cluster of chairs, where the three of us sat together and waited.

CHAPTERNINETEEN

Colton

"GOT IT," FINN YELLED ACROSS THE GYM, WAVING MY PHONE IN THE air. I realized I'd forgotten it when Coach sprung it on us at the last minute that he was extending practice and I'd gone to call Alex to let her know. I'd never memorized her number, even though it'd been the same for years. I knew that she'd worry when I didn't come home. I'd never been late since she'd arrived, and without my phone, Alex had no way to reach me either. Coach couldn't run the drills he had planned without me, so he'd agreed to let Finley make a quick trip to the house to let her know that we'd be late.

"Thanks, man. What's Allie up to?" Leaving her naked in my bed this morning was difficult, to say the least, and I kinda hoped to find her where I left her when I got back. I was already getting worked up for when she'd have to return to Texas. I had plans to do whatever I could during her last two weeks to convince her to transfer here to UCLA. We'd spent too much time apart already. Alexis was finally mine, and I had no plans of letting her go.

Finn slapped the phone into my palm, taking a moment to catch his breath from the jog from the parking lot. "Lexi's not at the house." His brow furrowed with concern, and I waved it off.

"She's probably out meeting her friend, Gertie, for brunch again."

"Hustle up, fellas!" Coach shouted to Finn and me over by the bleachers, stabbing at his watch.

I held up a finger, indicating that I needed a minute, to which Coach begrudgingly nodded his head.

Finley jogged onto the court, and before I'd even unlocked my phone, practice had resumed. My first call went straight to voicemail, so I hung up and tried again...three more times. All voicemail. *Where the hell was she?*

"Everything okay?" Blex asked, tapping me on the shoulder.

"Huh?"

"Is Alex okay? Coach has been calling you, and you're just standing here staring down at that phone. Did you get in touch with her?"

"No. It keeps going to voicemail," I answered, clearing my throat. My chest felt tight, and my heart was racing. I couldn't explain the anxiety I felt over not being able to reach her because even I didn't understand it. Odds were, her phone had died. I knew that. But for some reason, probably because I was so afraid to lose her now that I finally had her, I was in a full-blown panic. "I'm going to go back to the house and see if she's there."

My buddy's brows furrowed. "You do realize her phone is probably just dead, right?"

I nodded, feeling ridiculous.

"Alexis is a grown ass woman. She's *fine*. Get back on that court before Coach has a fucking coronary."

Practice lasted another hour, and my performance was less than stellar. I couldn't shake the feeling that something was wrong. As soon as we were dismissed, I ran for the bleachers where I'd left my phone to try Alex again, but it was no longer where I'd left it. "Hey," I shouted at the guys who were making their way to the locker room. "Did any of you pick up my phone by mistake?"

A chorus of "no" and grunts followed.

"I'll keep an eye out for it during cheer practice," Lyla offered, batting her lashes as she smacked on her lime green gum. *Where the hell had she come from?*

"Thanks."

Lyla's hand darted out, clutching my bicep as I started to move past her. "So, I couldn't help but overhear that Alex is missing...Lemme know if you need any help looking for her, okay?"

With my free hand, I pried her fingers off my arm. "I've gotta go."

"Allie?" I walked around the first floor calling her name before heading up to my room, hoping I'd find her there. When I stepped through the door, it felt like I'd been kicked in the stomach. All of the air whooshed from my lungs. *No.* I broke out in a cold sweat as I took in the empty hangers in the closet. I pulled open her drawers, already knowing I'd find them bare. I made my way into the bathroom, and all of her girlie shit was gone from the counter. "No!" I yelled, pacing back and forth, trying to make some sense out of this. *Why?* Why would she leave? I replayed our weekend in Santa Monica. Every amazing minute. Did I misread her? Could I have been that off?

"Fowls?" Finn shouted, rushing up the stairs. "Did you find her?"

"She's fucking gone."

"Yeah..." he drew out. "But did you find out where she went?"

I felt a burn in the back of my throat as I shrugged my shoulders, walking back to the closet and waving my hand over her empty side. "I don't know, but she took all of her shit, so I'd have to assume back home."

Finley's eyes widened as they darted around the room, noticing the lack of Allie's things. "What the fuck? She just left without saying anything?"

"Did you two get into a fight?" Blex asked, his big frame filling the doorway.

I shook my head, pinching the bridge of my nose to try to ward off a headache.

"Well, what happened? Think, man. Something had to have happened to have her packing her shit and taking off like a bat out of hell." Blex stared at me with accusing eyes. A few weeks ago, I'd have accepted full responsibility for behaving like a complete jackass. Something had happened all right, and this the last reaction I ever expected.

My roommates stared at me expectantly.

Oh, for fuck's sake. "We had sex!" I shouted, banging my fist down on the dresser. My body started to shake with anger, with barely restrained emotion.

Finn and Blex both stared at me at a complete loss for words. Finn finally opened his mouth to speak, and Blex immediately got in his face. "Don't you even fucking think about it," he warned, knowing as well as I did that Finn was about to make some stupid remark about Alex leaving after we'd finally had sex.

I felt like a caged animal, clenching and unclenching my fists to try to work out a little of the tension building up inside. "I don't understand," I muttered, pacing the room.

"Maybe she got scared," Blex offered. "Girls do weird shit when they're all up in their feelings."

"Maybe," I agreed, sifting through my memories again, unable to come up with a single time where she'd given any indication that she was having second thoughts. "But to just up and fucking leave without a word, Blex?" I shook my head. "I never expected this from her." Alex hurt a hell of a lot more than my pride with her little disappearing act.

—

"You have to at least call home and check on her," Finn suggested, passing me his phone. "None of us will be able to relax until we know for sure where she is."

Reluctantly, I took the phone. "What the hell am I supposed to say? My mom will be loaded with questions...Beginning with why the hell I don't know where she is considering she's supposed to be with me for the next two weeks."

"Just tell your mom what happened. She's cool as shit," Finn offered. He had an almost disturbing obsession with my mother.

Blowing out a long breath, I shook my head. "My parents can't know that anything happened between Alex and me." I eyed them both. "Got it?"

"Make the call, Fowler," Blex ordered, crossing his arms and leaning back against the wall.

Fine. I knew they were right. As pissed as I was at Allie just then, I was equally worried. I dialed mom's number and waited for her to pick up, praying I could pull off a good enough performance to keep her off our scent.

"Hello?" she answered with hesitation in her voice.

"Hey, Ma," I greeted, trying to sound upbeat. "It's me. I'm on Finn's phone."

I swear I felt her mega-watt smile all the way from Texas. "Hey, baby, it's so good to hear your voice. Everything okay? Where's your phone?"

"Yeah, everything's fine. It went missing at practice today. If I don't find it tomorrow, I'll have to get a new one...Save Finn's number in case you need to get in touch with me until then, okay?"

"I sure will. When are you coming home for a visit?"

It was the same question every time we spoke, and I almost always gave the same answer. "Soon." I did visit, just not near as often as she'd like. It was hard to see Allie with Dean before, but I wasn't sure I could handle seeing her at all after this.

I hated this part. The part where she stewed in silence over my brushing off her request. "Hey, Mom?"

—

"Yeah, baby?" Her voice was thick with disappointment.

"Have you, uh...Have you spoken to Allie, by chance?" My heart raced with nervous anticipation. If she wasn't there, I'd have a slew of questions fired at me, and I was in no way prepared to deal with the force that was my mother.

"Not yet...she's been with Dean since her momma picked her up from the airport. I should see her tonight, though."

I didn't know it was possible to feel so relieved and angry with one person at the same time. I didn't know whether to breathe a huge sigh of relief or break every fucking thing in sight. "Awesome," I choked out, trying not to reveal how angry I was. "I've gotta go, Mom. I just wanted to make sure she got home...You know, since I can't find my phone."

"Okay, Colt. I love you so much. Please think about that visit, okay?" Her voice cracked. "Dad and I would like to see you."

"Soon," I lied. "Love you too, Mom." I ended the call, dropping the phone back in Finn's hand.

"Well?" he asked, looking to me for the play by play.

"She's been with Dean since her mother picked her up from the airport," I repeated, feeling nausea churn in my stomach.

Guess I had my answer.

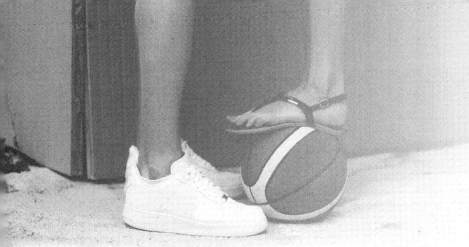

CHAPTER TWENTY

Alexis

"I'LL BE BACK TO SEE YOU TOMORROW," I WHISPERED TO MR. RYAN, bending to place a kiss on his cheek. "You get some rest, okay?" He squeezed my hand, mumbling something I couldn't understand, as he drifted off. I stared at him a moment longer, still shaken by how close we came to losing him today. By the grace of God, he'd survived the most difficult surgeries, and the doctors were now saying that although he still had a long road ahead of him, they were expecting a full recovery.

"You mean a lot to him," Dean said, scaring me half to death.

"Jesus! You scared the crap out of me." We were only allowed in one at a time, and I wasn't expecting anyone else to be in the room. I was already so on edge with the accident and the flight. And this unfinished business with Dean.

He smiled a lazy half smile. "It's so good to have you back, Alexis." He walked over to his father's bedside, taking my left hand into his, and twisting an invisible ring around the third finger. With a shake of his head, he blew out a breath.

Gulp. I wasn't ready for this. Not here. Not now. "Dean, I don't—"

His smile returned, but this time it didn't reach his eyes. They were sad, defeated, resigned. "It's okay, babe." His head tilted to the side, his lips flattening into a straight line. "I took a risk, and I lost...but I'll never regret us." A lone tear crept down his cheek as he squeezed my hand.

I could hardly breathe. "I don't—I don't understand," I stammered.

"He was the wildcard..." Dean sulked, playing with my fingers as he explained. "Everyone could see the connection the two of you shared, but I was foolish enough to take my shot anyway...I knew it that first summer at the beach. I watched the way you watched him with Chelsie and caught every dirty look he threw my way. I fell hard and fast for big brown eyes and a broken heart. Actually, I think it was your heart that attracted me the most. If you could love the guy who broke your heart so fiercely, then I wanted to be the one who put it back together. Surely, you'd love him more..."

My lips started to quiver. "I'm so, so sorry, Dean."

"I'm not mad, Alex." He trailed the back of his hand down the side of my face, rubbing his thumb along my lower lip before pulling it away and fisting it at his side. "How can I be mad over something you didn't even realize when deep down I knew it all along?"

"I loved you, Dean," I whispered, needing for him to know that.

"I believe you," he said with a sad smile. "I felt it. That feeling's what's kept me holding out hope that maybe someday your love for me would surpass the love you had for your best friend. But you can't choose who to love. You can't just turn it off. You were never going to stop loving him because that's not the type of person you are, and ironically, it's one of the things I will always love most about you."

I could no longer see through the tears flooding from my eyes.

"When I proposed...you ran right to him. I knew then that

—

it was truly a lost cause. But I still wanted to fight for you...to fight for us."

"Dean, I—" He held up a finger, asking me to wait. So, I zipped my lips and let him get out the rest of what he needed to say.

"I sort of had a rough day after we spoke while you were in California." His handsome face flushed with embarrassment. "I drove myself crazy wondering what was happening between the two of you every minute of every day until one night my dad and I had a few beers and I confessed everything. He made me promise to let you go. Not only for me but for you too." He looked over to his sleeping father and smiled. "And he was right, Alex. We had a good run, but it's time for you to go get your happy ending...and who knows, maybe someday I'll find one of my own."

God, I wanted that for him so much. "You will," I whispered, fighting back tears, "and she will be the luckiest girl in the world."

"There's my girl!" Mr. Fowler announced when I ambled into the house feeling like I was carrying the weight of the world on my shoulders. "How was my boy? He lookin' okay?"

"Yep, it's me," I sang as he enveloped me in his big arms, the scent of his coconut lotion filling my nose. "Colton's good, Mr. Fowler. Really good actually..." As drained as I felt from this never-ending emotional rollercoaster of a day, speaking about Colton had my pulse racing and a smile stretching from ear to ear.

"How good?" Mrs. Fowler broke in, waggling her eyebrows. "Did anything happen while you—"

"Hey," my dad barked, cutting her off. "That's my baby girl." He glowered her way as he walked into the room, placing a kiss on the top of my head. "None of that matchmaking business."

Colt's mom ignored him, looking at me expectantly.

—

"What happened is...we had a *wonderful* time."

"That's it?" she asked in mock horror. "That's all you're going to give me? A *wonderful* time. What's that even mean?"

"It didn't suck," I shot back, sticking out my tongue.

Momma shook her head, giggling. "Told you. Either there's really nothing to tell, or Allie here is keeping secrets." She aimed her first two fingers at her eyeballs then pointed them at mine.

"Y'all are ridiculous," I laughed, feeling the heaviness of the day beginning to lighten with each minute that passed in their presence.

After dinner, I excused myself for a shower and sleep. But what I really needed was some alone time to call Colt. The separation was wearing me down. I needed to hear his voice. I was anxious for a response to the letter I'd left this morning. I felt like throwing up because I really laid it all out there, feeling pretty confident that he shared my feelings to some degree. Still, there was always the possibility that I was completely off base.

I grabbed a quick shower to wash the rest of the day away before plopping down on my bed and digging my phone out of my purse, which I'd just realized I had never turned back on since the plane ride. With all of the excitement at the hospital, it had completely slipped my mind. As I powered it up and pressed my finger down on Colton's name, I hoped he wouldn't be too upset with me for completely falling off the grid today.

"Hello." My heart sunk when I heard a familiar, high pitched voice that did not belong to Colton. Pulling the phone away from my ear, I looked to make sure that I'd called the right person.

"Is anyone there? Hellooo?" My heart rate sped up to an alarming speed. Taking a few deep breaths, I mentally tried to talk myself down from the ledge. Maybe there was a good reason—nah, I couldn't even come up with one. He knew how I felt about her. He'd seen the way she treated me.

"Lyla," I deadpanned, feeling every hair on my body rise.

"Where's Colt?"

Her responding giggle set my blood to boiling. "He's in the shower right now...should I tell him to call you back?"

Breathe. Breathe, Alex. "Whose shower?" I asked, biting back tears. Like it even fucking mattered. They were together. She had his phone. And he was in. The. Shower.

"Mine, why?" she asked, playing coy.

I had nothing. Not a single word as tears pooled in my eyes and my heart shriveled up and died in my chest.

What the fuck was happening? I mean, we hadn't discussed exclusivity, but if we were together...*Shit*. Were we together? We hadn't had a chance to discuss that either...But we *slept together*. Wasn't I worth more to him than this? I told him I was in love with him and his response was to climb right back into bed with her?

"Wait, are you crying, Alex?"

The broken heart I thought I'd lived with all these years had shit on the pain of this moment. It was crippling. I couldn't have answered even if I wanted to.

"You are, aren't you?" She sighed loudly into the speaker. "You didn't think a man like Colt would sit around licking his own wounds, did you?" Another giggle. "Trust me, girl, he's got plenty of us lined up more than willing to do it for him."

Despite my best efforts, a sob escaped.

"Oh, honey." She tsked. "You have so much to learn about life."

She hung up, and the screen darkened. I hated to admit that she was right.

I knew nothing. Apparently, not even my best friend. About the only thing I was certain of at that moment was that Colton and I were through. Completely. I might not have been able to control who my masochistic heart decided to fall in love with, but I had a brain smart enough to shield myself from the pain. Loving Colton Fowler came at a price I could no longer afford.

—

CHAPTERTWENTY-ONE

Colton

WEEKS WENT BY WITHOUT A SINGLE WORD FROM ALEX. NOT A CALL. Not a text. Radio silence. I'd even been dodging calls from my parents because no part of me wanted to know what was going on with her and Dean. Our lives were so intertwined that there would be no way around it. Avoid. Avoid. Avoid, was the name of my game.

School and ball were my go to excuses and a welcome distraction from my thoughts, which never drifted very far from Allie. Her dark hair splayed across my pillow. The scent of her shampoo embedded in my sheets. Her smile. Her laughter. Hell, I even missed her bitching and whining. My life was empty without her in it. It was a sad existence, and I needed to snap out of it. That's why after nearly a month of sitting around waiting for her to realize she'd made a huge mistake I was throwing in the towel. There was a life for me out there that didn't involve Alexis Mack, and it was high time I went out and found it.

"Colton?" Finley shrieked when I descended the stairs

dressed in clothes that didn't consist of cotton and mesh. He rubbed his fists into his eyes dramatically. "Are those...dare I say it, *jeans?*"

"And buttons," Blex added, slapping his hand on the front of my shirt. "I do believe he's risen, Finley, my man."

"Praise God, Allah, Buddha, and all the other saints." Finley steepled his hands in front of his chest, taking a dramatic bow.

"Gods," I corrected, rolling my eyes.

"I said God first, numb nut."

"They're all gods, idiot," Blex corrected, hooting with laughter.

Finn scrunched his face in disgust as he slid his foot into his shoe. "You two can go right ahead and laugh your way straight to hell." He rolled his eyes upward to make eye contact with us towering over his hunched form. "There is only one God. It's like the deadliest of sins to believe in others."

Blex and I looked at each other briefly before bursting into hysterics. "Fuck, Finn. Your dumb ass makes getting out of bed worth it."

"I try," he muttered, rising from the couch and stomping his feet a few times to make his pants fall over the tops of his shoes.

"No, you don't. That's the best fucking part," Blex added on our way out the door.

Thursday night was ladies' night, and the club was jam-packed with, you guessed it, ladies. Normally, I felt right at home in a sea full of women, but since sex with Alex, I felt guilty even glancing their way. Which was stupid. We were not together.

"See anyone you like?" Finn asked, saddling up next to me at the bar. "I think I want that one." His finger pointed toward the dance floor to a redhead with huge tits and a big ass, both spilling out of her barely-there outfit.

"Nah, you go ahead. I'm gonna sit here and have a drink."

"Good idea," he said, passing his card to the bartender. "Beer goggles first, then they'll all start to look like Alex." He did the little finger snap point as he rose from his seat. "I like it, Fowls."

Finley had no clue how the mere mention of her name sent my heart racing. How much of a chore it was to simply draw air when she was occupying my thoughts. That's why when he slapped me on the back, tapping the neck of his Bud Light to mine, before hauling off to secure his woman of the night, I didn't punch him in his fucking face for bringing her up.

I spent the next hour stewing in memories of the girl I'd come here to forget, losing count of how many drinks I put down. Always hoping that the next would be the one to wipe my brain clean.

"Hey there, sad and lonely...Is this seat taken?"

My eyes drifted from the label I'd been picking at to the direction of the voice to find *tits*. Tits as far as the eye could see. I'm sure there was a nice face attached somewhere, but right in my line of vision was an enormous pair of chesticles. "That is an amazing rack," I muttered, appreciating God's work of art, or maybe it was a surgeon's doing. These days it was hard to tell. Whatever the case, I admired them all equally.

"Why, thank you...I'll take that as an invitation."

I thought I'd said that low enough so only I could hear, but apparently, I'd just given this fine woman a compliment without even trying. Maybe I hadn't lost my touch after all. "Go right ahead, gorgeous." And she was...gorgeous, that is. Sky blue eyes and long black hair. I wasn't even sure she was human. It was quite possible I dreamed her up. Apparently, I was good at that...imagining things that weren't real. Like I'd imagined the earth-shattering connection between Alex and myself.

"So, what's a fine man like yourself doing drowning in a bottle all alone tonight, huh?"

I shrugged. "Drinking to forget." With a wink, I tipped

the top of my bottle to her procured glass. "Shooting for beer goggles. You?"

She pulled her lower lip between her teeth, biting down. "Gosh, you're a cutie—" She paused, waiting for my name.

"Colton," I offered, filling in the blank.

"It's nice to meet you, Colton. I'm Coco."

"My pleasure." After another long pull from my beer, I realized she hadn't answered the question. "What's a beautiful woman with bazoombas like that doing all alone at the bar tonight?" Her face flushed with a shy smile. *And I was worried about my game?* I was *killing* it tonight.

"I'm on the prowl, honey." *Well, all right then.*

"For?"

Coco took a sip from her cocktail. "Funnily enough...beer goggles."

I was convinced that it was a stroke of fate that her tits showed up in my face when they did, delivering the antidote to my problem. Beer to numb the pain and breasts big enough to make you forget your name. *Allie who?* Okay, so obviously I hadn't forgotten her, but I was having a good time, and that was something.

After a few more drinks and lots of chatter, Coco and I were becoming fast friends. I felt comfortable enough to ask the question that had been weighing heavily on my mind since her arrival. "Can I ask you a personal question, Coco?"

"Go for it."

"Who gets credit for the tatas?" I asked, sizing them up with my hands in the air.

A loud laugh boomed from her chest. The deep, rich sound threw me for a moment. "One hundred percent credit goes to my surgeon."

"Well, the next time you see him, you can tell him your new friend, Colton, approves of his work. And that's a high compliment. I'm sort of a connoisseur of tits."

The apples of her cheeks turned a deep crimson. "You wanna feel?"

Did I wanna—? Was this chick for real? "You sure?" I asked, stupefied.

"Sure, why not. Knock yourself out, cutie."

It started out lightly with a little poke, and before I knew it, there was groping and boob shots, and we'd gained a small audience. It was the best night ever. Or, at least that I could remember because my memory was blessedly a blur. Beer goggles accomplished.

"For fuck's sake," I heard Blex growl as I was yanked from my stool by the back of my shirt and dragged out of the club.

"What the hell?" I shouted, fixing my shirt. "Why'd you do that?"

It took a minute for me to focus enough to realize that Blex and Finn were about to piss themselves laughing. "What's so funny?"

"She's a dude," Blex said, enunciating each word as soon as his obscene laughter permitted it.

"Huh? Who's a dude?"

"Your new buddy in there," Finn supplied, guffawing on the side of me.

Nooo. "No way," I challenged, deep in denial. *So, her laugh was a little deep...that didn't mean—*

"She had an Adam's apple and feet the size of a small country," Finn mused.

Bile churned in my stomach, burning its way up the back of my throat. "Why'd you assholes let me play with man titties?" I shouted, on the verge of losing the buzz I'd worked so hard to achieve all over the parking lot.

Blex shrugged. "You were having a good time. I didn't see any harm in it." A shit-eating grin crept across his face. "Well, until you started getting frisky with the man's jugs." He spit out another laugh.

"Does licking another man's nipple make you gay?" Finn asked, his face suddenly super serious. "Asking for a friend," he added, holding his palms out before his composure cracked and the hysterics resumed.

—

181

I was never speaking to either of them again.

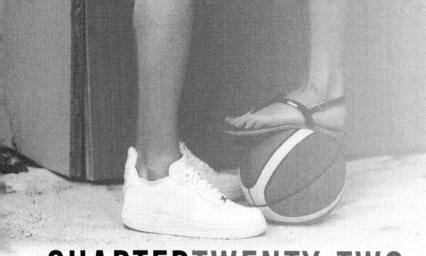

CHAPTER TWENTY-TWO

Alexis

I WAS IN A DEEP SLEEP WHEN A SOUND I HADN'T HEARD IN WHAT felt like ages had me popping right up in bed. For half a second, I debated whether to read it or not. I'd been a wreck, barely functioning since Colton annihilated what was left of my heart. Hiding the reason for my depression from my parents had not been easy, but I was dead set on not allowing this mess to cause friction between our families. I'd be civil when we saw each other, but beyond that, I had to quit him. Cold turkey. That part had been easy thus far, because not once had he even tried to contact me. Until now.

My body went nuts, acting as if it were a live grenade cradled in my palm rather than my phone. As I swiped right, I held my breath, anticipating the explosion.

Colt: I licked a man's nipple tonight bcuz of you. Thanks for ruining my life.

What the hell? I had no idea what that message was about. It was weird, even for Colt, but I stared at it for hours, imagining his fingers as they moved over the screen. There wasn't a doubt in my mind that he was drunk. It was two in the morning on a Saturday. He was probably lying in bed, thinking of me, just like I was lying in bed thinking about him. *Always thinking about him.* I didn't care that he was obviously pissed. My heart raced just knowing that he cared enough to send that message. It proved that he wasn't indifferent where I was concerned, and that thrilled me to no end. I hoped I haunted his dreams, keeping him up at night. It's the least he deserve for what he was doing to me.

I almost broke, typing out countless messages, and deleting them all, unsent, between the time I got his and my alarm going off at eight. It was time to get ready to go shopping with the moms, and I was running on little to no sleep.

After I was showered and dressed, I went downstairs, finding my father on the computer, messing with his stocks. "Hey, Daddy."

His head popped up, a worried smile on his face. "Hey, princess. How're you feeling?"

"Good," I lied, rushing off to the kitchen to grab a granola bar before he could see my tired eyes. I hated making my parents worry, but I didn't know how to pull myself out from the dark cloud I now existed within.

As soon as I sat to eat, my dad walked in. That same crooked smile aimed my way. "Mind if I join you?"

I shook my head, even though I'd have preferred to be left alone because pretending to be fine when you're not is exhausting, and I was tired.

Dad pulled out the chair across from mine, staring silently over my head as I ate. He waited until I'd swallowed the last bite before speaking. This time there was no beating around the bush. "What did that boy do to you?"

His directness caught me off guard. "Wh—huh?" I stammered, looking around the room. "Who?"

Dad's fist came down on the table, causing me to jump back in my seat. "Goddamnit, Alexis. I'm not stupid. You haven't been the same since you got home from California. I haven't heard you talking on the phone with him. Haven't seen you messaging each other."

Warm tears streamed down my face, but I said nothing. I couldn't. This was what I was afraid of. No matter what Colton did to me, I didn't want my family at odds with him. Didn't want our parents getting caught up in the middle of our problems.

"I know that it has something to do with Colton, and by you not saying anything, you're making me think the worst...I want to fix things for you, but I can't do that if you won't talk to me."

"I don't want you to b-be mad at hi-him," I cried, hugging my arms to my chest.

His face softened, marginally. "I love that boy like my own son, Alex, but *you* are my daughter, and I'll be damned if I just sit by and watch you self-destruct. You barely eat. You don't leave the house anymore but for school or if one of us drags you out...Is he in some kind of trouble?"

His questions were making me dizzy and adding to the stress that was already more than I could handle. It was all too much, and I broke. "You can't fix this!" I shouted, slamming my fists down onto the table.

"I can try." His hands covered mine, squeezing gently.

Shaking my head, I looked him right in the eyes and gave him what he wanted, because I was done. And because I had absolutely no fight left in me. "H-h-he doesn't l-love me back, Daddy," I cried. "I-I-love him s-so m-much, and he doesn't l-love me b-back." The next thing I knew, I was in my father's arms, crying on his shoulder. It was loud, and it was ugly. But freeing in a way.

I'd never seen my father look so helpless in my life. "I'm so sorry, Allie."

"I'll be okay," I assured him when my tears had dried. "I'm not the first person to suffer a broken heart. Just...give me a little time."

He nodded, the worry lines on his face seeming to age him ten years.

"Don't say anything to Mom or his parents, okay? It won't help anything."

After my breakdown with Dad, things actually got a little bit better. Having one person who understood my mood swings—who didn't look at me like I was headed straight for Crazy Town, USA, made me feel a little less alone. But I still missed him. *So much.*

Thanksgiving break was creeping up quickly, and Colton's mom was heartbroken because he'd made up some bullshit excuse for why he wouldn't be able to make it, which translated to he didn't want to be around *me*. It was going to be the first Thanksgiving they'd ever spent without their only child, and knowing that it was my fault that he wouldn't be there was just one more thing weighing me down.

My biggest fear when I wrote that stupid letter was that he wouldn't feel the same. Never did I imagine he'd be too disgusted to have anything to do with me. So disgusted, in fact, that he'd shunned his own family.

In a moment of weakness, I pulled up his name in my messages, rolling my eyes at the one he'd sent a few months ago about licking some guy's nipple, and then I broke the promise I'd made to myself.

Alex: Please come home for Thanksgiving. Your mom keeps begging me to talk to you. I promise I'll make myself scarce. You're breaking your mother's heart.

CHAPTER TWENTY-THREE

Colton

"GREAT GAME, FOWLS," MY BUDDY JASON SAID, CLAPPING ME ON the back of the shoulder on the way to his locker.

"Thanks, man, you too." We'd just won our last game until after Thanksgiving, which was in just three days, and the reality of being away from my family was really sinking in as all of my teammates discussed their travel plans, most of them leaving tonight.

After reading Alex's text last week, I'd really started to feel bad about the lie I told my parents. I couldn't use school or ball as an excuse. At the time, it seemed the only way to get out of spending the holiday at the same table with Alex and Dean was to make other plans. As far as Mom and Dad knew, I was spending Thanksgiving with a girl I'd been dating named Madison at her parents' house.

But there was no Madison, and I was really spending it home alone, which I was okay with, before that damn text. I knew Alex wouldn't have messaged me if Mom wasn't really having a hard time with this. She'd acted fine with it on the phone, but knowing that I was hurting her had me almost ready to hop on a plane. *Almost.*

You see, there was still the issue of Alex. It may have seemed petty, but I couldn't go back and pretend that nothing had happened. That she hadn't ripped my fucking heart out when she left my bed and went running back to *his.* I was in love with her to the point that it was making me crazy, and I didn't know how to deal with it. So, I chose not to deal with it at all.

As I was shoving the last of my things into my duffle bag, my phone started to ring. When I saw the name that was lighting up the screen, my heart dropped to the floor.

Mr. Mack hadn't called my phone since I was still living with my parents, and only ever to get in touch with Alex when we were out together. Something had to be wrong.

"Hello?"

"Long time no see, son."

I cleared my throat. "Uh, yeah. How's it going, Mr. Mack?"

"Not too great actually, but that's nothing for you to be concerned with just yet."

"Okay." I laughed, nervously. "What can I do for you, sir?"

"You can stop making my baby cry, Colton, and get your stubborn ass on a plane in...uhhh, three hours."

"Uh, I—" *What the hell was he talking about?*

"I know about you and Allie, Colton."

"*Shit.*"

"Listen, I'm not calling to blame you for her broken heart. If you don't love her...Well, then you don't love her, but you will not treat Alexis or your mother this way, do you understand me?" *Her broken heart?*

"No, actually I—"

"A real man faces his problems head on, son. He doesn't hide from them."

"I'm not *hiding.*" *I was absolutely hiding.*

"Great! Well, since you've decided in the last five seconds to grow a pair, I'll forward your itinerary to your email and see you at the airport at two a.m."

—

"But—"

"What was that?" he asked, talking over me. "Did I hear, 'See you at two, Mr. Mack'?"

"See you at two, Mr. Mack."

He let out an exaggerated laugh. "Atta boy, Colt. We're gonna make a man outta you yet. See you soon."

What the hell had just happened? I didn't understand half of what was just said, but apparently, I had a plane to catch.

I got to the baggage area a little after two, and sure enough, Alex's dad was sitting on a bench, waiting to take me home. He'd never made me this nervous before. Something had changed between us. I guess a man finding out you'd had sex with his daughter shifted things.

Rubbing my sweaty palms against my shirt, I walked over to meet him.

"All set?" he asked, rising from his seat. It'd been just a few months since we'd last seen each other, but the change in him was noticeable. He'd aged. Maybe it was just the late hour, but he seemed stressed. He'd always struck me as a man without a care in the world.

"Yeah, I didn't check any bags."

"Great!" Mr. Mack offered me his hand, pulling me in for a hug when I reached back. "Welcome home, Colt."

"Thanks, and, uh, thanks for the ticket too." I had absolutely no clue why I'd just thanked him for a ticket I didn't even want. Because as much as I looked forward to seeing my parents, I dreaded seeing Alex more. *Way more.* This was a disaster in the making.

When we pulled up to their house, I grabbed my bag and started in the direction of home.

"Colton," Mr. Mack, whisper-shouted, waving me back. "They don't know you're here. You'll crash on our couch since it's so late and we'll surprise everyone in the morning." He nodded, all too pleased with himself, while I was on the verge of a full-blown panic attack.

"Nah," I said, shaking my head. "I'm just gonna go—"

His hand hooked around my shoulders as he guided me to the back door. "Sleep on our couch?" he urged.

"Sleep on your couch," I agreed, laughing to myself.

Mr. Mack grabbed a pillow and blanket from the hall closet, setting them on the coffee table before heading off to bed. I'd slept in this house almost as many times as my own growing up, and I'd never taken the couch. This was weird.

As if he could read my thoughts, Mr. Mack called back over his shoulder on the way to his room, "Alex's room is always an option...But something tells me you're safer out here."

Mr. Mack had jokes.

"What the hell is he doing here?" Alexis was fuming.

"Surprise!" her dad chimed.

She snorted. "Surprises are supposed to be good, Dad," Alex hissed.

"You've been upset for weeks that he was missing Thanksgiving. I thought bringing Colton here would make you happy."

Alex sighed. "Him at *his* house...that would make me happy. Him...here, in *this* house? Not so much." *Ouch.*

"Relax, Allie. He's only here because we didn't get back 'til nearly three. As soon as he wakes up, I'll give him the boot."

"Perfect. I'll be in my room 'til then. Come get me when he's gone."

It took every ounce of restraint I possessed not to lift my head and have a look at her when I heard her footfalls on the stairs behind me. I was supposed to be avoiding her, and at the first sound of her voice, I was fighting the urge to chase after her. I guess old habits are hard to break. It felt like I'd been chasing Alex my entire life.

—

"You heard the boss, Colt. Get up. Let's go make your mom's day," Mr. Mack announced as soon as her door slammed shut. That man never missed a beat.

"Mind if I use the bathroom first?" I sat up on the couch, rolling the stiffness from my neck.

His lips curled into a slow smile. "You sure you ready to take that on, son?"

"Guess we'll see."

"Good luck, Colt."

On the way up to Alex's room, I made a brief stop at the hall table to retrieve the pin. Without warning, I picked the lock, swinging her door open.

"Is he gone..." She trailed off when she spun around to find me standing just inside her room. "What do you want, Colton?" Her face was red and splotchy, wet with tears. Allie's tears were my kryptonite.

"I'm not sure," I answered, my heart racing as I shut the door before stepping further into her room.

"You should go," she whispered, wiping at her cheeks.

"We need to talk."

Her hand lifted to her chest. "It's been three months," she choked out. "Three months, Colton. And *now* you want to talk?"

"Yeah," I rasped, taking another step toward her. "Yeah, Al, I wanna talk." My chest was tight, my heart racing. All I could see was my beautiful, broken girl, and all I wanted was a chance to fix us.

"Talk," she said, her jaw ticking, her arms crossed defensively on her chest.

"I miss you." A million other words needed saying, but those felt most important. Because suddenly all of the other shit felt trivial.

She nodded, touching her fingers to her trembling lips. "Me too."

"I need you, Al," I choked out, emotion thick in my throat. "I need you in my life."

—

191

"I can't." Her head shook rapidly. "It hurts too much, Colt."

Closing the last few steps between us, I tucked my finger beneath her chin, bringing her eyes to mine. "Not like this. It never hurt like this."

Her tiny frame began to shake with sobs as she fell into my chest, fisting her hands into the front of my shirt. Wrapping my arms around her brought an inexplicable peace. We had a lot of shit to work out. But this girl was my life, and this felt like the first step to getting it back.

"Shhh," I whispered, burying my face in her hair and inhaling the scent of her flowery shampoo. "We can fix this, babe."

"H-h-how?" she sniveled.

"I don't know," I answered honestly. "But this feels like a good place to start."

CHAPTER TWENTY-FOUR

Alexis

"AH, THERE YOU ARE. I WAS ABOUT TO GO UP THERE TO MAKE SURE you were both still alive," Dad teased, beaming from ear to ear as Colt and I descended the stairs.

Colton chuckled behind me.

"We're gonna go next door," I said, lifting onto my toes to plant a kiss on Daddy's cheek.

"Sounds good...You two sort everything out?" he asked, a hopeful glint in his eye.

"We're workin' on it."

Colton and I held hands while crossing the yard to his parents' house in silence. There was so much to say, but neither of us were ready to open that door. My insides were a mess. I wished we could start over right there and pretend that the past few months hadn't happened, but they had. And the pain of his rejection wasn't something I could bury and forget about. But I knew that we had to find a way to fix things because loving Colton might hurt, but losing him was unbearable.

"Oh my God!" Mrs. Fowler mumbled, covering her mouth

with her hands as we walked through the front door. She was shaking with excitement.

"Surprise!" Colt shouted, releasing my hand to embrace his emotional mother.

"Alexis, did you do this?" she asked when the two of them finally separated.

"No," I said, clearing my throat. "It was my dad."

I laughed when her face twisted in confusion. "Really?" she asked, looking to Colton.

His broad shoulders shrugged as he scrubbed at his chin, dipping his head in confirmation.

"How? When? Just yesterday you still had plans to go to Madison's parent's house."

Oh God. Who was Madison? My heart lodged in my throat, and I felt the urge to run. This was never going to work.

Colton went white as a sheet, his eyes holding mine as he answered his mother. "There's no Madison," he rushed out. "I made her up so I wouldn't have to come." He was answering her but talking to me.

"Why would you do that? Are we so horrible, Colton?"

Colt's hands fisted into his hair, tugging in frustration. He didn't want to call me out. He didn't want to hurt her. He was stuck.

"It wasn't you. Colton didn't want to come home because he didn't want to have to see me," I spoke up, tired of walking on eggshells.

Mrs. Fowler quit her pacing, her face fraught with confusion. "What?"

It was time to rip off the band-aid. I was so tired of hiding. "Colton and I haven't spoken since I returned from California."

"Well, that doesn't make any sense. You went on and on about how great of a time you two had when you got back."

Colton stood there, watching our exchange with a look of bewilderment.

"I did, but stuff happened after that."

Mrs. Fowler advanced on her son, finger pointed. "What.

Did. You. Do?"

"Me?"

"Yes, you," she shrieked. "I wondered if maybe...but then I thought...There's no way it had anything to do with you because you are the one person who would never hurt her."

"What are you talking about?"

"She has been a fucking mess, Colton," she shouted like I wasn't standing right next to her on the verge of full-blown hysteria. "Look at her." She waved a hand in my direction, putting me on display. "She doesn't leave the house, barely eats. She's failing all her classes. Her mother has been sick with worry...and you've been ignoring her all this time?"

"This doesn't make any sense," Colt muttered, his chest heaving. "Allie left me," he rasped. The emotion on his face made it clear that he believed what he was saying. "I went to practice that morning with her asleep in my bed and came home to an empty house. She was gone without a word. All of her shit...gone."

"I left a note."

"I didn't get any damn note!" he shouted. "I figured it out on my own that you'd gone back home when I realized you'd taken all of your things, so I called mom to make sure that you were safe and she said you were with *him*." Colton's whole face tightened with anger. "You went running back to him."

"No," I cried. "Dean called that morning. His dad was in an accident, and they didn't think he would make it. So, I...I packed my things and tried to call you, but you'd forgotten your phone, so I left a note."

"You two," Mrs. Fowler said, face red and flustered, "better figure this shit out." She eyed each of us individually. "I'm going next door. My heart can't handle this."

The door shut behind her and Colt, and I stood in silence, piecing together the mess that had just unfolded around us. That fucking letter had been the source of so much pain, and he'd never even read it. "I wrote you a letter," I repeated. "I put it on the nightstand underneath your phone so you'd see it."

—

His head moved in a slow nod. "Come here, Allie," he whispered, beckoning me with his hands.

But I was caught up in my feelings, and there was still one more thing I needed to address. "I called you that night." My heart raced at the memory. "Lyla answered your phone. You were in the shower." My voice cracked. "I wasn't even gone a day, Colton...You didn't even wait a day."

"I never found my phone," he muttered, thinking out loud. "Finn went back to the house to pick it up and let you know we had to stay late, but you weren't at home. I tried calling and it went to voicemail, so I put it on the bleachers, thinking you must've been out with Gertie and your phone had died. When I went back to grab it after practice to try calling you again, my phone was gone. I never found it."

"I don't understand what that has to do with you hooking up with Lyla the day I left."

"I didn't hook up with Lyla, Alex. I haven't been with *anyone* since you," he said, setting me straight before continuing his story. "Lyla was there, at the gym. She offered to help look for you," he sneered.

"She took your phone."

He nodded.

"That fucking bitch."

Colton and I spent the rest of the day lounging on my parents' couch, watching old movies. After such a long separation, it felt amazing to relax in the comfort of his arms. Plus, it was a good excuse not to have to talk, and after all the talking we'd done that morning, it was a welcome reprieve.

Occasionally, Colt would place a kiss on the top of my head, but beyond that, we'd done nothing more than cuddle. There was an awkwardness that came with being apart for so long, with being angry for so long, even if that anger was completely misplaced.

"Well, look who decided to show his face," Mr. Fowler announced, walking into the room.

He eyed the two of us cozied up on the couch together, and his face lit up. "Glad to see the two of you worked things out."

I whipped my head around, eyes narrowed. "You told your dad?"

"What?" he asked, running a hand through his curls. "*You* told *your* dad!" he laughed. "And you told him *everything*. I only told mine we weren't getting along."

My mom came in from the kitchen, having just returned home from work. "What'd I miss?"

"Nothing," we answered in unison.

"Oh, come on," she said, "I'm curious about that *everything*."

"Me too," Colt's mom said, coming up behind her husband. "Does *everything* entail the four of us becoming grandparents someday?" she asked, brows waggling.

"Hey!" my dad yelled from the kitchen, peeking his head out. "That's my daughter!"

I buried my face in Colton's chest, my body shaking from the vibration of his laughter.

Embarrassing and dysfunctional as they may be, those four nut jobs were ours.

—

CHAPTER TWENTY-FIVE

Colton

THE BREAK WAS FLYING BY. I'D SPENT NEARLY EVERY MINUTE WITH Alex, and it wasn't enough. It would never be enough. I was at my parents' house getting ready for our annual Thanksgiving dinner, stressing the fact that I had to leave in the morning—more specifically that I had to leave Allie.

Our adult relationship felt like a pendulum, always swinging, highs and lows. We'd never found an even keel.

"Ready, son?" my dad called, tapping his knuckle on the door.

I gave myself a final once-over before opening the door and returning with them to Alex's house.

The Macks always went all out for Thanksgiving dinner. I could smell the food cooking from the porch, and my stomach rumbled.

"Come on in," Alex's dad said, pulling the door open. "You know you don't have to knock."

"We like to pretend we have manners from time to time," Dad joked.

"Well, your manners made me have to get up out of my

chair," he laughed. "You really don't need to knock."

Their conversation faded into the background when Allie came down the stairs. My breath caught at the sight of her all made up. She wore a short sweater dress with tall boots and smelled amazing.

Alex walked right into my arms, lacing her fingers behind my neck. "You look so good," she whispered in my ear. Then she pressed her lips to mine, right there in the living room... in front of all four of our parents. It was the first time our lips had met since I came home and the first time we'd ever kissed in front of our families.

"Mmm," I moaned as she pulled back. "You are so beautiful."

"Thank you," she piped, rubbing her lipstick from my mouth with the pad of her thumb. She had my blood pumping with that one simple move.

"*Ahem*," Mr. Mack cleared his throat. "Let's eat!"

Alex and I made eyes at each other throughout dinner. Up 'til now, we'd been taking things slow, but my impending departure had apparently gotten us both worked up. I wanted her. Desperately.

Her hand resting on my thigh beneath the table made it hard to focus on anything else.

"Colton," she hissed, giggling, "my mom asked you a question."

"I'm sorry, what was that, Mrs. Mack?" My cock stirred as Allie began to slide her hand higher on my leg.

Mrs. Mack took another sip of her wine, hiding a smirk behind the glass. "I asked what time you leave tomorrow."

"Oh, ummm," Goddamn that girl was distracting.

"Ten-thirty tomorrow morning," Alex's dad supplied. Having been the one to book the ticket, he would know.

"Would you two like to be excused?" my mother asked, teasing, as all four of our parents gave us knowing looks.

"Yes," Alex said, standing from her seat, shocking every last one of us. "Actually, I think we would." I nearly choked on my turkey at the determined look on her face.

—

"Allie," I mumbled, eyeing our families. "What are you doing?" I gritted beneath my breath.

"Thanks for dinner, Mom and Dad, it was delicious." Alex tugged at my hand. "Get up, Colton," she practically growled before painting an innocent smile on her face and addressing my parents, "Happy Thanksgiving, Mr. and Mrs. Fowler."

Ah, what the hell? It's not like they didn't know all our business anyway. I adjusted myself beneath the table before standing and pushing my chair in. "Dinner was great, thank you." It took a concerted effort not to laugh at the blank stares I was receiving from all four of our parents as I made a quick glance around the table before taking off after Allie, without looking back.

My adrenaline was at an all-time high when we entered her childhood bedroom, both of us panting before we'd even set hands on each other. I let my eyes rove over each of her feminine curves as she gripped the bottom of her dress, lifted it over her head, and tossed it across the room. I sucked in a deep breath as I stared at her pink nipples that were just barely visible through the sheer black lace. My throat grew thick, my dick hard.

Alex bit her lower lip, staring at me for a moment, watching my face as I drank her in. Then, she pounced, backing me up against the door with a loud thump, her hungry eyes fixed on mine. She reached around me, turning the lock. Allie taking charge like this, going after what she wanted, was such a fucking turn on. My pulse raced out of control, and I could feel my cock already straining against the inside of my zipper.

"Shhh, Alex," I laughed low in my throat. "Just because they have a pretty good idea what's going on doesn't mean we need to give them the play by play."

"Whoops," she blushed, leaving me standing there as she walked over to the computer that sat open on her desk. Saliva pooled in my mouth as I stared at her round ass while she clicked away. Not a full minute had passed when the opening chords to "Thinking Out Loud" by Ed Sheeran drifted

—

through the speakers. "There," she said with an accomplished smile as she increased the volume to the max setting. Her hips began to sway to the beat, her hand reaching out, her finger beckoning me over. "Dance with me?"

Alex looked like a wet dream, dancing for me in nothing but her matching bra and panties. With my heart lodged in my throat, I walked to the center of the room to join her. "You are so sexy," I rasped, placing my hands on her bare hips, trailing them along her spine, brushing over the strap to her bra and back down again, our bodies moving in time to the music. I dipped my head to the bend of her neck, kissing her softly, inhaling the sweet smell of her perfume as she began to tremble in my arms.

Allie laced her fingers behind my neck, the pads of her thumbs rubbing slow circles at my nape. Her breath was hot in my ear when she whispered in a shaky voice, "I used to dream of this."

"Dream of what, babe?" I asked, spinning her out slowly and reeling her back in.

"Dancing with you..." Her voice trailed off as I nipped at her earlobe. "Without our clothes," she finished, her fingers slowly working at the buttons on my shirt. Her cheeks flushed with a light blush.

"Yeah?" I asked, smiling as I remembered the many times she'd gotten me so worked up I'd had to hide in the bathroom to rub one out. Our chemistry had always been off the charts, even before we understood what it was. "Me too." I tugged at her bottom lip gently before sucking it into my mouth. "You used to leave me with raging hard-ons," I laughed, pressing the proof into her waist as I reached around her back, unhooking her bra and sliding the straps down her arms.

Alex pulled my shirt open, her icy cold fingers slipping inside, tracing the muscles that lined my chest. "You made me so hot, Colt," she admitted, her voice heady with desire as she stared up at me through hooded eyes. Chest to chest. Skin to skin. Heartbeat to frantic heartbeat.

—

202

"How 'bout now?" I rasped, cupping her breast in my hand, kneading the soft flesh. "Do I make you hot now?" I felt my throat bob as I swallowed hard.

She nodded, grabbing my other hand and lowering it into her panties, letting out a loud gasp when I ran my finger through her slick folds. "So hot," she moaned, her head rolling back as I dipped a finger inside, finding her more than ready for me.

Lifting the finger to my mouth, I sucked it clean. "So wet," I growled, my dick throbbing as I walked us over to the bed, laying her in the center before stripping off the rest of my clothes and climbing in over her.

Lowering my lips to hers, I kissed her long and slow, making love to her mouth, never losing our rhythm. Our tongues continued to dance as I parted her thighs, lined up our centers, and pushed forward, giving her all of me in one hard thrust.

Allie's mouth formed an O, her eyes widening as she let out a sharp cry. Every muscle in my body tensed. Every nerve ending set on fire.

She felt so good. So fucking perfect. So *mine*.

"Come with me, Allie," I whispered, brushing sweat-soaked hair from her forehead as we came down from our climaxes.

She giggled, lazily trailing her fingers up and down my chest. "I just did, *multiple times, actually*. I don't think I *can* come again, Energizer Bunny."

"Was that a challenge?" I asked, flicking the tip of my tongue over her still erect nipple, relishing the way her body writhed beneath me. "Cuz I'm more than willing to give it another go."

Alex hissed, moving my hand away. "I *can't*. Are you trying to kill me?" she laughed. "Death by orgasm...hmmm. On second thought, it has a nice ring to it, whatdya think?"

I wrapped my arms around her still naked body, pulling her

to lay on top of me, her face inches from mine. "I want you to come home, to live with me," I clarified, placing a kiss on the tip of her chin.

She drew back a little in surprise, her heart speeding up, pounding against my chest. "Like, as a roommate?"

"Like, as *mine*," I answered, holding her stare.

Her body shook. "As your...what, exactly?"

"Everything."

"Everything..." she repeated, swallowing hard.

"Every. Single. Thing."

CHAPTER TWENTY-SIX

Alexis

knowing smile. "You and Colt have a good time last night?"

Heat flooded my cheeks. "Mmmhmm," I nodded, walking over to join her and my father at the breakfast table.

"Were you safe?" she continued, making this awkward situation even more uncomfortable than it already was. She did this shit on purpose.

Dad's fork landed hard on his plate as he began to choke on his scrambled eggs.

"I've been having sex for years, Mother. I'm pretty sure I know how babies are made by now...*and* how to avoid them."

"Enough!" Dad grumbled when he stopped coughing long enough to speak. "Jesus, woman," he added, glaring at my mother, who simply rolled her eyes, resuming her interrogation.

"So, you two are...?"

Here we go... "Actually, that's why I'm up so early. I have some news," I announced, biting my lip nervously.

Mom rested her chin in her hand that was already propped on

the table, leaning in with eager anticipation. Dad, on the other hand, froze mid-chew. I'm not even sure he was breathing.

"We're moving in together."

And the choking resumed as Dad beat a fist into his chest. His eyes were about to pop out of their sockets. *Poor Dad.*

"You're moving in—umm, where exactly?" All playfulness vanished from her demeanor.

"I'm going back to California with Colton...*today.*"

"Today? What about school?" Mom asked, looking like she was about to hyperventilate as she tugged at the neck of her tee.

Taking a deep breath, I shifted in my seat. "I'm going to drop my classes and transfer my credits to UCLA. I'll start this semester over in January. I'm failing everything anyway," I answered, looking over to my father to gage his reaction. His stone face gave nothing away as he listened intently.

"What are you going to do for money, Alex? You've never lived on your own...You—you'll lose your scholarships."

"She'll get a job, honey, like everyone else does. Or she can take out bigger loans," Dad chimed in, finally seeming to find his voice. "She's not the first twenty-year-old to move out on her own...and she'll be with Colt." As he added that last bit, Dad looked to me and winked.

My mom's bottom lip started to quiver, her eyes filling with tears. "But, she's our baby. How can you be so calm about this?"

My heart sank. I'd known she'd be upset. The longest I'd ever been away from home was last summer when I'd visited Colton, and she'd had a hard time with that. Still, expecting it didn't make it any easier. Along with Colton, she was my best friend. Pathetic, but true.

My dad's hand reached out to hold hers across the table. "She's in love, Momma. Would you rather Allie be miserable, the way she's been these past few months?" The concerned looks they shared made me feel awful for worrying them so much, but it had brought dad and me closer than ever. I couldn't be upset about that.

—

"No," Mom whispered, sniveling into her napkin, her head shaking and her eyes locked on mine. "But I'm going to miss you so much."

"I'll miss you too, Mom." I got out of my seat, walking over to wrap her in a hug, emotion thick in my throat. "I'll visit, and you can come check out LA. It's going to be great, you'll see."

I'd made it onto the plane and into my seat without much event, but when we started taxiing, all bets were off. It felt like I'd taken a shot of adrenaline straight to the heart. We were going to die. Colton had finally asked me to be his everything, and we were going to blow up in this fucking plane and never get our happily ever after. *Oh God. I couldn't breathe.*

"You okay?" Colt asked, dipping his head to whisper into my ear as he used the hand that wasn't currently being squeezed to death to rub my arm.

"Mmm mmm." I shook my head.

Colt did a shit job of trying not to laugh. "You're a pro at this now, babe. It's your third flight."

Shit. I was going to throw up. My eyes started watering. "Get...get my purse, Colt," I begged, fanning myself with the flight travel pamphlet from the seat pocket in front of me.

"We have to keep all items stored ri—"

My grip on his forearm tightened. "Just get it," I gritted out, focusing on my breathing. I did not want to spend the rest of this flight covered in vomit. I was sure he didn't either.

"Hurry up," he said, depositing the bag in my lap. Probably the only thing good to come out of losing my mind for the past few months was the bottle of Xanax I just pulled from my purse.

"What is that?" Colt asked with a look of concern as I dropped one into my palm before slipping it beneath my tongue.

"Crazy pills...you want one?" I teased, capping the bottle

and shoving it back into the bag, which he quickly returned to its rightful position.

A loud gasp slipped through my lips as the wheels drew up and we began our ascent. I laid my head back with my eyes shut tight and held on to Colt's arm for dear life as the medicine dissolved in my mouth. Sometime between then and the time our plane had leveled out that little miracle drug had kicked in and my fucks had left the building.

"Feeling better?" Colt asked with a lazy smile as my hand slid down his arm, moving to his thigh. There were only the two of us in our row, and I was suddenly feeling bored, and Colt was looking like fun. It wasn't even fair how gorgeous he was. I'd had to spend my whole life controlling myself around him, but I didn't have to anymore, and I was going to take full advantage of my new freedom.

His body jerked as I stretched my pinky out to the side, running it gently over the bulge in his mesh shorts. "Much better," I answered, turning a little in my seat, using my body to block anyone's view from the aisle.

"Fuck, Alex," he hissed under his breath as I slipped my hand up the leg of his shorts and began stroking him.

The harder he got, the wetter I became. Jesus, the way he looked with his head thrown back, his face puckered, and neck corded with tension as he tried to hide his pleasure had me clenching my legs together.

Colt's hand reached forward, and the tray fell over his lap, hiding my hand from view. *Good thinking.*

"Can I get you two a beverage or a snack?" Oh fuck.

I kept my head turned down, resting on Colton's shoulder as he answered for us. "Nah, we're uh...we're good. Thanks."

"No problem," the stewardess replied. "Enjoy your flight."

"Oh, we intend to."

When I heard the cart roll away, I squeezed his dick, causing him to jump. "Why didn't you warn me?"

Colton laughed. "Cuz you'd stop."

"Well, yeah."

He bit down on his lower lip, his Adam's apple bobbing on a swallow. "Don't stop."

I resumed stroking his cock until it was at full mast. My blood was hot with desire, and I was in desperate need to take advantage of my hard work.

"I'm going to the bathroom," I whispered, slipping my hand out of his shorts. "The one on the right side."

Confusion furrowed his brow as he stared at me, panting. "I mean, really?" he said, looking down at his lap. "You couldn't hold it for like thirty more seconds?"

I rolled my eyes. "I'm telling you so you can follow me, idiot."

"Really?" Colt looked around to be sure that no one was paying us any mind.

"Unless you're scared," I said as I stepped into the aisle and headed for the restroom without waiting for his reply.

Closing myself in the closet sized restroom, I sized it up, trying to formulate a plan of action. If we were going to join the mile-high club, we had to be quick about it. And smart. We basically had two options. I could ride him, reverse cowgirl on the toilet seat...ew. Or, I could sit on the edge of the sink, and by the looks of it, be at the perfect height...Yeah, that was definitely the way to go.

When the door started to push open, I had a moment of panic, hoping that I wouldn't have to explain to some stranger why I was propped up on the lavatory, because, well...I had absolutely no possible explanation other than the obvious. But that panic was short lived when I saw his mop of golden brown hair squeeze through the crack in the door.

"Are you sure—" I shut him up with a finger on his lips, shushing him.

Gripping a hand full of curls, I pulled his face to mine, pressing my lips right to his ear. "No noise," I hissed, barely above a whisper. "Get in, get out."

He nodded, biting his lip with a smile and a shake of his head.

—

Every part of my body prickled with desire as he slid his shorts just low enough for his erection to spring free. Colton wrenched my legs apart, pulled my panties to the side, and positioned himself right at my entrance. Heart racing, I gripped the edge of the counter as he looked to me for permission. With a slight nod of my head, Colt gripped my hips and thrust forward, and, my God, I saw fucking stars as he pulled out, slamming into me over and over. Just as I felt him spasming inside, just as I was on the cusp of what I knew to be the best fucking orgasm of my life, there was banging on the outside of the door.

"I'm going to need you to open this door. Only one person is allowed in the restroom at a time."

"You have got to be fucking kidding me," I mouthed to Colt as he pulled his shorts up and righted my underwear, helping me to stand on wobbly legs. I got a glimpse of myself in the mirror as Colton unlocked the door before quickly turning away. Every person on this plane would have zero confusion as to what we were just doing.

"I'm sorry," he said, sounding completely unaffected by our current case of blue genitals, as he pulled the door open. "She isn't feeling well."

"Colton?" The blond flight attendant's hand went to her chest. A slow smile spread across her face. "It's been a while."

Colt's eyes darted to the side to look at me as he answered. "Yeah, it has...How've you been, Jill?"

"I'm good. Looks like you're, umm...doing okay yourself," she mused, eyeing me.

He cleared his throat. "Yeah, this is Allie, my girlfriend. Allie, this is Jill."

I nodded, trying to force a smile and keep my lunch down at the same time.

"So, it's so good seeing you again, but you'll have to go back to your seats." Her cheeks flushed as she batted her lashes at Colt like I wasn't standing right here.

"Sure, no problem," he said, starting for our seats before

turning back. "Hey, Jill. You think we could get our wings?" he winked. "We earned 'em." *I hated him.*

When we returned to our chairs, I was humiliated, horny, and fuming. "Really, Colton?" I asked, shaking my head when he looked at me with his shit-eating grin.

"It was a long time a—"

"Don't," I said, cutting him off. "I can't even deal with you right now."

Colt's lips pressed into a flat line, his body shaking with suppressed laughter as he rested his head against the window and left me to stew by his side.

"Welcome home, Lexi!" Finley met us at the door to the apartment with a grin that spread clear from one ear to the other. My heart was racing with nerves. I knew that Colt had said they were fully onboard with my moving in, but it's not like he'd have told me if they weren't. After slapping Colton on the back, he reached for my arm, pulling me into his chest and squeezing the breath from my lungs. "I'm so happy you're back," he said, rocking us from side to side. "It's been so much less sexy around here without you!"

I snorted out a laugh, my jitters already beginning to dissipate. "Missed you too, Finley."

"Should I be worried about the two of you?" Colton teased, lugging the suitcases in from the porch, his eyes bouncing between us.

"Duh," came Finn's response as he waved his hands over his body. "What girl wouldn't want this?" He was joking. But with that blond hair, those crystal blue eyes, and a body like his, he'd be hard-pressed to find one. Finley was going to make some girl very happy someday.

"It'll be hard to refuse," I answered, unable to wipe the smile from my face, and I didn't want to.

"So, don't fight it, sexy." He winked, bursting into laughter when Colt shoved his chest, knocking him off balance.

"Pistols at dawn, motherfucker." Colt made one hand into the shape of a gun, aiming it at his friend and cocking it with his other.

"Hey, new roomy," Blex called, walking in from the kitchen, dismissing the other two idiots in the room with a shake of his head as he passed them by. "Don't you ever disappear like that on us again, young lady...You caused quite a commotion around here," he said, enveloping me in his arms as he placed a kiss on the side of my face.

"Right?" Finley agreed, jumping in on our conversation. "Had Colton here so fucked in the head, he was licking on man titties and shit."

"Oh my God!" I busted out laughing. "I forgot all about that message."

Colton's face blanched. "Guys, seriously, that's enough."

"Don't listen to him...*Tell me everything.*"

Every so often while Colt and I were unpacking my things, I'd burst into hysterics, picturing his run-in with the cross dresser. Let's just say Colton was highly unamused. It was quite possible he was already regretting his decision to invite me to move in.

"Colt?"

"Yeah?" he called from the dresser, where he was busily arranging all of my underwear and bras by color.

"If I ask you something, do you promise to be honest with me?"

He stopped what he was doing, looking back at me with a nervous frown. My heart skipped beats at the sight of *my man* with his mussed hair, furrowed brow, and his fingers draped in satin and lace thongs. "Sure, what's up?"

"Whose tits are better?"

Next thing I knew, I was flat on my back on the floor beside

—

the bed, Colt's hard body towering over mine. Shrieking with laughter, I slapped at his chest. "What're you doing, maniac?"

"Shutting you up," he growled against my lips before thrusting his tongue into my mouth, ripping our clothes off, and fucking me senseless.

The very next morning, ball practice resumed, and a few days later, classes. With the start of school came added afternoon practices and games. Colton hadn't been exaggerating how little downtime he had. His life was hectic, to say the least, and I lived for the nights when he would fall into bed and show me he'd been missing me just as much as I had him. Those moments more than made it all worth it.

Nonetheless, my days were long. I'd dropped all of my classes at Texas State and enrolled for the spring semester at UCLA, but until then, I had nothing to occupy my time. A girl could only sleep so much, and since our time was already so limited, neither of us was too keen on the idea of me getting a job. But I needed something to do when I wasn't following him to games or popping in to watch him practice, which I did regularly. Colton Fowler always was a sight to behold on that court. I hadn't realized just how much I'd missed watching him play.

Finley of all people suggested I find a place to volunteer, and that's when I found Saint Anthony's homeless shelter. It was only a few miles away from the apartment, and I was able to pop in to help out as little or as often as I could. I became fast friends with the other volunteers. There was always plenty to be done, from serving meals to handing out clothes and toys to children.

My new life in California was busy, but it fulfilled me in ways I never imagined possible. And for the first time in a very long time, I was truly happy.

CHAPTER TWENTY-SEVEN

Colton

WHILE ALEX WAS OUT VISITING GERTIE, WHO'D COME BACK TO LA TO spend the Christmas holidays with her family, I was rearranging our room so we could fit another dresser. After sliding the bed over to the other wall, I went on a scavenger hunt, foraging through the crap that had somehow migrated underneath, and that's when I found it—the letter.

Dear Colton,
I miss you already, and I haven't even left...
As soon as I finish writing this, I'll be on my way to the airport to catch the next flight home. Dean's dad was in a bad car accident this morning, and it doesn't look good. I know that you understand how much Mr. Ryan means to me, and why I need to be there right now. Still, I hate leaving without saying goodbye-truthfully, I hate leaving at all. The past few weeks, especially last weekend, were the happiest I've been in years.
    This is a conversation I hoped we'd have in person, but I don't want you to come back, find me gone, and assume the worst.

So, this letter will have to do. I've made my decision. Hell, if I'm honest, I made it the minute I hopped on that plane to come to LA-to come to you. You're the reason I couldn't say yes. I know that now, without doubt. There's no way that I could ever marry Dean feeling the way I do for you. I'm in love with you, Colton Fowler. I think maybe I always have been.

Thank you so much for everything. The summer, this weekend, your big cock-the shirt, you perv. I'll call you later tonight when I get settled.

Love always,
Allie
xoxo

I sat at the foot of the bed, reading it over and over again. My heart broke as I imagined the pain she must've felt after baring her heart like that and then thinking that I'd run off and slept with Lyla.

I couldn't believe that girl pulled such a juvenile stunt, but I let her know in no uncertain terms that if she even looked my or Alex's way again, I'd report her to the coaches and have her ass banned from the gym and thrown off the cheer squad. Lyla hadn't been a problem since.

Mine and Alex's relationship had been perfect since she moved in a month ago, but I walked around with a knot the size of Texas in my chest, constantly feeling like this was all too good to be true. Like it wasn't going to last because it never had before. Our parents always said we were destined to be together. But, it felt like fate just really liked fucking with us.

"What're you reading?" Allie asked, plopping down beside me on the bed, so engrossed in my thoughts, I hadn't heard her come in. When I turned to look at her, my heart sped up. *Fuck, she was gorgeous*, I thought, staring down at her windburned cheeks and bright red nose. At her teeth biting her lower lip.

"Hey," she said with a giggle, cupping her icy cold hands on my cheeks. "Are you okay?"

"You look really nice today, Al," I rasped, unable to focus on much else. She was here, and she was mine. But for how long?

Alex's eyes narrowed as she searched mine. "Thank you, Colton...You're acting weird. Did something happen while I was gone?" *Jeez, I needed to snap out of this.*

"Well, I found about five hundred pairs of dirty panties under the bed," I chuckled, glaring at her.

"Hey, you can't blame me for those. You're the one who's always rippin''em off of me. You should clean up after you eat," she teased, scrunching her nose at me.

"I also found this," I said, passing her the letter.

My beautiful girl's face flushed with embarrassment. "Told you..." She folded it up, setting it on the bed behind us. Her eyes darted around the room as she crossed her legs, the top one swinging rapidly.

"I'm in love with you too, Allie," I said, moving to kneel in front of her. Alex and I had been saying the words 'I love you' to each other since we were kids, but loving a person and being in love with a person were not the same thing. I felt the earth shift when I read her words, so I got it. I understood when her shoulders started to shake and her eyes welled up with emotion. It was the relief of knowing that when I said those three words to her now, they meant something more.

She blew out a long breath. "You are?"

"Alexis Mack, I've been in love with you since we were in high school, maybe even before that," I said, reaching up to tuck a lock of hair behind her ear. "All it took to make me realize it was seeing you with Dean, and by then I was already too late."

"Why didn't you say anything?"

"You seemed so happy, and I was afraid that if I told you and you didn't feel the same, things between us would change, and I'd lose you."

Realization dawned on her. "So, the move to California was because of Dean and me?"

I shrugged. "It was easier when I didn't have to see the two of you together."

"We really screwed this thing all up, didn't we?" she asked, running her fingers through my hair.

"I don't know, Al. Maybe if we hadn't tried with other people, we would've always wondered if what we had was real, you know? It was all we'd ever known." Growing up, I'd always assumed Allie would be mine. I'd learned the hard way never to take her for granted.

"Well, you sure sampled enough of the female population to make sure." Alex's eyes twinkled with mirth. "Were blowjobs your way of coping?" She snorted.

"A man's got needs, Al." I shrugged, rising to my feet, which were starting to cramp from sitting on my heels so long. "I didn't know that you'd ever leave Dean. But, yeah, I guess you're kinda right. Girls get less emotionally attached from sucking dick than they do from fucking."

"Hmm," she said, twisting her lips to the side. "Guess I never thought about it like that."

"See, so every time I let a girl put her lips around my cock, it was for you."

"You're too kind."

It was Christmas Eve, and we were getting all decked out to go celebrate with my coaches and teammates. I felt awful for not being able to take Alex back to spend the holiday with our families, but we were in the middle of a big tournament, and I couldn't leave. Allie refused to go without me, so here we were.

"Your girl about ready, Fowls?" Finn griped, pacing the living room in his three-piece suit. "I'm starving."

It was after 5:00 p.m. and Alexis had been getting ready since early that morning. When I'd told her this dinner would be a formal affair, she'd worked herself into a mini panic attack. Unlike myself, who'd grown accustomed to the lavish productions the program put on, Alex hadn't worn a formal dress since our senior prom. So, as an early Christmas gift, I'd set her up with an appointment at a designer boutique a few days ago and then surprised her this morning with a day at the salon—hair, nails, makeup, waxing, the whole shebang. All she had to do when she got back *two hours ago*, was put on the dress, which she had yet to allow me to see, mind you. I was *dying* to get a look at her.

"She's coming," Blex announced, rushing down the stairs. "Just needed a little help." That asshole smirked, waggling his brows.

"What kind of help?"

"Zipper...titty tape..."

My eyes narrowed across the room at my best friend. "You touched my girl's tits?"

Blex burst out laughing. "No, I just helped her figure out how it worked and zipped her up when she was through."

Our conversation ended when the sound of Allie's heels echoed off the stairs. Time stood still as I watched her step into view. Her dress was floor length with a slit that came up to mid-thigh. The skirt was red and trailed behind her, even in her sexy as hell, four-inch silver stilettos. The top was sheer silver with rhinestones that clustered in the shape of a bra to cover her breasts and were dusted lightly over the rest of the see-through top. She looked like she belonged on a runway.

"Well?" she asked nervously when I stood there gawking, unable to formulate words.

"Jesus, Alex," I rasped, loosening the knot on my tie. "You look...*wow*." I closed the few steps between us and lifted my hands to her shoulders, lightly trailing my knuckles down her arms. "So fucking beautiful, Allie."

"Thank you," she whispered, placing her dainty hands on my chest. "This suit is—" she closed her eyes, growling low in the back of her throat "—so hot," she added, her eyes fluttering open.

"You two lovebirds ready?" Blex called from the door. "Car's here."

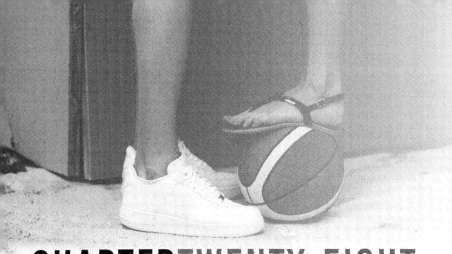

CHAPTER TWENTY-EIGHT

Alexis

I FELT LIKE A MOVIE STAR WALKING INTO THE BALLROOM ON Colton's arm. So in awe of my surroundings, I practically floated in on a cloud. The ceiling had been draped in white netting with twinkling lights that set a romantic ambiance. It gave the feeling of being under a blanket of stars. Four-chair tables with white cloths and chair covers to match filled one half of the space. Each chair was adorned with a huge gold bow tied around its back. The place settings were white with gold trim. It was all so fancy, no expense spared. On the other end of the ballroom sat a stage where a four-man band filled our ears with classic Christmas music. Beside the stage was an enormous tree, decorated elaborately in red and gold. A dance floor was set up just in front of the stage and to the right of it, an open bar.

"Colton and Alexis, don't you two clean up nice?" Coach Grady boomed, coming up behind us as we navigated the room in search of our seats. "I'm sorry you're missing the holiday with your family," he said, his concerned eyes locked on mine. Colt must've mentioned how difficult our first Christmas away from home was for me. It's not that I didn't want to be there because I did. It was just hard. "Well, just know I appreciate the sacrifice you're making to be with our Colt here." His hand clamped down on Colton's shoulder. It was obvious he cared for him a whole lot, and it warmed me to him.

My lips stretched into a slow smile. "Being with Colt is never a sacrifice, Mr. Grady." Colt's hand squeezed mine gently. "I'll be fine."

Coach beamed. "He is one of a kind, isn't he?"

"He sure is." I turned toward Colton as I answered, and our eyes locked. My heart did a little dance. I couldn't stop staring at my man in his Armani suit. I never understood why a person would pay such an enormous price for a name, but I was certainly glad for Colt's expensive taste tonight. And for Grandpa Fowler, who seemed to have no limits when it came to spoiling his only grandson.

"Well, you two kids enjoy the party." He walked off in the direction of his table, but before we had even taken two steps, he turned around and was headed right back.

"Forget something, Coach?" Colt asked, smiling.

"Yeah, I did, actually." His attention turned to me. "Alexis, I wanted to see if you'd do me a huge favor and take part in the halftime show on New Year's Eve?"

My eyes turned to the side, meeting Colt's. He shrugged like he had no idea what this was about. "Me?" My hand came to my chest, pulse racing with nerves.

"We thought it would be fun to have a couple of the players' girlfriends come out and shoot blindfolded." *Ugh. Why me?* My first instinct was to tell him no, but he was such a nice man, and he looked so excited about the whole thing. He'd also just referred to me as Colt's girlfriend, so I was really liking him just then.

"You should do it, babe." Colt nudged my arm with his elbow. "You've got a hell of a shot for a girl," he teased.

"For a girl?" I countered. "I seem to remember beating a

222

certain someone at horse a time or two."

Colt chuckled, his green eyes glistening. "It was one time, and we were like twelve."

I dismissed him with the wave of a hand. "Semantics."

Coach Grady watched our interaction with an amused smile. "So, how 'bout it, Alex? Can we count you in?"

"Sure," I said, already regretting my answer. "Why not?" *Why not?* Was I serious?

"Great. I'm gonna get back to Mrs. Grady. She hates when I leave her alone at these things."

I waited until he was out of earshot before growling at Colt. "Why'd you let me say yes?"

His arm curled around my waist, pulling me snug to his chest. "Shush." Colton rested a finger against my lips. "It'll be fun," he whispered, his mouth hovering a breath away from mine. My heart began to flutter when his warm tongue lightly traced over my lips, easing inside. He kissed me long and slow, stealing my breath and making me dizzy with want.

Ahem. Blex cleared his throat, drawing us from our trance. "Everyone is in their seats waiting on the two of you. Coach wants to say a few words before we eat." *Oh God.* How embarrassing.

Colton's teeth bit into his bottom lip as he huffed out a deep sigh, shaking his head with laughter. "Sorry, guys." He shrugged, holding his hands up. "My girl's a little distracting tonight." Then he fucked me with his eyes right there in front of the entire basketball team, coaching staff, and cheer squad.

A chorus of hoots and cheers rang in my ears as I shielded my heated face with my hand, allowing Colt to lead us to our table, where we were seated with Finn and Blex.

"Damn that was hot," Finn announced. "I'm gonna need you to teach me how to do that smolder thing, Fowls."

Colt chuckled. "Sorry, bro, some things can't be taught. You either got it...or you don't," he jeered just as Coach stood, blowing his whistle to silence his players.

"Merry Christmas, everyone." Mr. Grady's eyes flitted from

one table to the next, making his way around the room. "I'd like to start the evening by thanking each of you for being here tonight. I realize most of you are missing out on festivities back home, and we hope you know how much we appreciate your dedication and your commitment to this team. Tonight, we want you to forget about the game and enjoy yourselves. We've got a great meal being brought out to your tables shortly. DJ Ritchie will be taking over in about an hour, and we hope you'll stick around to enjoy a couple of drinks." His eyes narrowed, trailing around the room, "Those of you of age, of course, and some dancing. Bon appétit!"

As if on cue, servers appeared with trays of food and pitchers of water, filling our glasses. Dinner was a feast of honey glazed ham, rib roast, garlic mashed potatoes, green bean casserole, and buttery rolls. The types of food you'd expect to find at a family holiday gathering. It was absolutely delicious.

"Would any of you care for a glass of wine?" a waiter asked, passing out wine lists to each of us. I stared down at the menu in my hand, waiting for one of the guys to tell the man we were underage, but Blex, Finn, and Colt started discussing our options like ordering wine with dinner was something they did every day.

"We'll take four glasses of the Cabernet Sauvignon, please," came Colton, collecting the wine menus and passing them back to the man.

"What are you guys doing?" I muttered when the waiter had walked off.

Colt's arm went around my shoulders, his lips to the shell of my ear. "It's a private party, Al. No one is going around checking IDs. They won't tell us anything if we don't draw attention to ourselves."

"I don't even know what you just ordered. I've never had wine. We aren't this fancy in Texas, Colton," I teased, poking fun at his new lifestyle, which, to be honest, was quickly growing on me. What girl wouldn't enjoy getting all dolled up for fancy dinner parties and weekends at beachfront mansions?

"It's a popular dinner wine," Colt answered. "You'll like it. It's strong, so sip it," he added with a sly smirk. "Remember, I said don't draw attention to yourself."

The wine was disgusting. I can't even explain the taste, but it wasn't sweet at all, and I was a sweet drinker, on the rare occasion that I did drink. I'd consumed more alcohol last summer with these boys than I'd probably ever drank before, combined. But I sipped that wine anyway because everyone else around me was drinking it and I wanted to fit in. I could be classy, damnit.

"You don't have to drink it, Alex." Colt laughed, watching my face pucker as I took another swallow between bites. I liked it better that way. The food erased the lingering yuck from my taste buds.

"It's fine," I said, forking a bite of ham into my mouth.

"You look like you just got a whiff of ass, Lexi," Finn argued from across the table.

"Shh," I hissed, looking around to see if anyone had heard him. "I'm trying to be sophisticated, Finley." I widened my eyes at him, indicating for him to shut up.

He shrugged, his shoulders shaking with a chuckle. "Well, I'm just letting you know, as your friend, that you are not pulling it off." He winked.

Glaring at Finn, I grabbed my glass, chugging the last of it while making a conscious effort to control my outward reaction. It burned the whole way down, and I felt my cheeks flush as I hurriedly chased it with a bite of potatoes, giving the jerk across from me a snide smirk.

Ignoring the boys' laughter, I concentrated on my plate, feeling relieved to have that wine business over with. Then our waiter returned while I had a mouthful of food and refilled that fucking glass. When he walked off, Finn raised his brow in challenge.

"Just drink your water, babe." Colt moved to grab the wine, and I swatted his hand away.

"It's really not that bad anymore," I insisted. "I think I just

had to get used to it. Leave it." I don't know why I felt the
need to keep up, but I wanted to fit in. Somehow in my mind,
that equated to drinking the nasty wine.

Colt shrugged. "Drink it slowly, Allie, or it'll sneak up on
you."

This time, I listened to him, figuring if I finished anytime
soon, that waiter would be back, topping it off again.

Halfway through the second glass, I got the warm fuzzies.
I was feeling hot everywhere, but it was an enjoyable heat, the
kind you get cuddled up in front of the fire on a cold night,
wrapped in your favorite blanket. My skin tingled.

"You need to just fuck that girl and get it over with," Finn
said to Blex, regarding the new cheerleader, Georgia, who he
couldn't seem to tear his eyes from. Georgia was a beautiful
redhead with freckles on the bridge of her nose and just under
her eyes, which were green like Colton's. And she was nice. I
sort of steered clear of the cheerleaders in order to avoid Lyla,
but she was always coming over to talk to me. I'm sure it had
more to do with getting close to Blex than her desire to be in
my company, but I didn't even care. I liked her, and I hoped
they ended up together. Blex deserved a good girl.

"I think I might ask her to dance in a minute, but I don't
want to be the only ones out there." His eyes darted to the
empty dance floor. DJ Ritchie had kicked things off about
thirty minutes ago, and it was still bare.

"We'll go!" I offered, all too eager to feel Colton's hands on
my body. Apparently, wine made me horny. It didn't taste quite
so awful anymore either.

"Will we?" Colt teased.

Lowering my bottom lip, I tilted my head to the side and
fluttered my big brown eyes at him.

"I was kidding." He winked, taking my hand in his. "Let's
go."

We were the first two out there, but I didn't even care.
As far as I was concerned, we were the only two people in
existence when Colt placed his hands on my waist and began

swaying our bodies to the sensual rhythm of "Slow Hands" by Niall Horan. Colton had amazing control and awareness of his body. The slight thrusting of his hips perfectly timed to the beat. His lips brushed my neck, setting my pulse to race just before swinging me away and reeling me back in. His moves were fluid, like the music moved through him, while at the same time each touch felt deliberate. Dancing with him was a constant building of sexual tension and the ultimate foreplay.

When the song switched to something more upbeat, I glanced around, noticing the dance floor had started to fill up. Blex was a few feet away with Georgia, and Finn was near the bar, cozying up to a girl I didn't know. Everyone seemed to be having a great time, even Coach Grady and his wife, who were tearing it up with the rest of us to "Salt Shaker" by the Ying Yang Twins.

"Ready to go?" Colt's whispered words came hot on my ear, causing my body to shiver.

"I thought you'd never ask." In reality, we hadn't been there but a few hours total and had only made it through a handful of songs, but I was ready to explode with how badly I wanted him.

Colton's eyes bore deep into mine, hooded with desire. I felt his stare in the pit of my stomach. "What d'ya say we pick this party back up at home?"

"Let's get outta here."

CHAPTER TWENTY-NINE

Colton

I AWOKE TO THE GREATEST CHRISTMAS GIFT I'D EVER RECEIVED: Allie asleep in my arms. The sun was barely beginning to rise, casting the faintest glow over her naked body. It was a sight that still blew my mind every single day. Her red dress was thrown over the back of the desk chair. My suit in piles on the floor. Alex's titty tape stuck to the headboard. I chuckled at the memory of the two of us trying to remove those things without ripping her skin off. Allie stirred at the sound of my laughter.

"Hey, Al," I whispered into her ear, knowing I should have let her sleep after keeping her up most of the night, but it was Christmas, and I was excited to give her, her gift.

Alex moaned low in her throat, swatting my lips from her ear as if they were a gnat.

"Merry Christmas, baby," I said a little louder, earning her back as she rolled over to her stomach, dismissing me. I knew that I could've gotten her up by fooling around a little, but I was afraid she'd be too sore after last night, so I decided to leave Alex in bed and grab a shower. As I was preparing to brush my teeth, I heard a loud banging on the bedroom door. I pushed the bathroom door open just in time to hear Finley tell Alex that her delivery had arrived. I'd never seen that girl pop out of bed as fast as she did in that moment.

"Shit! I'm still naked," she announced, ambling over to the dresser for some clothes.

"Expecting something important?" I asked, lurking in the doorway with my arms crossed over my chest as she scrambled around the room.

Alexis slipped the "Big Cock" tee over her head. "Yeah," she answered, all out of breath as she stepped into a pair of my boxers.

"Want me to go get it?"

"No," Allie said, shaking her head. "You stay put. I'll be right back."

It took her more than five minutes to return. I was tempted to go down there and make sure she hadn't forgotten about me when the door opened and Alex walked in carrying a wiggly ball of wrinkles with a red bow tied around its neck. "Merry Christmas, Colton!"

The only thing I'd put on my Christmas list for three years in a row when we were kids was an English bulldog puppy. After the third year, I gave up. Today I understood that the reason I never got it was because my father was severely allergic to dogs, but back when I was eleven, twelve, and thirteen-years-old, it was the end of the world. I'd been devastated.

"You bought my puppy," I said, stunned. Getting a dog hadn't even crossed my mind since I'd moved out here, and honestly, I wasn't home enough during the season to give one the attention it deserved. But now I had Alex. And she was standing in my bedroom wearing a shirt with a big cock on the front, her hair looking like she'd stuck her finger in an electric outlet, makeup melted down her face, holding a little piece of my childhood. She was the most beautiful thing I'd ever seen.

My chest tightened as I took the puppy from her hands.

Only Alex would know to do this. She literally knew everything there was to know about me. "Thank you, Allie. I can't believe you remembered."

Her smile was radiant as she watched the dog lap at my face. "I remember everything, Colt."

"Do you remember his name?" I challenged, quirking my brow.

Her lips puckered as she tried not to laugh. "You're not still calling him Bacon?"

"What do you think, huh?" I asked, scratching the top of his head. "Is your name Bacon?" His tail wagged at the sound of my voice, and I shrugged, looking back to Allie. "Bacon it is."

"That's an awful name."

"Watch your mouth, woman," I teased, sitting on the floor and setting him on his feet. "You're going to hurt his feelings."

Alex rolled her eyes. "Be right back. I need to grab his things."

She came back in with a dog crate filled with toys, bowls, and dog food. After setting it on the ground, she dug out a collar with a green nameplate on the front that said, "Bacon." "Told you I remember everything." She smiled, fastening it onto the puppy's neck.

"How'd you get a dog and all this stuff delivered on Christmas day?"

"I had all of his stuff hidden in Blex's closet, and I got the puppy from Gertie's son. When I met with her last week, she told me his dog had puppies, and when I found out they were English bulldogs, I mentioned possibly getting one for you for Christmas."

My stomach knotted when it dawned on me how expensive these dogs were. Alex was living on student loans and whatever money her parents put in her account each month. "Babe, I can't believe you spent this much on me for Christmas."

Her head shook. "You shush. I have money. I've saved the extras from my grants and scholarships while living with

—

231

Mom and Dad, and my grandparents give me way too much for every holiday. Plus, Gertie's son practically gave him to me, and you never let me pay for anything anyway. What else do I have to spend it on?"

It was true that Alex and I had both lucked out in the grandparent department. Our fathers were both their parents' only children, and Alex and me their only grandchildren. They threw money at us like it grew on trees. "I love you, Allie."

"I love you too, Colt—" Alex's head pulled back, and she let out a scream as Bacon played tug of war with a lock of her hair, growling and whipping his head from side to side.

"No, Bacon!" I shouted through a laugh, prying his jaws apart to free Allie's hair.

Rubbing at her scalp, she rose to her feet. "I'm gonna go grab a quick shower. You should probably take the Baconator out to potty." Just as the words left her lips, Bacon popped a squat, relieving himself on my bedroom carpet.

"No, Bacon!" Alex and I yelled in unison. Something told me being puppy parents was going to be a lot of work.

"Yeah, so the guy at PetSmart said we should keep him on the tile 'til he's potty trained." Her mouth pulled into a frown. "I didn't think he'd have to go so soon. I took him out before I brought him up here."

"It's fine, Allie," I laughed. "Go get in the shower, and I'll clean this up."

"Where's Bacon?" Alex asked, coming out of the bathroom, followed by a cloud of steam.

"Finn and Blex are playing with him downstairs," I said, patting the bed next to me for her to sit. "Time for your present."

Allie's face lit up as she sat with her hands laced in her lap, bouncing on her knees.

I handed her the small box, watching intently as she ripped

the paper off, eager for her reaction.

"Tiffany's?" she shrieked. "You got me Tiffany's!"

"Are you going to open it and see what's inside?" I laughed.

Allie pulled the top off the blue box and lifted the black velvet one from inside. She pried it open slowly, gasping when she found the heart-shaped locket. Her eyes welled up with tears before she'd even seen the best part.

"Take it out and open it, Al," I urged

Her thumb rolled over the words engraved on the front side, "Our love story." Then she opened the locket. One side held a picture of two chubby babies and the other a photo my mom had taken of us on Thanksgiving Day.

"It's perfect," she rasped with tears dripping down her face as she fingered the photos inside. "I love it so much, Colton. Thank you."

"You're welcome," I said, taking the necklace from her hands and fastening it around her neck. "All set," I whispered in her ear. "Two decades down, Al, and we're just really getting started."

Alex spun around to face me, her hand clutching the locket to her chest. "Kiss me, Colton."

"Yes, ma'am," I answered with a salute before taking her chin with my thumb and forefinger and molding my mouth to hers. My tongue pressed against the seam of her lips and they parted, granting me entry. Alex let out a whimper. Her hands lifted from my chest to cup the sides of my face as she began smoothing her fingers through the day-old scruff. I worshiped her with every thrust of my tongue, pulling her tighter into my arms until I could feel her heart beating with mine. Until my own felt as if it would burst, incapable of containing the overwhelming love I felt for this girl.

"Colton," she breathed, rocking into me.

Bang. Bang. Bang.

A fist pounded on our bedroom door. "Colton, your present just dropped a deuce on the kitchen floor. I'm not dealing with this shit…Literally. I'm not. I'm gonna puke."

—

Alex and I pulled apart, resting our foreheads together as we shared a breathy laugh.

"Are you two doing the nasty?" Finn whined.

Alex burst into a fit of giggles.

"No," I said, "we're coming."

"I didn't ask all that now," he grumbled through the door. "Hurry up. The whole house smells like a turd."

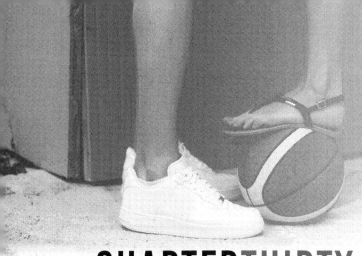

CHAPTER THIRTY

Alexis

"WHERE THE HELL IS COLTON?" I ASKED, COMING INTO THE HOUSE from walking Bacon. He was supposed to be practicing my shot with me for that damn halftime show I'd stupidly agreed to, which was *tomorrow night*.

"Coach needed his help with some things. Come on, Alexis," Blex said, getting up from the couch. "Put Bacon in his crate, and I'll go practice with you."

"Blex, he's been gone like all day, and yesterday too," I whined. I missed him like crazy, and everyone was acting so weird, not giving me any real reasons for his absence. I hated that my mind kept going to very dark places, but I just couldn't help it.

"You swear he's not cheating on me, Blex?" I finally asked, gnawing my thumbnail down to the skin.

"I promise," he answered, looking me right in the eyes. "That boy's got it bad, Alex. Trust me, he is not interested in anyone else. I swear he's with Coach Grady." That made me feel a little better, if only marginally. I didn't think Blex would lie to me, and honestly, I knew in my heart that Colt wouldn't either. I just couldn't help the paranoia creeping in.

Just then, Finn came trudging down the stairs wearing nothing but a pair of boxers and toting a massive erection. Living with three guys was, ummm, interesting in that department for sure. I spent a lot of time averting my eyes, wishing I could un-see *things*. And by things I meant boners. Every time I turned around one of those boys was sportin' wood. They had no shame, and they didn't tell each other either. Guys should have some secret sign for, "Your dick is hard." I couldn't have been the only person in the room who saw that shit.

"Where are your clothes?" I asked, looking off to the side.

"I was napping. You two assholes woke me up. Now gimme that mutt so I can put him in his cage and you go practice that shot." Finn made grabby hands toward the pup in my arms. "You better not embarrass me by losing tomorrow, Lexi. People know we're friends."

"I don't see you doing anything to help me." My brows shot up as I passed Bacon over to him. "And don't let me find him in your bed when I get back. He has to sleep in his kennel, Finn."

My heart swelled when that big blond jock started baby talking to the dog. "Your momma's just a mean old bitch, ain't she, Bacon?" Holding him up with his lips puckered, he let that puppy lick all over his face. "I know. I know she is..."

"Finn," I growled. "I fucking mean it. He's just starting to sleep most of the night without crying to get in our bed."

"So, let him in!"

"We sleep naked," I huffed, feeling my cheeks heat. "And I don't want dog hair in my vagina or him to lick me in places his tongue should never see."

Finley dismissed me with a sigh as he turned to climb the stairs, muttering to the little ball of fur, "It's okay, Bacon... Uncle Finn loves you." Who knew a dog would soften the testosterone levels in this house so drastically?

—

"Widen your stance, Alex. Your feet should be shoulder width apart." Blex bent down, physically turning my feet to point a little to the left. "Like that. Every. Single. Time."

"Got it."

"This is where you'll be standing when you make your shot." He put the ball in my hands, adjusting their position. "Now, you'll wanna bend those knees just a little with each shot."

"All right, let's do this. Where's the blindfold?" I asked, bouncing a little on my heels to get a feel for the knee bend.

Blex laughed. "Just practice your shot. You need to learn it with your eyes open first." I nodded as he did a little shimmy. "Show me what'cha workin' wit."

Closing my eyes, I took a deep breath, wiggling around to shake the nerves out. Then I opened them, zeroed in on the rim, and...missed by a fucking mile.

"That's okay," came Blex's response to my little stomp/groan as he went after the ball. "Your form was really good. Just give it a little more oomph this time."

"I haven't shot in a long time." As if he couldn't tell.

Blex repositioned the ball in my hands. "Bend a little more and really fire that ball, Alex. I've seen some of the punches you've thrown at Fowls." He chuckled at my narrowed eyes. "Go again," he instructed, moving to the side.

I bent a little lower this time, and my shot bounced off the rim.

"Much better. Now this time don't cup the ball. It shouldn't sit in your palm, let it rest on the tips of your fingers, like this."

"It feels like it's going to roll out of my hand," I complained. All of this formal training was so different from my usual method, which was to just toss it out there and pray.

"That's what your other hand is for. Use it to help guide the ball, and right before you shoot, move it. The only hand on the ball when you fire it off should be your shooting hand."

—

I tried to remember all the things he'd just taught me with my feet, knees, and hands on every shot. It felt like he was telling me to pat my head and rub my stomach while standing on one leg. But what started off as a seemingly hopeless endeavor began to come together once I'd found my groove, eleventy-billion throws later. I was actually sinking shots. Not all of them, but sometimes two or three in a row. When it was time to get back so Blex could get to practice, I was feeling a lot better about things. Even if I didn't land my blind shot, I was pretty confident that I could at least get it in the vicinity of the basket.

"You're a natural," Blex said on the walk back from the courts to the apartment.

"I don't know about that," I laughed. "But I'm definitely better than before. Thanks for helping me." I couldn't help but feel a little angry with Colt for standing me up.

"Anytime," he said, racing up the steps ahead of me and calling back over his shoulder, "You coming to watch us practice?"

"Nah," I answered, having just read the text I'd missed from Colt letting me know he wouldn't be able to make it home before practice. "I'm exhausted. Gonna have a bubble bath and chill with Bacon at home."

I was lying in our bed with Bacon curled into my chest when I heard the guys' loudmouths. Despite my greatest efforts, I never could fall asleep 'til I knew they'd made it home. At the sound of Colt's voice, my heart clenched, begging me to run downstairs and jump into his arms, seeking the comfort I'd been longing for all day, but I was upset and too stubborn to give in to its demands. It wasn't as much his being away that had me so emotional, but his complete lack of communication. I was sure that Colton was hiding something from me, and that hurt. *It hurt a lot.*

Colt called out my name on his way up the stairs. Purposely, I buried my face a little deeper into my pillow, making it easier to feign sleep. The creak of the door opening was followed by a disappointed sigh, and then I felt him looming over me. Colton brushed the hair from my face, causing my insides to shake. The scent of leather on his skin assaulted my senses, weakening my resolve. I'd always loved the way his hands smelled after playing ball. His thick lips pressed a whisper-soft kiss to my forehead, and I fought the urge to tilt my head, bringing my mouth to his. I couldn't even breathe for fear that I would give myself away by bursting into tears.

When I heard the bathroom door shut and the shower turn on, I released the breath I'd been holding, freeing a steady stream of tears along with it. Missing Colton while he was away hurt, but nothing compared to the pain of missing him while he was right here.

I must've finally dozed off while Colt was in the shower, because the next thing I knew, Bacon was being lifted from my arms. After locking him in the kennel, I felt Colton climb into the bed. He snuggled up behind me, curling his hard body around mine.

"I love you, Alex," came the whispered voice of the man I loved as I drifted back to sleep, blanketed in his touch.

When I awoke the following morning, Colt was gone, as were Blex and Finn. It was game day, so I wouldn't be seeing them much, if at all.

My chest ached as I reached to his side of the bed, finding the puppy where I knew he'd be. Colton had been taking Bacon out before practice and dropping him in the bed with me on his way out so that I could sleep in. He'd always done little things like that without my asking. Even when we were growing up and "just friends," Colton went out of his way to ensure my comfort.

After taking the pooch out to potty, we made our way into the kitchen for some breakfast. Immediately, my eyes found the vase filled with lilies in the center of the table—my favorite. Beside it sat a box of the raspberry filled donuts that I had an unhealthy obsession with from the bakery down the street with a note taped to the top. I couldn't help but laugh at the effort he'd taken to prevent another mishap with this letter.

Good morning, beautiful!
Hope you slept well. I figured you could use a good breakfast on the morning of your court debut. Also, I'm groveling. Is it working?
Blex tells me the girls' team will be begging for you to join after they see you shoot tonight. ;P I'm so sorry I missed practicing with you yesterday. I know that you're upset and with good reason. I also know that you weren't asleep when I got in last night. You're really not as good of a faker as you think.
I've had a lot of things to take care of over the past few days, but I promise to fill you in on everything tonight. It was never my intention to hurt you. God, Al...You have to know, that's the last thing I ever want.
Can't wait to see you tonight. Love you so much.
XOXO, Colt
And just like that, my anger melted away.

The Lyft dropped me off at the front of the gym at 6:30. The place was packed. I couldn't believe how many people were spending their New Year's Eve at a sporting event, although I really should've expected it seeing as tonight's game was against one of their biggest rivals, the Arizona Wildcats. It made me nauseated to think that all those eyes would be on me in a little over an hour. I had really been hoping for a small crowd due to the holiday, but that did not appear to be the case.

It was five to seven by the time I found my seat, courtside, right beside the Bruin's bench. Jamie and Desiree, the other two girls who would be shooting during halftime, were already in their chairs, welcoming me with huge smiles. They didn't look even a fraction as nervous as I felt.

"Hey," I said, forcing a smile, a little surprised by their warm welcome. Both girls were good friends with Lyla, so we really hadn't interacted much. They'd never been rude to me or anything. I guess I shouldn't have assumed they'd dislike me by association.

"Isn't this great?" Jamie asked, referring to our seats.

"It's incredible," I agreed. My heart raced with excitement at the thought of watching Colt play from this close. I just wished it wasn't overshadowed by the massive case of stage fright I had going on. "You aren't nervous?"

"Pshh. Nervous?" came Desiree's voice on the other side of Jamie. "Girl, ain't none of us gonna make that shot. Just enjoy the royal treatment and stop worrying about it. Half the crowd will be up using the restroom or grabbing snacks anyway."

God, how I wished I could be as relaxed about the whole thing as she was.

"We had a few drinks to ease the nerves before leaving to come here. Don't let that bitch fool you," Jamie laughed, elbowing her friend in the ribs.

"That too," Desiree agreed, turning her palms up with a shrug. "Desperate times."

My heart started pounding against my ribcage as the packed house went wild when our guys took their bench. Colt's eyes found mine before he sat, giving me a sexy wink that sent the butterflies swarming. I missed him to the point that it was painful. He was so close, and I couldn't do anything more than smile his way.

My eyes welled up when they announced the starters and his name was called. Colt was by far the crowd favorite. Sometimes I forgot what a big deal he was to everyone else because I'd been with him from the start. It was surreal to watch his dreams coming true. I couldn't have been prouder.

"So, you and Colton haven't been together very long, right?" Jamie asked as the players went to the court and the centers prepared for the jump.

"We've been together our whole lives," I answered with my eyes still fixed on the game. "But, yeah. We're a new couple."

If she said anything else, I didn't hear it, too engrossed in the action. The Bruins had won the jump and were already down court. With a white-knuckled grip, I bit my bottom lip and tensed as Colton shot an impressive three-pointer to start the game. Nothing but net, and I was up out of my seat, hands cupped around my mouth, screaming like a maniac.

My anxiety over the halftime show was forgotten as adrenaline took over. I loved the fast pace of the game, the way you could be up one minute and down the next. It was an emotional rollercoaster, and it thrilled me just the same.

Before I knew it, the first half had ended. The Bruins over the Wildcats, forty-five to thirty-seven.

While the guys filed out to the locker room, the cheerleaders took the court, performing their halftime routine. I tried really hard to behave like an adult and not sneer at Lyla, but a part of me wished that on one of those basket tosses they would forget to catch her.

"Hey, sexy," Colton whispered into my ear as the black blindfold came down over my eyes. His breath on my neck made me shiver, and I could smell the deodorant he must've just reapplied. I wanted to cry with how badly I needed to be in his arms, and my anxiety had returned tenfold. I was a fucking mess as he led me out onto that court. "Stay here."

"Ladies and gentlemen, we have something really special planned for our halftime show this evening," Coach Grady announced. "Let's lend these kids a little moral support, eh?"

Great. If they weren't all paying attention before, they certainly were now. "Colt," I whispered, hoping he was still nearby. *Fucking crickets.*

—

I heard movement and hushed voices. The crowd was reacting to something, but I had no idea what because I couldn't see. Oh my God, why wouldn't they just give me the ball and let me get this over with before I puked?

"Hey," Jamie said, tapping my shoulder. "It's just me. There's been a slight change of plans. I'm just going to untie your blindfold, okay?"

I nodded, unable to speak past the nervous lump in my throat. What the hell was going on?

I blinked a few times once my eyes were uncovered to clear my vision. My whole body started to shake when I saw our parents' smiling faces staring back at me, our mothers with tears in their eyes. The entire basketball team, the mascots, and the coaches were all on the court with them, standing right behind Colton, who was down on his knee at my feet. *Oh my God.*

"What are you doing?" I whispered, feeling warm tears trickle down my cheeks because I already knew. There could only be one explanation for the scene laid out before me, and all of my dreams were about to come true. My hands lifted to cover my nose and mouth. *I couldn't breathe.*

Colt smiled up at me, his emerald eyes glistening as they fixed on mine. "I love you, Alexis Mack." His voice sounded through the speaker system, heavy with emotion.

"I love you too," I whispered.

A chorus of "awes" rang out from the crowd following our exchange.

"I know that we've only been a couple for a few months now, but I have been chasing after you for my entire life." He chuckled. "I'm tired, Allie." His voice cracked, hitting me right in the heart. "I'm so tired of living with this constant fear that I'm going to end up having to spend the rest of my life without the only person I could ever imagine spending it with."

My head shook, emotion clogging my throat. At that moment, everyone else in that room disappeared, drowned out by the sound of his beautiful words and the beating of my heart. "Only you," I rasped as he opened the black box in his hands.

"When I said that I wanted you to be my everything, I meant it. Now I'm asking to make it official. Allie, I've loved you for as long as I can remember, and I will love you 'til my last breath. *Nothing* would make me happier than the honor of spending the rest of my life with you as your husband."

My body shook. I couldn't believe this was actually happening.

"Will you marry me?"

"Yes," I sobbed as he slid the princess cut solitaire onto my trembling finger. "Yes," I repeated as he lifted to his feet, enveloping me in his arms. "I love you, Colton Fowler. So. Fucking. Much."

I was brought back to reality by the loud laughter that followed that statement, which quickly morphed into cheers and whistles. Leave it to me to go and forget that the boy was mic'ed.

"I can't take you anywhere," Colt joked, bringing his lips to mine, and sealing our engagement with a kiss.

CHAPTER THIRTY-ONE

Colton

IT WAS JANUARY FOURTEENTH, TWO WEEKS AFTER OUR ENGAGEMENT, and six months since the last time we'd hiked up this hill. I'd forgotten all about Allie's journal entry until the reminder on my phone sounded yesterday. Since then my girl had been trying to convince me not to come up here to read it. Of course, that just made me even more curious.

So, here we were, sitting on the same rock with the journal open in my lap and Bacon curled up in hers.

I flipped through the pages until I came to an entry written in a familiar swirly handwriting I'd recognize anywhere. "Found it," I whispered, nudging Allie's shoulder.

She let out a groan, covering her face as I started to read.

July 14, 2017

Just Friends
Our souls were matched before we met—a bond like ours I can't forget.

But for all of you that I adore—I don't want to be your friend anymore.

The love I feel for you is real—your heart is all I need to heal.

It hurts too much, the pain a chore—I don't want to be your friend anymore.

Always just friends, I need so much more,

If you don't feel the same, please <u>close</u> this door.

"Wow," I muttered, feeling like I'd been punched in the gut. Alex and I had spent years hiding behind friendship, terrified of what we'd always felt boiling beneath the surface, but our attempt at playing it safe was exactly what almost drove us apart.

Her face turned bright red. "I told you not to read it."

"It's beautiful," I said, kissing her lips softly. "I'm glad I read it." I snapped a quick picture of her poem with my phone before packing the journal away.

"You are?"

"I am. It was your veritable 'shit or get off the pot,' and I shit. So, it's all good."

Alexis laughed so hard, she woke the dog. "Is that what this was?" she asked, twisting the ring around her finger. "You shitting on me?"

"I feel some excellent vows in the making here, 'I promise to shit on you, all the days of our lives,'" I teased. "We are writing our own vows, right?" I asked, taking Bacon's leash from her with one hand and holding her hand in the other as we started making our way back down the trail.

"Colton Fowler, if you say anything about shitting on me at our wedding, I will run out of there so fast..."

"It's romance, in code, babe. No one else will get it. That's what makes it *awesome*."

"You're a mess," she chided, giggling to herself.

"But you love me anyway."

"God, help me...I love you <u>anyway</u>."

THANKYOU

Thank YOU for reading my words. To write is my dream and I get to live it every day because of my readers. Your messages, your reviews, your support mean more to me than you will ever know.

As always, thank you to my husband Adam and to my children who sacrifice a clean house, cooked meals, and so much more so that I can pursue this crazy dream of mine. You put up with my mood swings and panic attacks and seemingly endless deadlines. You are my strength, and I love you more than words.

A HUGE thank you to my betas: Nicole, Danielle, Kate, Lauren, Karin, and Franci. You girls volunteered your time to help make this book the best it could be and I am so grateful.

Nicole, my brain, you have been here with me from the start and I wouldn't know how to do this without you. Your friendship, your support, and your honesty are invaluable. Even when my characters are pissing you off, you are there to keep me from losing my mind, supporting me every step of the way. I'm so lucky to have you by my side. I love you!

Danielle, thank you for your love and enthusiasm for these characters. You were always there, willing and eager to help me and you have no idea how many times your encouragement kept me going. You've become an integral part of my team, but even more importantly a dear friend. I love you.

Kate Farlow...GURL, I don't even know where to start. From reading my words and hashing out scenes to making asers and helping me market this book, you have gone above and beyond. I'm so thankful that you came into my life and blessed to call you my friend. I love you, Dick! #tripod

Lauren, my wifey...send me the therapy bill. Just kidding, I can't afford it. :p Thank you for loving my babies and talking me off the ledge so many times. I thought that damn blurb was going to do me in, but you swooped in and set me on the right track. You've done this more times than I can count. Breakaway wouldn't be what it is without you, and that's a fact. You are the left to my right and I love you so much. #tripod

Edeerie, my editor and my friend. Thank you for encouraging me to finish this book and for polishing and perfecting my words. I love you so very much.

Juliana, you rocked this cover, woman. Thank you for always being here for me. You are more than my designer. You are my friend and I love you.

Kate Stewart. Gosh woman. You've believed in me from day one and you will never know just how much that means to me. You are my unicorn, my mentor, and my friend. The memories we've made this year, I will never forget. You are stuck with me for life, because you know too much. Thank you for not letting me drown. LOL I love you to bits Katymin!

Shanora, my favorite Felicia. You have no idea how much I love and admire you. You are talented, selfless, and genuine. You are my sounding board and my friend.

Thank you to my proofreaders, Amy, Danielle, Nicole, Donna, Misty, Sandie, and Melissa.

HUNNIES!!! You are the BEST author group there is. Thank you for loving my words, supporting my dreams, and entertaining me daily. I love you ladies so freaking much!

Kylie, Jeananna, and Jo of Give Me Books, THANK YOU for all that you do for me. I'm so happy to have found a place in the GMB family.

Thank you to all the bloggers and authors who've read, shared, or helped support this release in any way.

To the friends and family who support my career and embrace this rollercoaster ride with me, thank you and I love you!

ABOUTTHEAUTHOR

Heather M. Orgeron is a Cajun girl with a big heart and a passion for romance. She married her high school sweetheart two months after graduation and her life has been a fairytale ever since. She's the queen of her castle, reigning over five sons and one bossy little princess who has made it her mission in life to steal her Momma's throne. When she's not writing, you will find her hidden beneath mounds of laundry and piles of dirty dishes or locked in her tower (aka the bathroom) soaking in the tub with a good book. She's always been an avid reader and has recently discovered a love for cultivating romantic stories of her own.

If you would like to connect with
Heather M. Orgeron, you can find her here:

Facebook: facebook.com/AuthorHeatherMOrgeron
Reader Group: facebook.com/groups/1738663433047683/
Twitter: twitter.com/hmorgeronauthor
Instagram: instagram.com/heather_m_orgeron_author

Made in the USA
Las Vegas, NV
12 October 2021

32169373R00142